A MURDER
OF
PRINCIPAL

A MURDER
OF
PRINCIPAL

SARALYN RICHARD

Encircle Publications, LLC
Farmington, Maine U.S.A.

Paperback ISBN 13: 978-1-64599-132-8
Hardcover ISBN 13: 978-1-64599-154-0
E-book ISBN 13: 978-1-64599-133-5
Kindle ISBN 13: 978-1-64599-134-2
Paperback Large Print ISBN 13: 978-1-64599-156-4

Library of Congress Control Number: 2020947901

Book design: Eddie Vincent / ENC Graphic Services
Cover design and digital imaging by Deirdre Wait / High Pines Creative, Inc.
Cover photographs © Getty Images
Author photograph by Jennifer Reynolds

Published by: Encircle Publications, LLC
PO Box 187
Farmington, ME 04938

Visit: http://encirclepub.com

Sign up for Encircle Publications newsletter and specials
http://eepurl.com/cs8taP

Printed in U.S.A.

For Bill O'Neal

*"Education is for improving the lives of others
and for leaving your community
and world better than you found it."*

—*Marian Wright Edelman*

Prologue

R.J. STOKER DROVE TOWARD HIS destiny through the Midwest neighborhood, whose heyday had come and gone, *en route* to the campus of a one-hundred-year-old high school. The car windows were open, the way he liked them. The brisk air and the smells of exhaust smoke, mixed with fast-food restaurant grease, invigorated him. He wanted to immerse himself in everything.

He wasn't thinking of the paychecks or prestige of being the new principal at Lincoln High. He wasn't thinking of the new two-story Colonial he had purchased, or the new 1993 Cadillac his wife had her eye on. He paid no attention to the train tracks, the abandoned industrial yards, or the untidy lawns and unkempt houses that had sheltered middle-class families decades ago.

Gang graffiti peppered the sides of buildings and viaducts. This scenery was a far cry from the posh Tennessee neighborhood where he'd served as principal for the past eighteen years, commanding one of the highest principal salaries in the South.

What Stoker *was* thinking about on this Indian summer day in 1993, the first day of school for faculty, was the challenge. Having accomplished his goals in Knoxville, he stood ready to tackle the big Midwestern city. Besides, he gained a certain gratification from being able to improve the lives of young people of his own race. Lincoln High School was predominantly Black.

Driving past the gym, one of the five campus buildings, he thought of the trophy cases and plaques inside, mementos of a rich and glorious past. During the research phase of his interview process, he'd learned that the school had been resting on its laurels.

1

Today a high school needed more than a proud athletic tradition to make the grade.

As Stoker had told his mentor in Knoxville, upon resigning, "There's a time in life to make changes, to conquer new horizons. I want to go where I'm needed, to be a catalyst."

Finally, Stoker pulled into the principal's parking space in front of the main building, the architectural oasis in the neighborhood. Its Ionic columns and solid copper trim spoke of better times, but today these sturdy, classical features bolstered the new principal into feeling he had made the right choice.

His heart swelled with anticipation when he strode into the building, his eyes taking in the cleanliness of the interior. While the President of the United States could drop in for a visit at any time and be impressed with the shine and polish, the order, those were merely cosmetic. Stoker intended to delve into the real substance.

Yes, the mostly African-American student body and the mostly Caucasian faculty displayed remarkable mutual respect. Yes, the school ran with the precision of a fine old clock. The people in charge of this school, the teachers and leaders, were intelligent. They cared about the students. But caring wasn't enough.

The accountability movement had blasted through traditional school success indicators everywhere. Unfortunately, the Abraham Lincoln High School Warriors, while well-loved in the classrooms and on the playing fields, had failed to meet academic competencies. When the school's last principal retired, the Board of Education had searched for a maverick, someone who would revolutionize teaching and learning. Who cared about whether everyone was happy? What the school needed was better numbers, more research-based strategies. What the school needed was R.J. Stoker.

* * *

An hour earlier, as Rebekah Stoker had rolled the lint-catcher over her husband's best charcoal wool-worsted suit for the third time that morning, she'd said in a sing-song voice, "You are going to be the best principal Lincoln High School has ever had." She sniffed the wood-and-spice of his after-shave. "Mmm—you smell great, too."

"What have I told you about talking in superlatives? You'll set me up to fail if you're not careful." Stoker re-tucked his shirt and adjusted the waistline of his trousers. The exercise program he'd followed all summer had worked wonders.

Rebekah set the lint-catcher down on the dresser and put her hand on a hip. "I can't help it if it's the truth, R.J. You're the best school-turner-arounder ever. Lincoln won't know what's hit it. Anyway, that speech you've been practicing is really something."

"Well," R.J. replied, the word rolling around in his mouth and coming out tinged with a Tennessee drawl. "Yes, I've had successes, but remember, this is my first inner city school. This could be a whole different ball game." He threaded a silver cuff link through the holes in his shirt and locked it in place. He glanced at the RJS monogram on the top of his cuff, embroidered pale gray on white.

"Don't tell me you're having second thoughts. I hope I didn't give up that nice big house and garden and all our friends in Knoxville for nothin'."

R.J. examined his face in the mirror. This was a warrior ready for battle. "No, no second thoughts. After all the books and articles and training, this is where I'm supposed to be." He knotted his striped silk tie, chosen to represent the school colors, purple and gold.

Satisfied with the way he looked on this first day of school, he kissed his wife, grabbed his briefcase, and left for work. He couldn't wait to dig in.

Chapter One

SALLY'S FIRST OFFICIAL DAY OF school as an administrator failed to live up to the hype. In her old kickboxing days, she would have called it a nine-pointer, an honorable loss.

First off, she had planned to get to school early. While she was getting ready, her bichon puppy, Archie, brought her a back-to-school gift—a nest of smelly, wiggly baby moles, whining for their mother. She returned the nest to nature and cleaned up the mess, but then had to rush to do her hair, burning it with the curling iron.

When her husband Ron popped in after his morning run to wish her luck, she'd turned her just-lipsticked mouth toward his for a kiss. "I guess I'm a little jittery. You should see the mess Archie made, and I'm late on top of everything." She paused to examine her face in the mirror. "At least I'm not new to Lincoln, like Mr. Stoker. I can't imagine how he must feel."

"Place like Lincoln with so many traditions, and that strong teacher's union, I bet he'll be looking to you for guidance and support."

Butterflies did a break dance in her stomach. "I never thought of it that way. Do you suppose that's why he hired me? I thought he liked my ideas for improving students' self-esteem."

Ron put his hands on his wife's shoulders. "You're probably the best assistant principal the school ever had, but the fact that you came from a leadership position in the union—that probably didn't hurt."

"I still think it was gutsy of him to hire me over the Black candidate." Sally sprayed each side of her neck with Obsession cologne and hugged her husband, careful not to mess up her makeup. "I'll work twice as hard to prove myself."

4

Ron followed his wife into the kitchen, where she grabbed her briefcase and a bottle of water. "You'll be great. You are exactly the right person for the job, and you know it. No one cares about the kids' learning more than you."

Sally stood on tiptoes to kiss him goodbye. "It'll take more than caring. To do this job right, I'll need a strong constitution, a helluva lot of fortitude, and a bucket load of luck."

* * *

By noon, Sally had given an opening day speech to 200 faculty members in the auditorium, outlining procedures for class lists, taking attendance, and reporting enrollment information to her office. Over the past eighteen years, she had sat through seemingly hundreds of these dry, dull speeches, so she'd tried to spice hers up with a light rhyming poem:

> Nobody doesn't love school's first day.
> The welcoming game we all will play.
> Turn class lists into seating charts.
> New students will enter all our hearts.
> In all reports, accuracy counts.
> As you complete them, efficiency mounts.
> Thanks for submitting your lesson plans.
> With professionalism, our kids are in good hands.

Okay, so she wasn't a great poet, and her efforts at originality and collegiality had fallen flat. A few polite applauders populated the audience, probably the last of Sally's teaching friends. She'd been warned that once her friends realized she couldn't do them favors or share hush-hush gossip with them, they would abandon her. At least she'd tried.

The worst part of the day, however, came right after her speech. Mr. Stoker introduced himself to the faculty and rolled out his agenda for improving the school. If he had consulted her, or anyone else on the staff ahead of time, he would have known how badly his plans would be received. Sally cringed with every, "We're going to…" This faculty enjoyed participating in decision-making. They hated being told what to do.

No sooner had Mr. Stoker delivered the ending words than Mr. Gottschalk, the calculus teacher, jumped up and waved his hands to speak. "With all due respect, I think you need to understand all the problems we face before you tell us what to do. We've got lots of challenges here—poverty, underachievement, misbehavior, lack of parental support, to name a few. You need to learn the ropes before you go changing things."

When Gottschalk finished talking, he drew more applause than she had with her not-so-clever poem. Appalled by the sheer audacity of this clear challenge to Stoker's authority, Sally looked to see how Stoker was taking it. She had to hand it to him. A smile played on his lips, a lion contemplating his prey, as he replied to the teacher with a swift, strong message.

"Let's be clear as we welcome back students tomorrow morning. This is a new day at Lincoln High School. I've done my homework here. You can be part of the problem or part of the solution. *We* will be strategic, well-prepared, and innovative. And *we* will also be kind. That is how *we* will, together, make a difference in the lives of *our* students."

* * *

Stoker may have rebounded, but the meeting had punched a gaping hole in Sally's self-concept as a Lincoln faculty member. Like a captured butterfly, she felt her whole world shifting, her loyalties flapping in the net. Mr. Stoker had chosen her as his assistant, and she owed him her support. Somehow, in being freed from the classroom, she had become captive to the administrative agenda.

After the meeting, everyone was given time to work in their classrooms, something Sally had always enjoyed in years past. This year, though, her time was not her own. A line of teachers formed at her door, waiting turns to complain about their schedules. And many of them hadn't paid attention to Mr. Stoker's instructions to be kind.

The afternoon brought a massive headache, and Sally had to conjure up some new friends: aspirin, endurance, and resilience.

Once the teachers had gone home, and the halls were quiet, Sally retreated to her office to decompress. She flopped into the rolling executive chair, took off her heels, rubbed her feet, and opened a bottle of water. Had she eaten anything since the granola bar she'd grabbed on her way out of the house this morning? She didn't think so. She dug into her purse for a package of peanut butter crackers saved for occasions like these.

As she munched on the snack, she considered how the day had fallen below her expectations. Having taught at Abraham Lincoln High School for so many years, she thought she knew all of the ins and outs of the student body, the faculty, the administration, and the community, but, judging by today's experiences, she had a lot more to learn. This job was way more than she'd bargained for.

Chapter Two

TYRONE NESBITT PEERED INTO THE mini-mirror in his locker, making sure his fresh haircut still looked good. Captain and quarterback of the Lincoln football team, he had about as much prestige as a student could get in this school, and he wanted to *maintain*. He'd always liked the first day of school. No homework, no grades, no eligibility worries yet. This year he planned to stay focused. There were seventeen colleges looking at him, so far.

"Hey, Tyrone." The unmistakable voice purred from behind.

"Oh, hi Shayla, what's up?" Tyrone closed the locker and flipped the combination lock, then turned around to hug his current lady love.

"Do you have practice today, or can you come over after school?"

The words and Shayla's sultry tone of voice conjured a pleasing image of afternoons spent in Shayla's bedroom while Mrs. Davis was still at work. Tyrone shook his shoulders and stood up straight. He knew for damned sure that afternoons at Shayla's would not get him into a Big Ten school. Besides, Shayla's twin brother, a local gang leader, had walked in on them a couple of times, and that dude was beyond scary.

The bell for homeroom intervened, as if timed to perfection. Tyrone put his arm around Shayla's waist and led her toward the classrooms. "Sorry, Baby. Football comes first; you know that."

* * *

The first day of school was usually fun for Assistant Principal Walter Welburton. His grip on Lincoln's discipline policies was tighter than a parachutist's hold on his ripcord. Good discipline was what made Lincoln a great school. These kids today needed to learn boundaries and self-control even more than they needed academics. Apparently they weren't getting much discipline at home, so the school needed to fill in the gaps before the real world swallowed them up.

Wally had spent twenty-two years as the right hand of the last principal. Really did the guy's job, truth be told. Last year when Mr. Morgan had announced his retirement, everyone thought for sure it would be Wally's turn. He went through the motions, updating his resume, applying for the job, and interviewing. He had been far and away the most popular candidate with all of the interview groups: teachers, parents, and other administrators. How was it, then, that he had lost the job to that outsider, R.J. Stoker?

Well, whatever. He was still in charge of discipline, and he knew he had the full support of the faculty, which was something Stoker would never have. And without that, he wouldn't accomplish a thing. Wally leaned back in his chair and played with the end of his tie. *One thing's for sure,* he thought to himself, *I'm not carrying another principal on my back. This time I'm out for one guy only, me.*

* * *

First day of school, and calculus teacher Ben Gottschalk was already muttering to himself. The quality of students just kept going down, down, down. This bunch had the lowest test scores he had ever seen, and their behavior was going to be terrible, too. He just knew it.

When he'd turned his back on his first class to write some formulas on the board, he could hear someone whisper, "What the f---?" He simply was not going to tolerate foul language, even if the offender was captain of the Lincoln football team. He would not lower his standards, no matter what new ideas this Principal Stoker had.

After the students left, instead of relaxing, he kept rehashing his worries. *I tried to tell our new principal at yesterday's faculty meeting, but, no, he wouldn't listen to me. I'm one of the finest teachers in the school, and*

I teach the best of the best. Well, I used to teach only gifted students, but these days, I might have just anyone in my classes. If the cut-off scores keep sliding down, I might as well be teaching calculus to my dog.

A soft rapping at the door interrupted Ben's ruminations. President of the Faculty Association, Norma Dunn, said, "Looks like we have the same planning period. May I come in?"

"Sure," Ben said. "Have a seat." He perched on the corner of his own massive desk. A visit from the attractive school leader was highly out of the ordinary. His comments to Stoker yesterday must have touched a bigger nerve than he'd realized.

Norma sat in a student desk, crossed her shapely legs, and opened a small leather-bound notebook. Ben's experience with her had been minimal, but he'd heard rumors about her, ranging from *tough cookie* to *veritable lunatic* to *faculty siren*. "I hope you don't mind my coming to you like this. I just want to ask you a few questions."

"What for?" Ben replied. "Am I in trouble?"

"No, not at all. It's about your comments at yesterday's meeting."

"I knew it. I should've kept my mouth shut. It's just that Stoker seemed so sure of himself, talking about all of the changes in curriculum and instruction he was bringing. It's obvious the guy hasn't got a clue about the way things are here." Gottschalk began to pace.

"You're not in any trouble, Ben. The faculty association just wants to make sure it stays that way." She patted her shiny hair and uncrossed her legs, leaning forward. "I wondered what made you speak out, though. Was there something in particular that Stoker said that bothered you?"

Ben stroked his goatee. "I didn't like any of it, his looks, his arrogance. Everyone knows Wally Welburton should have gotten that job."

"Easy, Ben. That kind of talk is going to get you nowhere, and it probably will label you as a racist."

"A racist? You've got to be kidding me. If I were a racist, why would I work in a place like this?" Ben's face and neck were the color of eggplant. "Look, Norma. We've got problems here, problems with *kids*. Stoker's coming in and trying to change *us*, the *teachers*, instead of the *kids*. I just couldn't hold in my disgust."

10

"The faculty association understands how you feel. We are watching Stoker very closely, too, and we will stand behind our good teachers one hundred percent."

"Well, that's a relief."

"Of course we will. But remember, we are a group of professionals. And professionals need to behave professionally."

"Are you saying it's unprofessional to speak my mind at a faculty meeting?" He twirled the Stanford ring around on his finger. "Stoker comes in here talking about some podunk school in Pennsylvania that was turned around by that mastery learning program. It wasn't even his school, and anyway, who cares? We have bigger problems that need solving. Student attendance, student discipline, bad parenting. Someone has to tell this guy."

Norma made a few notes and looked up at her colleague. "Your point is well-taken, but I'm afraid you've placed a target on your back. From now on, let the faculty association do the talking for you." She closed her notebook and stood, smoothing out the wrinkles in her tight skirt.

"And something else," Ben said, his voice an octave higher. "I'm not a racist. I'm sick of everyone thinking a white teacher is a racist if he disagrees with something a Black administrator says. It's not about race; it's about ideas—intelligence, following the rules. Maybe you don't see it, because you're Black. Except—" He held out his tanned forearm next to Norma's, "I'll be damned if your skin is any darker than mine."

Norma turned on her heel to leave. "Just remember what I said. The faculty association supports its teachers, but you have to chill, Mr. Gottschalk. You have to behave like a professional."

Chapter Three

THROUGHOUT THE SCHOOL DAY, R.J. Stoker pursued a single agenda: he made himself accessible. He walked the halls during passing periods, stopping to speak to teachers and students. He visited the cafeteria for all four lunch periods, listening to students as they reviewed schedules and classes with their peers. He even sat in on a few classes, trying to get a sense of Lincoln's *modus operandi*.

When parents and community members came to the office, the secretary had been instructed to ask them to please come back at four p.m. after student dismissal. Mr. Stoker would be observing classes in the building until then. He wanted to show everyone that he was not the kind of principal who sat in his office and issued policies and procedures. He was not Mr. Morgan, and this was not business as usual.

During the lunch periods, he noticed Mr. Welburton and the faculty members on duty, hovering over the students as they ate. Just the first day of school, and already he could sense the tension. He nodded at the faculty members as he passed by, but he made it a point to engage in conversation with several students. One of them was Tyrone Nesbitt, who was surrounded by friends, both male and female. Stoker walked over to the table and introduced himself, shaking hands as if running for office.

* * *

Welburton snickered when he saw his new boss cozying up to the students. *Making friends with the inmates already? Whatever he's up to, it's just going to come back to bite him on the butt.*

"What do you suppose he's doing over there?" Gottschalk, the calculus teacher, asked, having finished monitoring the cafeteria line and moving to his post near the doorway.

"Looks like he's introducing himself to the students," Welburton replied. He wasn't going to start bad-mouthing the new principal. In fact, he shouldn't be seen talking to this guy either, after he'd harangued Stoker at the faculty meeting on Monday.

"I wish you had gotten the job, Wally. You deserved it after all you've done to keep order at Lincoln High."

Welburton looked around, wishing he could run from the man who, he assumed, only meant well. More than anything, he hated to be pitied. "Yeah, well, thanks, man. We'd better watch the doors now. Bell's about to ring."

Not for the first time, Welburton felt worried. Not only did he sense a wind change coming in the way Stoker approached administration, but he also wondered whether Stoker would be looking for a way to replace him with someone who wouldn't be a constant reminder of the "old regime." Now, it seemed, being liked by the faculty could be a detriment.

* * *

"Oh, shoot," Sally Pearce exclaimed, having snagged her pantyhose on the corner of an open desk drawer. "Another run." The day was almost over, and she hadn't even had time for lunch.

One of her primary job functions was to take care of the master schedule, and that provided her with constant complaints from teachers on the first day of school. "Why do I have so many students in my homeroom?" "I don't like having a first period plan." "The students you gave me aren't qualified to be in this class."

When Sally was a teacher, she never in a million years would have complained like this about her schedule. She was always grateful to have a job, eager to do her best to make a difference in her students' lives. Having no children of her own, she threw herself into her work as a teacher. Maybe it wasn't such a smart move to go into administration. At least in the classroom, she could be the boss.

Sally remembered the saying from administration classes: the higher you go in the chain of command, the lonelier you are. Long-time friends of Sally's were now expecting preferential treatment or inside information from her. In taking this job, she had flipped a switch. Once her friends saw that she couldn't grant favors, she would feel the isolation.

On top of that, Sally was worried. It seemed all of the faculty members were predisposed to not accept Mr. Stoker. When they complained about their schedules, they also dropped little remarks about him, fishing for a reaction from their former colleague. It concerned her that Mr. Stoker appeared to be off to a bad start with the faculty. The way he'd responded to Ben Gottschalk's comments at the faculty meeting seemed like a declaration of war. Maybe he wasn't used to dealing with such a strong faculty association in Tennessee. Here, the teachers had a fifty-three-page professional negotiations agreement, and there were a jillion ways he could violate it.

Sally walked over behind the file cabinet where no one passing by the office could see her. She removed her pantyhose and threw them in the trash can. Then she dug into her handbag for a peanut butter granola bar that she kept for emergencies. She took a bite and chewed while she opened a bottle of water on her desk.

Before she could sit down, Mr. Stoker approached. She motioned for him to come in and have a seat.

"How was your first day of administration?" he asked.

"Busy," she replied. She pointed to the granola bar. "Too busy to stop for lunch. I have another one if you'd like it."

"Thanks, but I just ate my sandwich a few minutes ago. Once things settle down a bit, we shouldn't have to skip lunch." He leaned forward. "How did the schedule work out? Any problems?"

"Ha. Not unless you consider a couple of dozen complaints from teachers who wanted me to cater to their personal agendas. Ms. Williams even called me a racist because her class loads were four students heavier than those of her white colleague next door."

"That's smoke."

"Pardon?"

"Don't engage in conversation with a Black teacher who calls you a racist. She was just blowing smoke, trying to get you upset, trying to put you in an indefensible position. Don't fall for it."

"So how should I have responded?"

"Just ignore her. Or tell her you won't dignify that statement with a response. You're going to have run-ins with teachers who try to use race to cover up their own inadequacies. Let them know you see right through it, and ignore the comments."

"Is that what you were doing when Ben Gottschalk harangued you at the faculty meeting?"

"To a certain degree, yes. I anticipate the faculty will challenge me, especially until they get to know me and know what I expect. That happens whenever there's new leadership. My style is very different from Mr. Morgan's. But that guy, Gottschalk—he was really rude, and I had to put him in his place."

"Sort of like a renegade student on the first day of class?" Sally smiled at the comparison, but she was thinking about martial arts. Many times her opponents had seemed menacing, only to cave under her strong mental and physical preparedness.

"Exactly. You have to show the faculty they can't come at you any old way. If you tolerate it from the first guy, you'll have nothing but misery." He leaned back and crossed one leg over the other. "I'm going to be asking for a lot of changes in the next few years, and I expect resistance, but I'm strong enough to withstand it to get us where we need to be."

Tiny drops of moisture dotted Sally's forehead. She loved the school just the way it was, but her loyalty would have to be to this new leader, the one who wanted to change it all. "Well," she said, "I'll be here to help you."

"I know that, Sally. That's why I picked you."

Chapter Four

THE HEAD FOOTBALL COACH, ROY Donovan, former quarterback at Lincoln in the days when the school was mostly white, lay face-down on the 50-yard line, pounding the grass and shouting. Real tears dotted his cheek, and his voice sounded like a bleating goat. "I'm crying, sweating, bleeding on this field. I'm giving you guys all I've got to give. Why? Because you have potential. You have smarts. You have energy. Most of all, you have the purple and gold winning tradition inside your hearts."

Tyrone elbowed his buddy DeWayne. He couldn't believe the coach was doing all this. The first game was in two days, but it was no sweat. In fact, Lincoln was predicted to win it all this season. So why all the drama? Everyone loved Coach D., but this was too much.

Donovan continued, rolling over and propping himself up on his elbows. He ignored the blade of grass stuck in his mustache. "Every last one of you has got what it takes to be a winner, to get a free ride to college, to leave this neighborhood for a better life. I don't want to see you waste it."

A murmur went through the line of players like a brisk wind brushing tall reeds. Tyrone extended an arm to the Coach. "C'mon Coach. Get up off that ground. We ain't gonna waste it. We ain't gonna let you down either. We'll be the best team you ever coached in your life." He looked at his teammates. A chorus of affirmative shouts peppered the air.

Now standing, Donovan brushed off his pants and made eye

contact. "That's what I want to hear, team. But there's something else you need to know."

A worry line formed between Tyrone's eyebrows.

"You all know we have a new principal, Mr. Stoker, right?"

"Yeah, what about him?"

"Well, he wants to see all of you be successful, too."

"What's wrong with that?"

"In the classroom, as well as on the field. He's going to be a stickler for making sure you stay eligible. No grades, no play. No exceptions."

A collective groan rose from the field as this news sank in. It was always difficult to balance athletics and academics. There wasn't a player on the team that hadn't had grade problems in the past, Tyrone included.

Donovan went on. "So I need you to push even harder this season. Give it your all, on the field *and* in the classroom. We can't afford to have any of you taken off this team for ineligibility."

Tyrone thought of his calculus class, the formulas on the board that could have been written in Mandarin Chinese, for all he understood them. First day of school, and he already had fifty problems for homework. The security of being sought after by seventeen colleges began to fade with the reality of the challenges ahead. At this rate, he would have to put thoughts of Shayla into the deep freeze till after football season.

* * *

Originally from New York, Derrick Johnson had a reputation at Lincoln, having taught social studies for eight years there. Tall and slim, he wore horn-rimmed glasses, a three-piece suit, and a close-cropped haircut. Except for being Black, one might mistake him for Indiana Jones in the college classroom.

Mr. Stoker was unfamiliar with Mr. Johnson's reputation as a stern taskmaster, but every time Stoker passed room B201, he saw Mr. Johnson standing at the front of the room, lecturing as if his life depended on it. The economics students, all seniors who needed the credit to graduate, seemed to be sleeping with their eyes open. Stoker shook his head, making a mental note to stop by often. Lecturing in this modern day was not going to cut it, especially in a school with low performance indicators.

Before he could pass the classroom, Mr. Johnson caught sight of him and rushed into the hallway. "Excuse me, Mr. Stoker. I wonder if you could help me. The class next door is making so much noise I can't teach my class."

"Really?" Stoker replied. "I hadn't noticed any excessive noise."

"Yes, students are talking constantly, and it disrupts the learning environment for my classes. Miss Singer is a new teacher, so I don't want to make waves, but—"

"I'll look into it," Stoker promised, still straining to hear the disruptive sounds. He walked toward the next room, pondering the statement about being new and making waves. *I'm new here, and that's exactly what I intend to do, make waves, lots and lots of waves.*

* * *

In Room B203, students were clustered into groups of four, and they were deeply engrossed in activity. At first, Stoker couldn't locate the teacher, because she was neither at the front nor the back of the room. She was sitting on her haunches next to a group of students, listening. Ms. Singer, too, had a reputation, though she was a new hire. She was young, gifted, and white.

When one of the students pointed at Mr. Stoker, Melody Singer went to greet him. "Good morning, Mr. Stoker. Welcome to our American history investigation."

"Glad to see you are using cooperative learning so early in the semester. How is it working out?"

"The students are really involved. They are supposed to come up with three higher level questions that modern day prosecutors would ask the perpetrators of the Salem witch trials."

"Sounds like an interesting assignment."

"Some of my colleagues," and Melody's eyes rolled toward Mr. Johnson's classroom, "think I'm crazy to use cooperative learning this early in the school year, but my students are juniors, and they're able to handle it."

"Obviously. The students are talking, but they are talking in an orderly fashion. Just be sure they don't become too rowdy."

"Yes, sir. That's my job—to be the guide on the side, not the sage on the stage."

"I'll let you get back to it," Mr. Stoker said. "Guide on."

Chapter Five

IF WALLY WELBURTON HAD ONE weakness, it was a love for ladies, ladies of all ages, sizes, shapes, colors, and persuasions. Being a school administrator for so many years, he had been treated to a constant parade of beautiful, attractive, and interesting specimens. He had enjoyed the view, occasionally flirting a bit, and even had a fascination or two along the way. But he had never succumbed to temptation to take it any further.

Wally was, after all, married, a family man, a churchgoer and pillar of the community. Not only that, but he was, as a school administrator, held to a higher standard of behavior than most. Any lapse in judgment, any shadow of impropriety, might taint his record, cost him his job, and even cause him to lose his license. No, there was too much at stake.

Under Mr. Morgan's principalship, Welburton had been given free rein to make decisions in managing the school. He was Mel Gibson to Morgan's Danny Glover. Since discipline was the pillar upon which their administration was cemented, and Welburton was Mr. Discipline, he had become used to the solid block of support and prestige he commanded at Lincoln High. Abraham Lincoln, himself, could not have been respected more.

This morning, as he sat alone in his office, sipping bitter coffee, he felt pangs of insecurity, the likes of which he had not felt in decades. He glanced around the room at the framed photos of himself, surrounded by Lincoln faculty, students, and other administrators. His eyes were drawn to the one with Mr. Morgan and Sally Pearce, taken at the Library Book Fair last year. Sally was making eye contact with him, as if he were the Crown Prince. He decided to give her a call.

"Hey, Sally. How're things going at your end of the building?" He leaned back in his chair and played with the end of his tie.

"Pretty busy here with schedule changes and lines of late-enrollees. It's going to be a neat trick putting twenty-seven hundred kids into twenty-five hundred seats without creating class overloads. Tell me again why I coveted this job for years." She gave a short laugh.

"You just wanted to be like me when you grew up." Welburton sipped his coffee.

"Maybe so. I do appreciate having this chance. As complicated as it is, there is something satisfying about creating and implementing a working schedule."

"I'll check with you in twenty-two years to see if you feel the same way."

"Is that how long you've been at it, Wally? And you're not burned out yet? I have new respect for you."

"Yeah, always the bridesmaid, never the bride. You know how that goes." The coffee's acid burned in his throat.

"I'm sorry for bringing it up. It must still chafe."

"No, I'm okay. Listen, how about lunch today after the student lunch periods?"

"Can't. There's a line of enrollments waiting to see me. Rain check."

Welburton hung up the phone and rummaged in his desk drawer for an antacid. He picked two cherry-flavored tablets and popped them in his mouth. He closed the drawer with a slam. Time for putting on a game face and doing lunch duty. He did a quick calculation; he had done 16,644 lunch duties.

* * *

While the students ate lunch under the supervision of assigned faculty, many of the teachers ate in the adjoining faculty cafeteria. The food was the same, and, just like the students, the faculty had separated into lunchtime cliques. With a few exceptions, the tables were segregated by race.

21

Norma Dunn was one of the exceptions. Light-skinned to the point of paleness, her full mouth and rounded nostrils worked together to make an attractive face, and her figure was slim, but curvy in all the right spots. President of the Faculty Association for the past year, she was all-business every moment that she was not in her classroom, and sometimes even then. Still, she enjoyed a reputation for being rather kooky.

Now she sat enthroned at the lunch table with two counselors and two department chairs, gossiping about the administrators. "What do the counselors think about Mr. Stoker so far?" Norma asked.

John Manning jumped to reply, *sotto voce*. "He's certainly shaking things up, letting so many late enrollees enter. Doesn't he realize these are not the kids who are going to bring good test scores in? Frankly I've seen several come in without proper documentation, just his signature."

Norma's ears tingled. "Do we have room in classes for these late enrollees? I thought we had no room at the inn."

"Have you ever heard of overloads?" John replied. "Sally's trying like crazy to keep classes at their contractual size limits, but this guy is the damn Statue of Liberty, 'Give me your tired, your poor—'"

"The teachers' negotiated agreement requires all overloads to be resolved by the end of this week. You'd better remind Sally of that, this being her first time to do the schedule. I would hate to file a grievance on her the first week of her administrative career, but of course, I will if it comes to that."

"It's really not her fault. Stoker's got this idea that the school's unfairly excluded people from enrolling. I've heard him in the enrollment office saying, 'We'll waive this requirement, and this one, and this one.' Pretty soon we won't have any requirements at all, and we'll have so many students, they'll be conducting classes on the football field."

"What could possibly be his motivation for that?" Norma wondered aloud. "It's not like he's being paid by the student."

"Who knows. All I know is I'm making schedules as fast as I can, and I'm running out of seats to put the kids in."

"Do me a favor, John. Remind Sally that Friday is the deadline for eliminating overloads. She'd better rein in our illustrious principal or hire more teachers, or else."

* * *

One of Shayla Davis's classes was office education. It was a double period with half spent in the classroom and half spent working in a school office. When she found out she would be placed in Mrs. Pearce's office, she was ecstatic. She had had Mrs. Pearce as an English teacher sophomore year. It might have been her favorite class in all four years. *That teacher had a way with students—she made me want to do my best. Too bad she's leaving the classroom to be an administrator.*

When Shayla entered the assistant principal's office, she was greeted with a melodious, "Shayla, I'm so happy to see you." Mrs. Pearce held her arms open for a hug. "I can't think of anyone I would rather have as an office aide."

Shayla showed a dazzling smile. "I'm happy, too. It's my lucky day."

"What have you been up to?" Mrs. Pearce asked. "Hey, whose senior ring is that around your neck, missy?"

"Tyrone Nesbitt. Remember him from sophomore year?"

"The captain of the football team? I sure do. You two make a darling couple, but I hope you aren't too serious. College first."

"Yes, ma'am." Shayla slid the ring back and forth on the chain, wondering whether college would really be in her future.

Chapter Six

ON THE THIRD DAY OF school, Wally Welburton arrived early, as was his custom, and parked in his assigned parking place. His was usually the first car in the parking lot, but that day there was a new green Pontiac sitting in the coaches' row, motor running, with a guy huddled over the steering wheel.

Wally turned off his engine, locked his car, and ambled over toward the other car. As he approached, he recognized the head football coach, Roy Donovan, puffing on a cigarette. Wally rapped on the window and motioned for Donovan to roll it down. When he did, the strong scent of tobacco assailed his nose. "New car, Coach? You're here early."

"I found this note on my windshield last night after football practice. Nothing like this has ever happened to me in all my years at Lincoln." Donovan's hands shook as he handed over a wrinkled piece of notebook paper.

Wally set his briefcase down on the pavement between his legs and held the paper up with both hands. On it was a smudged message printed in pencil:

BLACK DEVILS HATE HONKY COACHES. STOP COACHING, OR DIE!!!

"Oh, no," Wally said, placing a hand on the coach's elbow. "Roy, this is the work of kids trying to scare you. It may not even be Black Devils, just wannabes. We'll find out who did it and we'll expel them."

Donovan stubbed out his cigarette and cut off the motor.

"Come to my office, and let's write up an incident report. Don't worry. We'll get these guys."

Donovan climbed out of the car. He stared at Wally with the intensity of a quarterback looking for a pass receiver. "How can you be sure of that? You know coaching is my life. I love it with all my heart. But I can't risk my family, my security, my existence. I didn't sleep all night."

Wally put his arm around the larger man in a gesture meant to be comforting, but feeling awkward. "Let me handle this, Roy. I'll get right on it, and hopefully we'll have a solution before practice this afternoon."

"I just don't get it. I've worked with Black players all my life, and I've never had any of them call me a honky, at least not to my face. Most of my players are like sons to me. Why would any of them want me dead?"

"Chances are this note has nothing to do with your players. Probably just some kids trying to act like badasses to impress their friends."

"Well, I can't just ignore it." The coach spit on the ground, as if to punctuate his thought.

"Nor should you. You were right to bring it to me. I'll take care of it. I promise." As Wally unlocked his office door and ushered Donovan in, he wondered whether this was a promise he could keep.

* * *

Tyrone stormed out of his economics class. Mr. Johnson was getting on his last nerve. All he did was talk and test, talk and test. It was the third day of school, and he'd already failed three tests. And economics was required for graduation. School was giving him a headache already, and his next class was calculus with "Mr. Stanford," Gottschalk. Another poor grade would come from that class, and he would not make eligibility for the big game against Madison next Friday.

As he reached his locker, he saw Shayla standing near the staircase, apparently looking for him. "Hey, Baby," he called.

She walked toward him wearing a smile that didn't reach her eyes.

25

"I was hoping to see you before second period," she said.

"Whassup?" He put his arm around her shoulders and leaned his face into hers. She smelled like that rosewater cologne on her dresser.

"Is there any way you could skip football practice this afternoon?"

He pulled back, dropping his arm. "Skip practice? I don't think so. Why?"

"We need to talk, and no one's gonna be home at my house this afternoon." A tinge of seriousness colored her words, and Tyrone suppressed the impulse to run away.

"Honey, you know Coach is very strict about not missing practices. Besides, I think we should find another place to be together. Your house freaks me out."

She grabbed his arm. "You don't need to worry about my brother. He won't rat us out."

"I'm not so much worried about him telling on us as I am afraid of *him*. He made it pretty clear last time that he was going to beat my butt if I ever showed up there again." He glanced at his watch—only one minute left to get to calculus. "Anyway, what do we need to talk about?"

"No time now. Meet me here after sixth." She stood on tiptoes to brush her lips against his before heading for the stairs to go to class.

Tyrone touched his lips, wanting to hold onto the warmth of the kiss, but all he could think of was the image of Shayla's twin brother Claude, hiding outside of the bedroom doorway, the Black Devils tattoo exposed and shining on his right bicep.

* * *

Mr. Johnson's economics class was good for a nap, if nothing else. Claude Davis knew more about economics from the street than he could ever learn from books, anyway. *I wonder how the homey would react if he knew I had three K folded and hidden in my sock.*

Careful to keep his upper arms covered by his t-shirt, he huddled over his desk, trying to drown out the tiresome droning from the front of the room. He was tired, but sleep eluded him. He was too pumped from last night's activity in the 'hood. It had been the lieutenant's idea to target the Coach. It solved the problem of how to stir up the new recruits, showing them who was tops on this turf, but for Claude, personally, it provided a way to get back at his sister's boyfriend. *Who does he think he is, disrespecting my sister?* Tyrone and all of the dudes on the team worshipped Coach Donovan. What better way to destroy the team, derail the projected winning season, and ruin dreams of scholarships than to take Donovan out?

Chapter Seven

AFTER HE TOOK A WRITTEN statement from Coach Donovan, Welburton knew he needed to meet with Stoker. For many years, Wally had been able to manage discipline matters independently, knowing he had the backing of Principal Morgan. But this was a new day, and Mr. Stoker didn't seem like the kind of guy who would take his hand off the stove, even if it were burning hot.

Welburton's plan was to question potential witnesses and several students known to be Black Devils as soon as possible. He would hopefully get enough evidence to shut the case down before today's practice. He knew he couldn't send Donovan onto the football field without having resolved the matter, ultimately setting up an expulsion hearing. Depending on what he found, he might call in the police liaison and file criminal charges, as well. He slipped Donovan's statement onto his clipboard and dashed out of his office to find Stoker.

Bursting into the main office, Wally created an air vacuum that caused papers to fly and the secretary's pet bird to caw. "Is Stoker in?"

"You just missed him. He said he was going to Ms. Pearce's office."

Without further comment, Welburton about-faced and threw open the door, repeating the paper-blowing effect. He dashed down the hall and around the corner to the other assistant principal's office, where he threw open another door.

The secretary and registrar slapped their hands on their desks to hold down loose papers. Mr. Welburton's entrances and exits were all-too-familiar. Wally breezed past both of them and knocked on the closed door of the inner office.

Stoker moved the Venetian blinds enough to see that it was Welburton, and he opened the door. "Whatever it is, it looks important. You've got the expression of a race car driver in the final lap."

"Sorry to interrupt, boss, but this is time-sensitive, and I thought you'd better know immediately." He looked at Pearce, who was poring over the master schedule, a pencil behind her ear. She rubbed her forehead as if to stave off a headache.

"You can speak in front of Mrs. Pearce. We're a team." Stoker touched his cuff links as if to make sure they were still intact.

Welburton gripped the clipboard. "There's been a threat made to Coach Donovan, apparently gang-related." He flipped a page on the clipboard to reveal the actual note found on Donovan's Pontiac. "Donovan has a great reputation with the team, always has. Nothing like this has ever happened to him, so he's freaked out."

A scornful guffaw issued from Stoker's mouth. "You call this a threat? This looks juvenile to me. You don't even know if it was our kids who did it. Or real gang members. It could just be some kids, wanting to see how the coach would react. If he shows his fear, he'll give them what they want."

"With all due respect, sir, even if it was a youthful prank, the note constitutes a threat, and as such, the perpetrators should be punished. We can't have our faculty threatened. It's hard enough getting good teachers."

"How would you suggest we handle it, then?"

"I've got a written statement from Donovan." He showed the statement to Stoker and gave him a minute to peruse it. "I'm planning to investigate, call in some potential witnesses, gather some evidence. Hopefully we can get enough information to nail the perps before football practice this afternoon."

"Nail them?"

"Recommend expulsion, sir."

"Expulsion? Oh, naw, Welburton. Teach them a lesson, but don't deprive them of the one thing that will get them a better life. Besides, expulsions are a black eye against the school."

"So are threats against teachers. What if something actually happens to Donovan? He's known throughout the state, maybe the nation. It is our duty to protect him."

"Nothing's going to happen to Donovan. Go ahead and investigate. When you get something to go on, let me know. I'll be the one to decide how far we take the punishment. Fair enough?"

"If you say so, sir." Welburton made brief eye contact with Pearce and swallowed a bushel of air. "I'm going to start the investigation now."

He shut the door behind him a tad short of a slam, causing a whoosh that rattled the scheduling paperwork.

Stoker turned back to Pearce and said, "Just as I was saying to you about these overloads, we aren't here for the faculty. We are here to do what's right for the students."

Chapter Eight

BEN GOTTSCHALK WAS STILL NURSING his anger over being put in his place publicly on opening day. *Who does that behemoth think he is? Just because he's principal and I'm a lowly teacher. He should be asking us what the problems are, so we can tell him how it is here. Instead, he's coming in here like a charging bull, telling us about what research says.*

He flipped through the latest set of calculus tests, mostly Fs. He muttered to himself, "These kids are going nowhere. They're already so far behind, I don't see how any of them are going to catch up."

Just in time to overhear these musings, Welburton entered the room. "Better not let anybody else hear you say things like that, Ben. You're politically incorrect."

Gottschalk reddened and turned the stack of graded papers upside down on the desk. "At least it's you and not our new empty suit barging into my classroom. I still wish you were the principal. The whole faculty was behind you, you know."

"Ancient history, Ben. I'm here on different business. Do you have these football players in your next class?" He showed a list of four names to the math teacher.

"Sure do. None of them doing very well, grade-wise, either. What's up?"

"I want you to send them to me, one at a time. I'll meet with each one for about ten minutes. When I send one back, send me the next one on the list."

"I hate for them to miss class and fall further behind. What's this about?" Gottschalk felt a prickle of excitement. Maybe something

31

was happening that would bring that arrogant SOB Stoker down.

"I can't say. You know that. And I'd appreciate it if you wouldn't talk about this with anyone either."

"Okay, boss. Glad to do whatever I can for *you*." When Welburton left, Ben pulled out the test papers of the four students being called down. All Fs. *Whatever's going on in the discipline arena, you won't be playing football much longer anyway.* He shook his head, trying to erase the echo of Norma Dunn's warning about being professional.

* * *

Johnson, the economics teacher, paced outside of Sally Pearce's office. He refused to sit down. That felt subservient, and if there was one thing he hated, it was feeling subservient to anyone. He was a proud Black man.

He'd seen Welburton leave, followed by Stoker, and he couldn't imagine what was so friggin' important that she couldn't see him now. He looked at his watch again. In ten minutes his planning period would be over, and he would have to leave.

His thoughts scattered when he heard, then saw the door opening, and the lady's white face peering out at him. "Sorry to keep you waiting, Mr. Johnson. Please come right in." Her smile seemed genuine, but he knew better than to trust it.

He entered the office, but instead of sitting down, he continued to pace. "Mrs. Pe-ahce, I've come to ask just how many late-entering students you are going to stick me with. My classes are overflowing with students. Every desk is filled with a warm body, and yet I am still getting new students every day."

"Won't you sit down? I can explain about the overloads."

"You needn't explain, madam. You just need to remove them. Besides the fact that there are no seats, the newcomers are so far behind that they will never catch up. They will fail in a class that is required for graduation, and it will be all your fault."

"Mr. Johnson, sir, I sympathize with your situation, but—" Sally opened her enrollment reports and studied them.

"I don't need your sympathy, I just need you to address the

situation, and quickly."

"—this is a public school, and we are mandated to accept students, no matter how late they enroll."

"Well, give them to someone else. I tell you I won't have them." The teacher felt his patience draining. Did he really expect satisfaction from this inexperienced woman?

"All of the classes are full. We are doing the best we can to place students in classes equitably. And one more thing. While we are balancing the classes, I hope you don't say or do anything to make your students feel unwelcome. It's not their fault that the classes are full."

"Then hire more teachers. Do something. I believe the teachers' contract provides for resolution of overloads by this Friday, does it not?"

She bit her lip. "Yes, sir, it does."

"Then you have three days, or else."

Sally's eyebrows leaped to the top of her forehead. "I hope you don't intend that as a threat, Mr. Johnson. That would be very unprofessional, unethical, and illegal."

* * *

During the next passing period, Tyrone hustled to his locker, where Shayla usually awaited him. This time, just when he really needed to talk to her, she wasn't there. For the past fifteen minutes, he had sat in the assistant principal's office, answering questions. It hadn't taken much to figure out from the questions that someone, most likely a gang banger, had threatened Coach Donovan.

Until Tyrone joined the varsity team freshman year, he had never had a male role model in his life. Not that he had missed it. His grandmother, mother, and four aunties and their families had made his family cool. But when he came under the influence of Roy Donovan, he realized that men were different. Different things were expected of them in society. He had long stopped thinking that Donovan was white. When he grew up, he wanted to be just like Coach D.

Hell, everyone on the team felt the same way. There wasn't a single

Saralyn Richard

guy who didn't respect, even love him. There was no doubt they all owed their sense of team, motivation to win, and college prospects to Coach Donovan. So the fact that someone may have threatened him was intolerable.

When Mr. Welburton asked whether he knew any members of the Black Devils, Tyrone shuddered, thinking of Shayla's brother Claude. If Claude had had anything to do with harming the Coach, it would be hard for Tyrone not to take it personally. *It's no secret that Claude hates me for messing around with his sister, and the easiest way to get to me would be through Coach Donovan.*

And anyway, where was Shayla?

* * *

Shayla was in the bathroom. It seemed she had to go almost every hour between classes. She hated it, because her favorite part of school was meeting Tyrone at his locker. *I wonder if he's missing me right now.*

Last period while she was sorting enrollment forms for Mrs. Pearce, she saw her econ teacher, Mr. Johnson, exiting the office in a big huff. Afterwards, Mrs. Pearce looked pale and shaky. She hated it that someone who wasn't good at his job could have such a negative effect on someone who was.

And now, it was time to get to Mr. Johnson's class, herself, or he would have a very negative effect on *her*.

34

Chapter Nine

STOKER SAT LIKE A BUDDHA, absorbing the information Welburton was giving him about the threat on Coach Donovan. He had to admit, Welburton had done a fine job of smoking out the details, leaning on certain individuals who "owed" him from previous disciplinary scrapes, and he had conducted more than fifteen interviews in three hours' time.

"So," Welburton concluded, "we have enough to file expulsion papers on Claude Davis. His dean has quite a list of priors on him. We need to proceed right away. We'll make an example of him, and it will deter future gang activity in the school."

The Buddha, who had sat with his eyes half-closed during the summary, sat up straight and uttered a sound like a half-shout, half-cough. "Hucshh! We will do no such thing."

"What do you mean? This is standard operating procedure, Stoker. It's how our discipline policy works."

Stoker fiddled with a cuff link before asking, "Are you a person who does things right, or does the right thing?"

Wally did a double-take. "What are you talking about? What's the difference?"

Stoker gazed at the assistant principal with an eye well-practiced in assessing hearts and souls. He replied, "Sometimes it's okay to break the rules, if it means doing the right thing for a person."

"Doing the right thing for whom? The perpetrators of a crime?" Welburton's face exploded with red, and he bared his teeth. "How about doing the right thing for Coach Donovan? The dean? The football team? The school?"

35

"Coach Donovan is paid to be here. I hear he does a good job with the team, but he can leave and go anywhere he wants whenever he wants. Likewise, the dean. My responsibility is to ensure that the future of every Lincoln student is the best it can be, and expulsion is not in my vocabulary."

Welburton bowed his head, whether in prayer for composure or to assimilate this radical departure from the *status quo*, Stoker could not tell. After a period of silence, accompanied by heavy breathing, he responded. "It appears you want a kinder, gentler Lincoln High School. I understand that. Coming from Knoxville, you might have been successful with that approach to discipline, but this is an inner city school. You are dealing with gangsters and hard cases who have been trying for decades to get a foothold in this building. The only way we've been able to hold them at bay, to preserve an orderly learning environment, and to keep quality teachers, is to hold firm to our policies. If you give in on one case, the whole system will unravel."

Now it was Stoker's turn to flush, his face turning the shade of mahogany. "I don't give a damn about policies and systems. We are dealing with people, young people whose lives and livelihoods depend on our ability to make a difference in their future. If you focus on the policy, you lose the big picture."

"But, the faculty—"

"Don't talk to me about the faculty. They have their educations, their employability, their comfortable lives. We need to do everything we can to make sure the students are able to do as well."

"Do you have experience with gangs, Stoker? These guys are hardened criminals. They poison the learning environment. They even discourage parents from sending good students to the school. Allow them free rein, and you will see a mass exodus of our best students. How will the test scores be then?"

"Let me deal with the gangs. I'll do it my way, without expelling students for a lapse in judgment. Give me the paperwork, and I'll take care of the rest."

"What do I tell Donovan?"

"Tell Donovan we've identified the students who put the note on his car, and we will make sure they are taken care of so it doesn't happen again." Stoker stood and punched his desk with a fist. "Oh, and Welburton, you did a good job investigating."

* * *

Within the hour, Stoker had Claude Davis in his office, a matador facing a bull. Good-looking kid, but full of attitude. He'd probably witnessed a lot of heavy stuff in his young life to make him so defiant, to make him fall to the gangs.

"Mr. Davis," he began, attempting to start off by showing respect for the young man. "I have evidence here that links you to a note that was placed on Coach Donovan's automobile during practice yesterday."

"What evidence is that?" Claude mumbled. He was pulling on the loose threads on his pants leg.

"I have sworn statements from two witnesses, who shall remain nameless. To top it off, the Coach's car was parked near a surveillance camera. You couldn't have picked a worse spot to commit this act." Stoker watched the student's face to see if he bought the bluff.

Aside from enlarged pupils, Claude didn't react. "I don't know anything about it, man."

"Cut the crap, Davis," Stoker replied. "You did this, and you know it. We've got enough to nail you and put some of your friends at risk, too. What I want to know is why."

"Why what?" Claude crossed his arms.

"Why does a senior risk his education to do something this stupid? What were you trying to accomplish?"

"It was a prank, man. That's all, just a prank."

"Does this have something to do with Black Devils? Because let me tell you something, *Mister* Davis, my school is not gang turf." He stood, his full six feet four inches towering over the seated student. "This school is *my* turf. Do you understand? If you want to do gang stuff, stupid though it may be, do it away from the school or school grounds."

"Am I going to be expelled?" Claude asked, a hint of a whine in his tough-guy voice.

"According to the district policy you should be. Threatening a faculty member is not only a serious offense here on campus, but it is considered an assault in the real world. One phone call, and I could have you locked up for a long, long time."

Claude stared at his feet. Stoker followed his gaze and noticed bulges in both ankles. "And another thing, young man, if those are bankrolls in your socks, they won't do you a bit of good in getting out of this mess."

After a period of reflection, Claude finally made eye contact. "Okay, I've messed up, and I'm sorry. Where do we go from here?"

Stoker knew Claude's apology and apparent concession were likely insincere, and possibly manipulative, but he leaned in close to whisper in Claude's ear. "I'll make you a deal you can't refuse."

* * *

When Welburton told Coach Donovan he had identified the student who'd put the note on his car, the coach got down on one knee, hands clasped, and shouted, "Thank you, Jesus!"

Though Donovan was known for such grand gestures, the reaction made Welburton uncomfortable, because he knew what was coming next. Sure enough, the coach stood back up and clapped Welburton on the back as if he'd scored a touchdown, then asked, "When will the expulsion hearings be?"

After Wally explained that Principal Stoker was handling the "punishment phase," and that he didn't know what Stoker would do next, Donovan exploded. "You mean my life isn't worth anything to this school? Why isn't Stoker going for immediate expulsion? How am I supposed to keep going out there every day with this threat hanging over my head?"

Wally put his hand on Donovan's shoulder. "Listen, Roy. We've got the perp. He knows he's been caught. What I can do is give you two security guards to protect you and the team during practice for the next week or so. Hell, I'll even personally watch your car while you're in practice, make sure no one comes near it again."

"You'd do that for me?" Donovan asked in a mollified tone.

"Sure, buddy. We are in this together, for better or worse—just like a marriage."

* * *

The parking lot was shaded by the building in the late afternoon sun, providing Welburton some needed cover as he crouched behind the car parked adjacent to Donovan's Pontiac. He had been in this location for a good twenty minutes, shifting positions every five minutes or so to get comfortable. He really didn't think anyone was going to bother the car, especially just after Davis met with the principal, but a promise was a promise, and Wally's reputation with the faculty had been built on such promises, fulfilled.

The breeze kicked in as the sun moved further westward, and Welburton zipped up his jacket. Just then a rock scattered on the pavement nearby. He inched forward to get a view of Donovan's car, and sure enough, someone was approaching it, someone wearing a jacket, collar turned up, and a knit cap, pulled way down. Whoever it was moved fast, and before Welburton could react, he had placed a note under the windshield wiper blade of Donovan's car.

Welburton leaped into action, and the young figure jumped, then sprinted away. Welburton chased him, yelling, "Stop." His forty-nine years felt like a hundred as he gasped for air, but the hours spent in the Lincoln weight room several evenings a week helped. After a hundred yards, the fugitive tripped on a broken beer bottle and went down. Welburton covered his prey, out of air, but victorious.

When he could finally speak, the assistant principal screamed, "What the hell do you think you're doing, messing with a faculty member's car?" He recognized Claude Davis from their interaction earlier that day.

Claude jerked his wrist away from Welburton's claw-like grip. "You don't get it, man. Stoker told me to do it. Just ask him."

"Stoker told you to put another threat on Coach Donovan's car?"

"Nah, man. It's not a threat. Just ask Stoker. Please?"

"You're coming with me." Welburton stood and grabbed Claude by the elbow.

Claude shook his shoulders, but he walked alongside the assistant principal without a word of protest. When they returned to the parking lot, Welburton led the way to the Pontiac with the note under the windshield wiper. He removed the note and opened it up. This time it said:

Sorry for the last note, Coach. I didn't mean it, and I won't ever do it again.

Chapter Ten

WHEN SALLY PEARCE HAD DECIDED to leap from the teaching pond to the administrative ocean, it was with a vision of being able to do larger, more global work. Instead of having 135 students per semester, she would have 2700. The importance of her daily tasks would increase proportionately, or so she'd thought.

Now she was thirty-six hours ahead of the deadline for fixing overloads, and she would be working throughout the night trying to find or create seats for new students without disrupting the schedules of old students. She hadn't had two minutes to herself on any day since school had started. She woke up in the middle of the night every night, bathed in sweat, worried about some detail, and her husband Ron was losing patience.

"I thought this new position was going to be a promotion," he said the morning after a particularly fretful night. "Seems to me you had more authority when you were in the classroom."

"Ironic, isn't it?" Sally replied. "I've got teachers telling me what to do all the time now. The kids never did that." She picked up her puppy, Archie, and scratched the tight curls on his head.

"What does Stoker say about that? I assume you've discussed it with him."

"Oh, yeah. He's part of the problem, in a way. He says the schedule is solely for the benefit of the students, and our duty is to give them the best resources possible. That means ignoring the faculty agreement and all of the complaints."

"Can you do that?" Ron asked. "Aren't you bound by that agreement just like a contract?" He knew all about contracts and labor law. "Sally, warning bells are tolling in my brain."

"Yes, but I can't make him see that. In Tennessee, where he's come from, there aren't strong unions, and the teachers have almost no say in their teaching conditions. Here it is a different universe."

"So what'll happen if the overloads aren't fixed by Friday?"

"Grievances, hearings, possible financial remedies, who knows? Norma Dunn has been breathing down my neck for days, checking the numbers. It's funny—I sort of admired her when we were on the same side, but now she's the Wicked Witch of the West."

Ron's gray-green eyes met his wife's in a moment of clarity. "Honey, you've got to make Stoker understand how crucial this is. Starting his tenure at Lincoln High this way would be an utter disaster, for him and for you. If he won't listen to reason, maybe you should talk to the superintendent."

* * *

Rebekah Stoker had also had a fretful night's sleep. She dreamed that someone in disguise had come up to R.J. and her at the furniture store. The man was covered in a white sheet with only eyes and mouth exposed. He asked R.J. for a favor, and when R.J. told him no, he stabbed him in the heart. In the dream blood was everywhere, and she was running around trying to gather it up and put it back into her husband's chest.

She shot up out of the bed, crying, "No, no—it can't be!" She was gasping for air, and the bed coverings were strewn around her. R.J. got up on one elbow and wrapped the other arm around his wife's shoulders.

"What's wrong? Calm down. You must have had another bad dream. Do you want to tell me about it?" He glanced at the alarm clock, which read 5:32. "I guess we'd better get up and get going anyway."

Rebekah felt the horrific action of the dream slipping away from her waking consciousness, but she was left with the one scene of someone stabbing R.J. in the heart. Should she tell him? He was already looking at her as if she were a hysterical lunatic. No, she would take deep breaths and calm herself.

Stoker rolled over and threw his legs over the edge of the bed, finding his slippers with both feet. He rubbed his eyes, ears, and beard stubble on his way to the bathroom to get ready for work.

Rebekah got up as well, making the bed immediately. She straightened the lamp shade on her side of the bed, where she must have flung an arm during her violent dream. She was glad her younger daughter was away at college this year, or she would have had to face an inquisition at breakfast. She stepped into the dressing area where she caught sight of herself in the vanity mirror. Her hair was wild, and her complexion had an unusual pallor.

Stoker was shaving at the opposite sink, his face encircled by generous globs of white foam. "That must have been some nightmare you were having. Care to tell me about it?"

"I can only remember a fragment, something about your new school." Again she wondered whether she should be more specific. If she thought hard enough, she could probably recall more of the dream, but to what end? "Tell me, R.J., how are you getting along with the people at Lincoln? Are you finding them easy to work with?"

Stoker drew his last strokes of the razor and bent to wash his face in the sink. "Easy? Not really. They're used to doing things a certain way, and they're resistant to change. I'm not going to win any popularity contests this week, but that's not why I came here anyway."

"I know. You came here to make a difference with—"

"The kids. And already I see some progress. It's going to take a lot of fortitude, though, to create the systemic change that's needed. The Lincoln faculty has it so good, and their union is unbelievably aggressive in keeping it that way."

Rebekah washed and dried her face, still shaken by the frightening image of her dream. "Well, try not to make too many changes in your first month, R.J. No sense getting everyone so angry that they sabotage everything you want to do."

"Thanks for the warning, but I'm afraid it's too late. I've already made some enemies."

"That scares me."

"Don't worry. I know what I'm doing. It's not like anyone's gonna kill me, or anything."

Chapter Eleven

BY 6:45 AM, STOKER WAS sitting at his desk, sorting through his mail, with thirty minutes to spare before the students arrived in the building. After that, he would be out of the office until late afternoon. He enjoyed this quiet time in the mornings. He liked to think of it as strategic planning time.

So he was a bit unnerved when he heard a loud knock on the doorframe and a booming voice with a New York accent. "May ah come in, Mr. Stoker? Derrick Johnson, social studies."

Stoker sighed, but tried to disguise it as a cough. "Yes, Mr. Johnson. Come right in and have a seat. How can I help you today?"

Johnson eased his tall frame into the upholstered chair across from Stoker. He removed his glasses, polished them with the end of his silk tie, and put them back on. "I feel I should tell you, one brother to another, that I am appalled with some of the white faculty he-ah."

Stoker cringed. The only thing he hated more than being referred to as a Black principal was being referred to as a brother by a Black faculty member who wanted a favor. "To whom do you refer?"

"Well, you might recall that I spoke to you last week about Ms. Singer, the new teacher next door. She teaches freshman social studies, and all day long she has kids talking, clapping, moving around the classroom, even singing. The noise is unbearable. It interferes with my lectures. I've asked her to stop at least a dozen times."

"And what does she reply?"

"She says that's the way she teaches. She doesn't know any other way."

"And what other faculty member appalls you?"

"Ms. Pe-ahce, the assistant principal. She persists in sending me new students, even at this late date. I have more students than desks, and they keep on coming in. I told her they couldn't possibly pass, and if they don't, it would be her fault."

Stoker leaned back in his padded executive chair and peered at Mr. Johnson, trying to decide how best to vivisect him. "So you want me to tell Ms. Singer and Mrs. Pearce to do as you wish them to?"

"Yes, of course, brother. You the man."

"I'm sure you will be disappointed, then, when I tell you that I thoroughly support Ms. Singer. She is using research-based and proven visual-auditory-kinesthetic instructional strategies to help her students learn. Perhaps you would benefit from taking a course in multiple intelligences. You would find that lecturing is the least effective means of presenting subject matter in the high school classroom."

Pausing for a breath, he went on. "As regards Mrs. Pearce, I am the one who has instructed her to provide all students, late-entering or otherwise, with complete schedules. Let me remind you this is a public school, Mr. Johnson. We must welcome every young man or woman who comes through the door, and we must provide each of them with the opportunity to learn and to earn credits."

Johnson's face was almost comical, eyes bulging and mouth agape. He started to speak, but only air came out. "Hnh, hnh. But what about the teachers' contract? Have you read the sections about teaching conditions? We can't tolerate overloads or late-entering students at this school. And I'll have you know I have a Master's degree in social studies. I'll not be insulted about my teaching methods by you or anyone else."

Stoker flicked an imaginary speck from his sleeve, refusing to become riled in response. "No insult intended, Johnson. You've hit the nail on the head: it's a new day at Lincoln High School. Business as usual is gone. Now we will do what is best for students, not what is best for teachers or administrators. Is that clear?"

* * *

Stoker was still shaking his head over the nerve of Derrick Johnson. *How could he expect me to cater to his requests, just because I'm a "brother"?* He made a mental note to visit Johnson's classes again soon. He was pretty sure the guy's teaching was ineffective. Otherwise, he would have been too busy to spend his planning periods in administrators' offices, complaining.

Sorting through the pile of mail on his desk before leaving for classroom observations, he noticed a lavender envelope addressed simply: *Stoker.* Never one for delayed gratification, he tore open the envelope. Inside was a brief invitation: *Meet me in A304 at 4:30 today. Much to discuss.* Stoker turned the note over and looked in the envelope for details, but that was all there was. He sniffed the paper and thought he detected a faint scent of raspberries and vanilla.

Intrigued, Stoker flipped through the master schedule, scanning the "room" column to see whose classroom A304 was. The closest room, A302, was assigned to the Business Department Chair, Christopher Buckley. Mr. Buckley was also the wrestling coach. Stoker couldn't imagine Buckley would be sending mysterious notes on scented paper.

The situation felt like a set-up, and Stoker was too smart to fall for it. He had survived similar invitations in Knoxville. He was, after all, still under fifty and although his athletic physique could now be described as stocky, he was not bad-looking. The first time he had received a note to meet a teacher, he ended up being involved in a sexual harassment case, with him as the victim. Ever since, he had been wary of anything that smacked of "feminine" and "mysterious."

He would, however, pass by A304 in his walk-through visits, and he might be able to figure out what was going on. On his way out into the hallway, he remembered Rebekah's admonition not to make people angry. *Oh, well, what will be, will be.*

* * *

After school, Stoker met with parents, returned phone calls, and dictated his walk-through notes onto a tape, so Ms. O'Malley could type them up the next day. When 4:30 showed on his desk clock, he thought about the lavender note. Room A304 was a computer lab, unassigned to any one teacher. However, he presumed the note had come from someone in the business department who would have a key to the room after hours. He had no intention of climbing the two flights of stairs to meet with an unidentified woman. He had folded the note, stuffed it back in the envelope, and secreted it in the bottom drawer of his desk, just in case it might become important later.

At 5:45 pm, he was loading his briefcase with paperwork to review and approve before tomorrow morning, when he heard the door to the outer office click and then open. He thought Ms. O'Malley had locked that door on her way out. He dropped the briefcase to walk the six steps to see who was coming in, and was surprised to see Norma Dunn, the shapely business teacher, also president of the Faculty Association. His thoughts went immediately to the lavender note.

"Am I intruding?" Norma said, showing a perfect row of straight, glistening teeth and looking around as if to see if anyone else were there.

"I was just getting ready to leave, Ms. Dunn. How can I help you?"

"May I come in and sit down? I have some business to discuss with you." Stoker thought of saying no, deferring whatever business it was until the next day, but it was possible that it might be something important, something that it would be irresponsible to put off. Besides, curiosity was getting the better of him. "Certainly. Have a seat." He pointed to the upholstered chair Johnson had occupied that morning, and he walked around to sit behind his desk.

Ms. Dunn was rummaging around in her Louis Vuitton knockoff handbag. She finally seemed to locate what she was looking for, and she drew it out, then handed it over the desk to Stoker.

"What's this?" Stoker asked, taking the shiny white box from her hand.

"Dark chocolates," she said, showing her teeth again. "They come from California where my sister lives. I thought you might could use a bit of energy to help you get through the long, hard days here."

"Thank you, Ms. Dunn."

"You can call me Norma."

"To what do I owe the gift?"

"Let's call it a 'Welcome to Lincoln' gift. You really have joined a unique and special faculty, you know."

"All public schools are unique and special in my view, Ms. Dunn. They are filled with opportunities to impact positively on the lives of young people."

Norma nodded as if she expected as much from the new principal. Shifting her legs to the opposite side of the chair caused her tight skirt to rise, showing a few inches of thigh. "Why didn't you meet me in the computer lab this afternoon?"

Stoker picked up a pen and tapped it on his desk top. "I have made it a habit not to respond to invitations to events hosted by unknown parties." He opened his bottom desk drawer and placed the chocolates on top of the lavender envelope. "Let me ask *you* a question. What was it that you wanted to discuss in the computer lab that you couldn't have made an appointment to discuss here in the office?"

She lifted her chin. "I've found a little bit of adventure can be a good thing. I was hoping you were of a like mind."

"Ms. Dunn, I am a married man who has accepted a very serious position in this school. I intend to do my professional best to improve exit outcomes and opportunities for our students. I don't have time for anything else."

Norma's eyes blazed in response. "Okay, let me put it this way, *Mister* Stoker. Lincoln High School has the finest faculty of any economically disadvantaged school in the nation. We are a finely tuned machine, with all the individual parts working in synchrony. The reason it all works so well is a solid dedication to traditional rules and policies that have stood us in good stead for generations. I've come to offer you my services. I can teach you all about the systems in place, how to get along with even the most difficult faculty member, and which are the red-button issues for our faculty." She rubbed the arm of the chair in a light caress. "We could even have some fun together along the way."

Having had enough, Stoker stood and grabbed the handle of his briefcase. "Time to go home, Ms. Dunn. I have a feeling your definition of fun and mine are very different."

Chapter Twelve

SHAYLA SAT AT THE KITCHEN table, using a pencil tip to twirl circles through her hair, without thinking much about the economics homework in front of her. It had been more than two weeks since Tyrone had been over, and she missed him with all her heart. She had come home every afternoon while he was at practice and sat by herself, staring at homework, unable to concentrate.

Yesterday had been her birthday, hers and Claude's, and except for the two sweaters her mom had bought her and the knock-off Louis Vuitton clutch Tyrone had given her at his locker, it had been kind of a dud.

Her mother worked downtown as a security guard for a big office building, so it was Shayla's job to fix dinner for Claude and herself, and put away a portion for when her mom got home, around nine p.m. This afternoon she had fixed two packages of macaroni and cheese, but when she started cutting up cooked hot dogs to mix into the casserole, she felt so nauseated she had to stop. She wasn't very hungry anyway, unless hunger for Tyrone counted.

And Claude hadn't been around much either. He wasn't much for hanging around the house or doing homework. Most of the time he was out with his homeys, probably drinking or smoking weed. She loved her twin brother, but she disapproved of his choices, and he didn't understand hers.

She knew she should have paid more attention to Mr. Johnson's lecture today. Econ was required for graduation, and all this business about supply and demand would probably be important in the real world, too. All she knew was that money was in short supply in this neighborhood, and if she was ever gonna rise above this shabby house and make a success of herself, she'd have to find a way to make herself in greater demand. She wanted a better life, and that was part of what attracted her to Tyrone. He was not only handsome and sexy and athletic and popular, but Tyrone was going places. And if she played her cards right, she would be going right along with him.

There were only two obstacles that she could see. One was Claude. Her brother was always trying to break her and Tyrone up. He kept telling her Tyrone was just using her, that he was seeing other girls behind her back. She refused to believe these lies—she knew Tyrone's only other love was football—but the tiniest seed of doubt germinated in her brain and sometimes kept her awake at night, worrying.

The other obstacle was college. While Tyrone had college recruiters chasing his ass all the time, Shayla knew she wouldn't have the funds to go to college, unless scholarship manna fell from heaven to help her out. If Tyrone went away to school in the fall and left her behind, what were the chances they would stay together as a couple? Probably zero.

Shayla pushed aside her nausea and willed herself to concentrate on the chapter in her economics book. She would have to learn this material. And tomorrow she would ask Mrs. Pearce to help her with scholarship applications. She reached for Tyrone's senior ring on the chain between her breasts and lifted it to her lips. A kiss for luck couldn't hurt.

* * *

Shayla's brother Claude was having his own run of bad luck, and it was all that new Principal Stoker's fault. Maybe some dudes would appreciate the kind of slack Stoker had cut him in order to keep from being expelled, but not anyone in Black Devils. *Give me Welburton any day over that.*

It was a Black Devil rule that when you got caught, you took the consequences like a man, even if it meant rotting in prison. You didn't go apologizing and saying you wouldn't ever do it again. At the same time, the Devils needed him inside the school to handle the Lincoln turf. The only reason he had accepted Stoker's offer for clemency is because of the money. His mother's minimum wage job didn't bring in squat. The only hope for him and Shayla to survive and maybe to get out of this 'hood was for him to continue doing the Devils' work. Getting expelled would bring him shame and worse punishment from the gang leaders, and it would cost him and his family.

Now the G.M. was in his face 24/7. He couldn't afford another screw-up. The gang practically invented the word retaliation, and he had witnessed some very violent and painful ones in the five years he had been involved. Now he had eyes watching him from all sides: Devils' eyes, Welburton's eyes, and Stoker's eyes, too. He felt like a trapped animal, just waiting to be killed.

To make things even worse, there were rumblings that the Devils were targeting Shayla's boyfriend. Tyrone represented all that a Black guy from a tough neighborhood could do to make it out the right way. He was all-American, rah-rah. Taking him down would be a show of force for the Black Devils. And Claude was terrified that he would be the one assigned to do it.

* * *

After practice, Tyrone helped carry a water jug back to the gym. He was picking up a couple of towels, too, when Coach Donovan clapped him on the back. "Good passing today, Nesbitt. Your dedication is starting to really pay off."

"Thanks. I've been trying something new this season."

"Yeah? What's that? Maybe we can bottle it and use it for the other team members."

"I've been visualizing each play as if I were seeing it from a bird's eye perspective. It gives me a sense of precision."

"I like that, Captain. I like it that you came up with it yourself. Shows you take the game seriously."

"Now if I could just do the same with calculus."

"Having trouble with the class?"

"So much that I might not be eligible for the first game."

"Say no more. I'll talk to Mr. Welburton about getting you a tutor. We can't have our star QB benched for grades, now, can we?"

"No offense, Coach, but I doubt Mr. Welburton will care enough about me to get me a tutor. I think Mr. Stoker would be a better bet."

A crumpling of the eyebrows gave Donovan a perplexed look. "Why do you say that? Welburton has always taken good care of our players."

Tyrone picked up a couple more towels and threw them over his shoulder. "Yeah, but I get the feeling that things are changing, and now Mr. Stoker is really the one in charge."

Chapter Thirteen

IT WAS THE ELEVENTH HOUR for resolving overloads, and Sally had convinced Mr. Stoker that meeting the contractual deadline would be good for the school—especially the students. Sitting in an overloaded class would limit the amount of interaction with the teacher, and students needed more, not less, of that. She had been working almost around the clock, first identifying who the "ghosts" were, students on the rolls, but who had never actually shown up, then removing them and balancing the sections. Even after that was finished, she had so many extra students that they would have to hire four new teachers, one for English, mathematics, science, and social studies.

Shayla had been very helpful during the class period when she worked in Sally's office, and Sally was grateful. "I don't know what I would have done without your help these past few days."

"Happy to help. It's tedious, but interesting work." As she commented, Shayla suppressed a burp and turned an odd shade of greenish-tan.

"Don't you feel well? Maybe I've worked you too hard."

"I think I need to use the restroom," Shayla replied, and before receiving permission, she ran from the room. When she returned, her face was slick with moisture, and her eyes had a faraway look.

"You look like a snowflake in the tropics. Let me give you a pass to the nurse."

"No, I'll be all right. The bell's going to ring in a few minutes, and I can't miss my econ class. I want to talk to you about scholarships, too. I'm going to need help if I have a prayer of getting to college next year."

"I'll be glad to help you. I write a mean recommendation letter, if I say so myself." Shayla's coloring was not yet returning to normal. "I still think you should go to the nurse and have her check you out."

"Thanks for your concern. If I'm not better in the next hour, I'll get a pass and go then."

Before Sally could argue further, the bell rang, and Shayla left for Mr. Johnson's class. Sally returned to her enrollment reports, taking and exhaling a deep breath. Whatever was wrong with Shayla, she had been a jewel in helping with the office work. Helping her get a scholarship would be a small price to pay in return.

* * *

Norma was not used to being rejected. She had taken a big gamble, putting herself out there with Stoker. Of course, she knew he was married. She had chaired the faculty committee who had hosted a meet and greet for the Stokers last spring. On the other hand, she had known many a married principal in her time, and almost all of them had been happy to know her, too.

Her position in the Faculty Association had afforded her many opportunities to interact intimately with administrators, and, as long as she conducted herself professionally in all other ways, she had found sexual dalliances with administrators to be exciting and interesting. They also gave her a sense of power that she would never have acquired from being just a business teacher. Once she lured the principal into the liaison, there was almost nothing he wouldn't do to keep her quiet.

Norma sat at her desk, while her students pounded away at their computers. She ruminated about yesterday's interaction with Stoker. *It's too bad he didn't fall for my seduction play. He could have used my connections with the faculty to his advantage, and I wouldn't have minded having closed door meetings with the new boss.*

Now, having shown her hand, so to speak, and failed to accomplish the desired outcome, she had lost big-time. Stoker would shun her, probably for the duration of his term as principal, and she would be less able to perform effectively as chief representative of the faculty.

She hated to admit it, but she had lost some self-respect, too. At the age of forty-two, she noticed unflattering changes in her creamy café au lait complexion, and though she had always prided herself on her tight abs and thighs, she had to admit it was becoming harder and harder to maintain them. The thought of being turned down by the stocky ex-jock brought stinging tears of frustration.

She dabbed at the inside corners of her eyes without disturbing her makeup. "Class," she snapped, "time to close up. The bell's about to ring." She walked among the computer stations, making sure everyone was following her protocols for shutting down the computers.

Shutting down is exactly what I'd like to do to Stoker. As she passed by the chair of the sole white boy in the class, a thought sizzled in her brain. *I know. I'll get Welburton to help me fix Stoker's ass. Before we know it, Lincoln High will have another new principal—and maybe it will be Wally Welburton.*

* * *

When Norma entered Welburton's outer office, she saw, even before Myrna, the secretary, pointed it out, that he was busy. The frosted glass door with the assistant principal's name stenciled on it in black, shiny letters, was closed, and the sounds of muffled male voices filled the air.

"Stoker is in there," the secretary mouthed and pointed, while she waited for a phone call to go through.

Norma had no intention of being there when Stoker came out. She didn't want to see him, and more importantly, she didn't want him to see her. "I'll come back," she mouthed back, and she turned around and left, leaving the strong scent of raspberries and vanilla in her wake.

Stoker opened the door to the inner office just as Norma closed the outer one. He sniffed the air. "Was that Ms. Dunn who just left?" he asked.

Myrna nodded. "Do you want me to try to catch her for you?"

"Oh, heavens, no," Stoker replied, as he stepped just outside of the inner office. He turned back toward Welburton and said, as if there had been no interruption in topic, "So let's go ahead and set up some tutoring for the football team. Just make sure we get some people who know how to work with our kids." He added, "Not Gottschalk or Johnson."

Welburton called out, "Understood."

As he left the office Stoker muttered, "No point in giving extra pay to the same teachers who are failing them."

Chapter Fourteen

I T HAD BEEN TEN DAYS since Tyrone and Shayla had been together for more than a passing period here or there. At the end of fifth period Shayla had placed a folded note into the palm of her love before hurrying off to her computer class. Tyrone tried to embrace her, but she was ten paces away before his arm reached the spot where she had been.

Tyrone's sixth period class was P.E. Conditioning, a euphemism for pre-football practice. Standing as close to the inside of his locker as he could, he opened the note, hoping that no one could see. Shayla's handwriting was as curvaceous as her body, and Tyrone was struck with the fact that he missed both. The note said: *Football or no football, we need to talk. Meet me in the hallway behind the cafeteria today after practice. Miss u, S.*

Re-folding the note and jamming it into the back of his calculus folder, Tyrone wondered whether Shayla was going to break up with him. He felt a stab of guilt as he realized how little he had paid attention to her lately. It wasn't that he didn't love her; it was just all the pressure of senior year: grades, practice, scholarships, and the upcoming football game. On top of all that, he was set to start tutoring sessions next Monday.

As he pedaled the exercycle at 35 mph, he considered how he might be able to fit in a date night. He wanted to offer something positive when he saw her after practice. Maybe they could catch a movie after Saturday afternoon's game, or after church on Sunday. He would give her a choice.

Fifty minutes and several machines later, Tyrone took the field for practice. He was sweaty and sore, but feeling strong and fit, just like a Warrior ready to do battle. Whatever exercises and plays Donovan had for them, Tyrone was ready, and for the next two hours, all thoughts of his girlfriend were benched.

After practice, Tyrone walked with some teammates back to the gym. He was carrying the water cooler and several towels, as usual. About fifty yards from the gym entrance, Coach Donovan called to him. "Tyrone, would you mind going back to the practice field? I left my timer on the ten-yard line."

Tyrone really didn't want to take the time to go back to the field, knowing that Shayla was waiting for him, but he couldn't tell the coach no after all of the trouble he had gone to on his behalf. He sprinted back to the field, grabbed the timer, and placed it around his neck.

He had just turned to head back toward the gym, when he heard a whistle coming from behind the bleachers. The day had turned dusky, and he squinted in the direction of the sound. Seeing nothing, he took off, tired, but eager to shower and meet with his girl. Something flashed black in his peripheral vision, and he felt a solid, muscular arm grip him in a lateral vise that threatened to crush his windpipe. The attacker brought him to the ground in a single movement so smooth it could have been a tango step.

Once on the ground, he struggled to break free, but none of his football moves worked to break the hold on him. He felt like he was suffocating, about to pass out, but then he heard, more than felt, a crunching blow to the side of his face. Lights flashed in his head, but he hung on, trying to get a look at his attacker. When he did, he felt his eyes bulge in shock.

He tried to shout at Claude Davis, Shayla's brother, but his voice malfunctioned, and all that came out was, "Yiiii—."

"Shh!" said Claude, as he used a four-inch blade to slice a diagonal rip in the back of Tyrone's practice jersey. "You're gonna be okay, man. Just lie there and let me mess you up. I'm s'posed to be killing you, but I can't do that to my sister's boyfriend. Keep us both out of trouble. You don't know who hit you or why. Got it?"

Tyrone groaned and closed his eyes. The last thing he thought of before losing consciousness was Shayla, waiting for him by the cafeteria.

* * *

Tyrone opened one eye, then the other, trying to assess where the disinfectant smell was coming from. After being in a state of utter darkness, utter quiet, the world seemed overly brilliant and raucous, although the only light was coming from the wall lamp behind his head and a few stripes of daylight from between the slats of the closed blinds. The offending noise came from the blood pressure machine, which had his arm in a vise at the moment.

Moving only his eyes, he assessed the room. He appeared to be in a hospital bed, his torso and legs under bed coverings; his head and face, all but his eyes, nose and mouth, covered with thick padding. In the chair at the foot of the bed, his grandmother sat, an open book in her lap and her eyes closed under her wire-rimmed glasses.

"Uh," he uttered. A sip of water would be heavenly. He tried to say the word, "Water," but found he was unable to move his mouth. A louder, "Uh" caused Granny to jump to her feet.

She moved to the bedside and leaned over, peering into Tyrone's eyes. "You awake, angel? You gave me quite a scare."

Tyrone could smell the scent of Niagara spray starch on Granny's blouse. It was one of his favorite smells of childhood. "Uh-uh," he answered, pointing to the pink plastic pitcher of water on the rolling tray.

"Don't try to talk, baby. Your jaw is wired shut." She poured a glass of water and placed a straw into it. "Here, I can just squeeze this straw between your teeth, so you can sip. Take it slow."

Tyrone sipped and swallowed, thinking that this was the best water he had ever tasted. He wiggled fingers and toes, enjoying the pleasure of movement. Aside from the pressure and pain in his head and a sharp pain in his upper left arm, he didn't feel too bad. He had a million questions threatening to burst, but talking was apparently out of the question. He raised his eyes to Granny's face.

"Been here since yesterday evening. Coach found you unconscious on the football field, no one else in sight. Broken jaw, pretty long knife slash on your arm, lots of cuts and bruises, but nothing life-threatening, thank the Lord. Doctors said you'll be back with the team before you know it."

Tyrone attempted a smile, but his face refused to cooperate. He let his eyes roam the room. Nobody in the other bed, no flowers or food. His eyes landed on the cork board, where a big paper heart was tacked at eye level.

Following his gaze, Granny supplied the words. "Oh, yeah, that sweet girlfriend of yours was here almost all night, holding onto your hand. She said she'd be back as soon as school was out this afternoon."

* * *

After school, Shayla took the bus to the hospital. She hoped Tyrone would be awake when she got there. He had been totally out of it last night, and she was frightened. Who would have wanted to harm Tyrone? He was practically the most popular guy at school, and he never did anything to hurt anybody. How badly was he hurt? Would he be able to come back to school, and when? What about playing football? A lot of Tyrone's future was riding on his being able to get a football scholarship.

It broke her heart to see him lying there, not responding when she spoke or squeezed his hand. She couldn't imagine her own future without him. He just had to get better.

When she pushed the door to Tyrone's room open, the soft whoosh echoed the one in her chest. Frown lines marked her smooth complexion, and her posture seemed like that of a much older woman. She was tired from being up all night, weak from being nauseated all day, and upset from worrying about Tyrone.

She perked up immediately when she saw Tyrone's eyes open, and the look he gave her when she walked in, as if she were a goddess, shimmering in the radiant sunlight. She practically skipped over to the bedside and, careful not to hurt him, bent down and kissed his hand, which was taped with an IV.

"Don't try to talk. I'll do all of the talking. Everyone at school asked about you. I waited in the cafeteria for the longest time, and when you didn't come, I thought you were mad at me or something. By the time I left to go home, there were sirens and flashing lights outside, and I was so scared it might be you. And then it *was* you." She paused to get a breath and turned to see Tyrone's grandmother sitting behind the door. "Oh, hi, Mrs. Nesbitt. I didn't see you there at first."

"That's okay. I'm going to the cafeteria for some coffee. I'll let the two of you be alone for a while." She winked at Tyrone, and he winked back.

When Granny had closed the door, Shayla pulled the chair she had been sitting in over to Tyrone's side. "Hi, handsome," she said. "I'm glad you're going to be okay." Her fingers outlined the pattern on the white blanket. "I was really worried last night. But now with your head all bandaged, you look like a bunny rabbit, instead of a victim of a plane crash."

Tyrone closed his free hand over Shayla's. After a few minutes of silence, he used it to beckon her to come close. She leaned her face into his, as close as possible without touching him. He caressed her cheek, reminding her of the first time they had kissed, leaning up against the flowering plum tree in the park. She closed her eyes and breathed in his scent. Broken jaw or not, he was her Prince Charming.

"Tyrone?" Should she tell him the reason she'd wanted to meet him after practice. Probably this wasn't the best time.

"Mmmhh?"

"As much as I love being with you after school like this, I'd much rather you were at football practice right now."

Tyrone sighed, squeezed Shayla's hand, and drifted into sleep.

* * *

An hour later there was a knock, and the door whooshed open. Granny had returned by then, and she and Shayla sat in the two chairs by the window. Tyrone raised his eyelids, surprised, as Principal Stoker entered the room.

Tyrone noticed the frown line between Mr. Stoker's eyebrows, the way he closed his eyes and took a breath when he saw the school's quarterback all bandaged up. For a moment he wished that Mr. Stoker were not his principal, but his father, coming to comfort and cheer him up.

"I hope I didn't wake you," Stoker said. "I heard what happened to you, and I've felt just terrible. I had to come tell you so."

"Uh, uh," Tyrone replied, hoping it sounded something like, "Thank you."

"No need to thank me, son. And don't try to talk, either. Looks like you'll be in for a bit of quiet time for a little while." Stoker walked over to the window. He extended his hand toward Tyrone's grandmother, introducing himself. Then he said to Shayla, "Aren't you the young lady who works in Mrs. Pearce's office?"

Shayla smiled. "Yes, Mr. Stoker. Shayla Davis. Tyrone's my boyfriend. It's very nice of you to come visit him." She slid Tyrone's senior ring from side to side on its chain around her neck.

Stoker turned back to Tyrone. "I'm very sorry about this. Something similar happened to me when I was in high school, so I think I know how you are feeling right now. The fact that it happened on school property makes it personal for me, as well." He shoved his hands, cuff links and all, deeply into his pants pockets. He bit his lips into a determined line, as if holding back a torrent of words.

Tyrone wondered what they all might be.

"I just want to know one thing right now. Do you know the person who attacked you?"

A small groan escaped from between Tyrone's teeth. His brain had been replaying the incident like an action movie. He could imagine the smell of his attacker's breath, hear his rough words, but he just couldn't bring up his identity. He had been trying off and on all day, and he'd come close, but even if he could talk, his mind was a blank.

Stoker continued, "I know you can't talk with your jaw wired, but maybe you could write his name. We can't let him get away with this."

Tyrone made the tiniest movement of his head from side to side, as if to say, "No."

"You don't know who attacked you?"

Tyrone repeated the movement.

"Okay," Stoker said, gently patting one of Tyrone's ankles through the bedclothes. "You just heal and get your strength back." He looked over toward Mrs. Nesbitt and said, "If there's anything I can do to assist you or Tyrone…" His voice trailed off as he glanced at Shayla, and as an afterthought said, "Or you either, Shayla, please don't hesitate to contact me. We can get your homework, start your tutoring, whatever you feel you can manage, as soon as you are ready."

Granny stood then, her eyes shining with tears. "Thank you so much, Mr. Stoker. We appreciate all you are doing for Tyrone. We're honored."

"No need to thank me. I'm just doing my job," Mr. Stoker said. Then he did something that made Tyrone's eyes water, too. He opened his arms and folded his little granny right up into a bear hug. He nodded to Shayla, patted Tyrone's ankle again, and departed, leaving behind a room full of good will.

Chapter Fifteen

AFTER FAILING TO KILL TYRONE, Claude didn't dare show his face at school or anywhere else. He needed time to think, get his story straight, maybe even run away. He had been an up-and-coming leader in the Black Devils, been running drugs since seventh grade, but he knew that falling short on the Donovan and Nesbitt assignments would change all that. In fact, his own life or that of a family member might be in jeopardy now.

He knew it was cowardly, but he had dressed and pretended to go to school. After the tardy bell, he'd rushed home and, fully clothed, gone to bed, pulling the covers over his head. He knew he had hurt Tyrone. The blow to his jaw had made a solid crunching sound. The knife wound was probably superficial, but hopefully it would be enough to convince the Devils that he had at least tried. Oh, who was he kidding? They'd never buy that, and he knew it.

Around eleven o'clock that morning, he heard a noise in the front room. He jumped up and ran into the room, shouting, "What's goin' on?"

His heart pounded triple time when he saw the First Lieutenant to the Grand Marshal standing in his living room, picking at his teeth with a toothpick, and scowling at him. "Nice of you to invite me over," the thirty-three-year-old drawled. He was dressed in jeans, a sweatshirt, and a long raincoat.

Claude knew better than to reply. Whatever he might say would be interpreted as provocative. What he did, instead, was to flash the hand signal and feel for the diamond stud earring in his right ear. His intended message was: brotherhood.

"You fucked up, Davis. Very disappointing. What happened to your balls?"

"I—I tried, I tried to kill him. I hurt him plenty bad."

"Hurt doesn't cut it, and you know it. You left him alive. Did he see your face? Does he know who hit him?"

"I don't think so. I had my face covered, and it all went down quick."

"We needed to make a statement, ya know? Show those Hispanic 'bangers whose territory this is. We wanted to scare Donovan, then kill Nesbitt. We have our eye on Assistant Principal Welburton, too. We thought you were the man for the job, but now we think you might be going soft on us." He raised his voice, "You goin' soft, Davis?"

"N-no. Not at all. Give me another chance, and I'll prove it." Claude's mouth went dry. All he could think of was to escape, move to another state.

The Lieutenant gave out with a hoarse guffaw. "How's that for a co-in-ci-dence? That's exactly why I'm here. You get one more assignment, Davis. One more, and that's all. Flub this one, and you're finished, and your pretty sister will be finished, too."

"What do you want me to do?"

"Kill the principal. Kill Stoker. We'll show him he can't buddy up with us. We'll show this city whose turf that school is on. Once he's dead, no one will want to be principal there ever again. Do this, and you'll be back in good graces."

Claude tried to swallow his fear, but his esophagus wasn't hungry for it. He wasn't going to have an easy time killing the principal, especially since the guy had cut him a break after the Donovan mess. "Is there a plan?" he asked, knowing full well there always was.

The Lieutenant pulled a .45 caliber pistol from his raincoat pocket. "Here. It's registered to a dead guy. Fully loaded. Take him wherever you see an opportunity, but do it quick, Davis. You might say there's a lot riding on it."

* * *

After school Norma Dunn met in her classroom with both Ben Gottschalk and Derrick Johnson. Each had requested a meeting with the faculty association president to complain about Stoker, but Norma decided it might be better to see them both at the same time. Usually these types of meetings were gripe sessions about things beyond the Association's sphere of influence, anyway. Not that she wouldn't love to find a way to stick it to Stoker. She was still chafing from his rejection of her sexual advances.

The men arrived as soon as the hallway had cleared of students at the end of the school day, Gottschalk in a plaid sport shirt and Dockers, Johnson in a three-piece suit. Norma greeted them at the door as if she were a party hostess, welcoming friends and family. She offered them bottles of Dasani water before they sat down at a long, rectangular table full of computers. The afternoon sun spotlighted the center of the table, creating an impression of warmth and hospitality. It almost made the litter and stale smells left behind by the students disappear.

"I hope you don't mind sharing the meeting," Norma began. "It sounded like your issues were similar, and in the interest of time, I thought we could all benefit from meeting together."

"Not at all," Gottschalk replied. "Nothing secret about my problems. Everyone already heard my confrontation with Stoker at the faculty meeting on opening day." He opened his lips in a quasi-smile, showing extensive dental work.

Johnson appeared to shrink into his wool-worsted suit, as if he wanted nothing to do with the math teacher or his issues with the principal. "Ah'd be glad to come back at a more convenient time, if you wish, Mrs. Dunn." He lifted himself up a fraction of an inch as if to stand.

Norma patted his cuff with her manicured fingers in an almost tender gesture, causing him to sit down again. "I'd rather you stayed, Mr. Johnson. Let's hear Mr. Gottschalk first, and then we will hear from you." She smiled at the economics teacher as she would have smiled at a student who had changed his errant ways.

Gottschalk took the floor then, both literally and figuratively. He stood and ranted, pacing and punctuating his sentences with frothy spits. "—I tell you, that man is up to no good. He is ruining this school."

"Calm down, Mr. Gottschalk. Can you be specific?"

"You want specifics? Okay, I'll give you specifics." He consulted a tiny notebook in the pocket of his shirt. "Twenty-seven times. There haven't even been twenty-seven days of school yet. He has stood at my door, observing my class twenty-seven times. I think that constitutes harassment."

Johnson straightened his posture in the chair. "I haven't been keeping track, but I'll bet he's been to my door that many times, too. Isn't that a breach of our contract, Ms. Dunn?"

"That does seem excessive. I'll have to read the section of the contract on formative evaluation, but technically, just standing at the doorway without interrupting or making comments is probably within the purview of the principal. Did he disrupt your classes?"

"Ha-ha," as if having the principal watch the class isn't a sure-fire way to make everyone uncomfortable. "To be honest, since I teach seniors, I think they aren't afraid of the principal anymore, and certainly not this one. He seems to think he's their big brother, protecting them from those big bad teachers. I think they are glad to have him watch the class. I think some of them are hoping he will bust me for something, and I'll go easy on them when it comes to homework and tests."

"Has he commented on your teaching, either at the door or afterwards in writing?"

"No, not yet, but I'm sure that's coming. I think he has targeted me since I challenged him on that first day of school. He's trying to get rid of me. Maybe he doesn't like me because I'm white."

Mrs. Dunn turned toward the very Black Mr. Johnson. "Is that your feeling, too?"

"Yes, it is." He faced Gottschalk. "It's not your color, man. It's the fact that you're a teacher, and he is using his pow-ah to keep you in your place." Looking back at Mrs. Dunn, he added, "I've asked him to speak to Miss Singer, the new teacher next door. Her classes are noisy and disruptive. He's done nothing, but support her—her playing with her students—they clap, sing, dance, move furniture around. It's absurd."

When Mr. Morgan was principal, Norma enjoyed taking petty complaints to him. It gave her a reason to hobnob with the administration, and sometimes that led to some very interesting experiences. With Stoker, she knew she wouldn't get to first base. She fanned herself, though it wasn't hot in the room. "Listen," she cut off Johnson as he was taking a breath. "I'm going to document what each of you has told me today. I'll research the contract to see if any terms have been violated. Then I'll meet informally with Stoker, as required in the grievance procedure. If anything else happens that you need to tell me about, please report it in writing with names, dates, times, and as many specific details as possible." She stood up and smoothed her skirt. "Meanwhile, gentlemen, I don't need to tell you to be very careful. Until we know what we are dealing with, it's important for all teachers to be very—"

"Professional," Gottschalk filled in the word. "I'm always professional, but now I'm going to be secretive, too."

"Not secretive," Norma corrected. "Just discreet. Professional and discreet. That's all your association asks of you."

* * *

Stoker had arranged with Sally to be "on call" in case Norma Dunn came in for another after-hours meeting. If he could avoid it, he didn't want to be caught alone with her again. So when Norma knocked on the open door frame after everyone else had left for the day, Stoker picked up his phone and punched Sally's extension.

Norma was wearing a tailored business suit, navy with lavender stripes, and a frilly handkerchief peeking from a jacket pocket. The way she was leaning into the office, showing her sparkling teeth, she looked as provocative as a hungry fox.

When Sally answered Stoker's call, he said just two words, "Seven up," and hung up the phone. He then stood and said, "Hello, Ms. Dunn. Have a seat."

Having heard the strange two-word sentence, Norma shot him a sideways glance. "I've come on Association business, strictly business."

"I don't doubt it. What is the problem this time?"

Before she could launch into her issue, the outer office door creaked, and Sally appeared, carrying a can of Seven-Up, and wearing the exact same pin-striped suit. The two women stared at each other for a moment, and uttered a simultaneous, "Nordstrom's."

"Here's your drink," Sally said, extending a can of soda pop to her boss.

"Sally," Stoker boomed. "Come in and have a seat." He turned to Norma. "It's okay with you if my AP hears this *business*, isn't it?"

"Sure. It's your turf. Basically, I've just come as the first step in the grievance process."

"Grievance?" Stoker's voice carried a tune of disbelief in its cadence. "It's only the second week of school. Give me a break."

Norma took off a shoe and rubbed her opposite calf with her stockinged foot. "Unfortunately, the contract doesn't call for breaks, and there is a bit of unrest amongst the teachers."

"The teachers? All of the teachers? Some of the teachers? Can you be specific?"

"Pursuant to Article XIV, Section 27, Working Conditions, teachers are entitled to notification prior to classroom observations by administrators. Evidently you have been observing teachers without notifying them in advance."

Stoker made eye contact with Sally and chuckled. "Well, if that doesn't cook my grits. What do you think about that, Mrs. Pearce? Do we have to notify teachers before we observe their classrooms?"

Sally's face flushed, and she shifted positions in her chair before she responded. "I think Ms. Dunn is referring to summative evaluation observations." She turned to address the association leader directly. "Is that right?"

Norma opened the booklet containing the professionally negotiated agreement in her lap. "The contract language says, classroom observations. It doesn't specify whether they are summative or formative."

"I'll be damned if I'm going to notify anyone before I walk through the halls of this building, observing what is going on in classrooms," Stoker almost shouted. "I am the educational leader of this school. I will damn well know what is going on in classrooms all of the time." He adjusted the right cuff of his shirt so that the RJS monogram showed. "I'll tell you what. I will put out an all-school memo notifying all teachers that I will be observing classrooms any day and every day of the school year. They should expect to see me at their doors frequently. That will be their notification."

"You don't need to get angry. You just need to follow the contract. Certain teachers feel you have been picking on them."

"Names, Ms. Dunn. Give me the names of the teachers who feel so persecuted."

"Okay, okay. Mr. Johnson and Mr. Gottschalk."

"I knew it. Those two sorry asses don't know if they're washing or rinsing half the time."

"Mr. Stoker, please. That's not professional. These are two very dedicated teachers who have been here a long time."

"And they both teach seniors, seniors who need their credits to graduate. They are boring the students to death with one lecture after another. They don't even allow for questions. Let me tell you something, and I want you to tell them this: I'm not only going to be watching them teach. I'm going to be watching their grading practices. If they fail too many students, I'm going to call them in to explain to me why so many of their students aren't passing."

He turned to Sally. "And Mrs. Pearce, here, and Mr. Welburton, too, they will be helping me in monitoring failure rates."

Sally shifted some more. Stoker had to remind himself that she was new to administration and probably hadn't experienced so much drama in the past.

"And I'll tell you something else," he went on. "I am not somebody who's going to go along to get along. Don't be bringing me little snippets from the contract every other week and think I'm going to kowtow to people who don't care about doing what's best for kids." The more Stoker thought about it, the angrier he was. "And don't be telling me what is and is not professional. You tell those teachers how to be professional, how to elevate students. Period."

Norma closed the booklet and put her right pump back on her foot. Without being dismissed, she stood and pivoted until she faced the door. "Yes, Mr. Machiavelli, I mean, Mr. Stoker. Whatever you say. But remember, the first step toward a grievance is a face-to-face meeting to discuss and try to resolve the issue." She bit off her next words, "We've just had that meeting."

Chapter Sixteen

WELBURTON WAS HAVING PROBLEMS OF his own. Years of experience as the school's disciplinarian and leader of the deans had given him a certain expertise in gang matters. He had gone to workshops led by criminal justice personnel, even the FBI, some featuring incarcerated gangbangers, and he himself had spoken at educational conferences about how to manage gang activity in schools.

So when he saw the signs of incipient trouble at Lincoln, and this so early in the school year, he knew what to do. He began by calling a meeting of his discipline team, the deans. There he stressed the importance of discretion. There would be no benefit in letting the gangs know the administration was on to them. He asked the deans to be vigilant throughout the school day, particularly before and after school and during lunch periods, and to report any suspicious activity immediately. The trick was to enlist the faculty in monitoring the building without unleashing a panic.

Welburton held up a photograph he had taken that morning outside of the gym. The graffiti showed a bloody pitchfork next to a pair of crying eyes. He had snapped the Polaroid shot before instructing the maintenance crew to scrub and paint over the evil message.

"This is the work of the Black Devils," he said. "See how the pitchfork has curlicues on its prongs and shading on its shafts?"

"How do you keep up with all of this symbolism?" one of the deans asked, shaking his head. "It seems they change every other day."

"I watch certain kids very closely. You know who they are. We've had them on our list for ages. Their behavior, their dress, the way they carry themselves—we take our cues from them. Right now the Hispanics are moving into the neighborhoods and starting to assert themselves. The Devils are getting anxious and acting to protect their turf. The result is like a chemical reaction—add the wrong catalyst, and we could have a huge explosion."

"Anything other than graffiti?" another dean asked.

"Yeah, there was a fight in the second lunch period yesterday. Black on Hispanic. Both were throwing signs before the fists came out." He nodded at the dean who had been on duty. "Thanks to your quick action, we were able to contain it."

Worried looks were exchanged around the table. "We can expect more of this, I'm afraid," Welburton went on. "So I'm bringing the police liaison into all lunch periods, effective immediately. Hopefully these mopes will realize that fighting will get them suspended *and* arrested."

Byron Witkowski, the most senior of the deans, raised his hand. "Boss, it's getting around that Stoker won't support us in cracking down on these guys. Some faculty members were talking at lunch about the guy who threatened Coach Donovan. He should've been expelled, but he's still on the class lists."

Welburton felt a stab in his gut. Truthfully, all of their diligence and hard work, all of the specific wording in the discipline policy, would come to naught if Stoker didn't back them up. Wally summoned his calmest, most confident tone of voice before responding. "Listen, we need to do our jobs the best way we know how. Leave Stoker to me. He's green in these matters, coming from Tennessee, but I will take responsibility for bringing him along."

"Good luck with that," Byron snarled. "So far it looks like the only people he cares about are the kids."

Ignoring the remark, Welburton said, "Thanks for reminding me, Byron. Let's all keep our eyes on known gangbangers, including Claude Davis."

* * *

After the lunch periods, where two fights had erupted, Welburton approached Stoker in the hallway. "Listen, Stoker, I've got some important information to run past you. When can we meet?"

Stoker didn't blink an eye. "What's wrong with right here, right now?"

"Well, um, usually we don't talk about things in the hallway, just in case we are overheard." Welburton thought this guy was going to take some getting used to. He was so different from Mr. Morgan.

"I like to be out and about in the building during the school day," Stoker said, "and I doubt anyone will hear us talking here in the science wing." He clapped Wally on the shoulder as if they were old friends. "So what's up?"

Wally struggled not to cringe from the familiar gesture. He concentrated on how to present the gang situation to his new boss. "Well, it's unusual for this to happen so early in the school year, but we've been picking up signs of gang tensions in the building and on campus."

"Oh, not that again," Stoker exclaimed. "What makes you think so?"

"We've had an influx of Hispanic families in the neighborhoods over the summer. About a dozen new Hispanics in the school. The police told us Los Lobos was recruiting heavily in these parts, and now we're seeing signs, graffiti, taunts, fights. That threat on Coach Donovan last week—that's typical gang stuff when they feel they have to assert power over their territory. It all adds up to trouble, unless we stay on top of it."

Stoker's eyes dilated, and he took a breath before responding. "I thought I told you I took care of that Donovan threat."

Welburton felt Stoker's unstated message: *You whites don't know shit about handling gang problems.* "Yes, you did, but this goes beyond just that one incident." He pulled the Polaroid photo from his jacket pocket. "This, for example, was painted on the outside wall of the gym this morning. We got it taken care of right away, but there'll be more. The Black Devils are trying to tell Los Lobos to get lost."

Stoker fixed Welburton with a stare. Wally shook his shoulders, trying to shrug away the odd feeling that Stoker wasn't buying any of this. "Look, I don't know whether you realized you were coming to a school where there was known gang activity. They probably didn't have this problem in Knoxville. We know the signs and symptoms of this disease here, and we know the treatment, too. We have to get tough, act fast, and show these guys that the school is off-limits as their playground for violence."

Stoker remained impassive, spurring Wally to grasp at another argument. "Listen, don't you think the attack on Tyrone Nesbitt was gang-motivated?"

"Nesbitt? What makes you think that?" Stoker dropped his crossed arms and made eye contact for the first time. Welburton knew he had hit his mark.

"The attack on Nesbitt had all the marks of a gang hit on a school hero... on school property... school team... knifing. It's a wonder Nesbitt wasn't killed."

"So what do you propose?" Stoker asked with apparent sincerity.

"We need to come down hard on these guys, issue ten-day suspensions for fighting, and warnings about recidivism. We need to increase the police presence, educate the faculty to look for and report anything resembling gang paraphernalia or representation. We need to monitor the halls and the campus before, during, and after school."

Stoker just shook his head, his mouth a straight line. "No, Wally. We aren't turning Lincoln into a prison. That would be over-reacting. It's that kind of general oppression that drives kids into gangs to begin with, and the cycle continues. You may know a lot about gangs from the administrative viewpoint, but I know a lot from the personal one."

"This isn't going to go away, Stoker. It's only going to increase until we have a major crisis on our hands."

"We'll worry about it if and when that happens. In the meantime, I'm going to hold higher expectations of our students than that. On the other hand, you have given me something to think about. Keep me up-to-date on this."

Welburton almost cried with frustration. In this dicey neighborhood, he and Mr. Morgan had built a rock-solid institution—a place where people weren't afraid to teach and learn. This new guy was going to tear down in two weeks' time what it had taken years to create, and there didn't seem to be anything Wally could do about it. He punched one fist into the other palm and pivoted in place, so Stoker wouldn't see the murderous look on his face. He would have to think of something.

Chapter Seventeen

"**I** WONDER IF YOU COULD DO me a favor," Sally Pearce said to her favorite office aide, as Shayla entered her office at fifth period. "I need to make sure all of the students in the freshman acceleration program have been placed with the right teams of English, math, science, and social studies teachers."

After Sally heard Norma Dunn threaten a grievance to Mr. Stoker, she realized that this was one last task she had to do to make sure all the students were in the right places. Since this was the first year of the acceleration program, there was a possibility that some of the counselors had rushed to put late-entering freshmen into classes, without regard to the careful teaming done over the summer. She certainly didn't want to incur a grievance her first month as an administrator.

Sally pointed to a color-coded chart on an easel. "Here are the teams of freshman teachers—orange, green, red and blue." She grabbed a pile of computer printouts colored orange. "Here are the orange students' schedules. When you check each schedule, you should find that the math, English, social studies, and science teachers are all orange. If you find one that is not, highlight it and put the schedule in an error pile." She pointed to a place on the table that already had two or three highlighted pages.

"Yes, ma'am," Shayla said, sitting down at the conference table and getting right to work.

"Do you have any questions?"

"No, ma'am. It looks easy to me." Shayla wiped her brow. She looked at the first schedule, then at the chart on the easel, back and forth. Tyrone's ring clicked on the table each time she bent over the schedules.

Sally sat at her desk, to the left of Shayla, and attacked the stack of green student schedules. The work was tedious, but necessary, and she was so grateful to have Shayla's help. Her other office aides didn't have the same sharpness and attention to detail.

The two worked side by side without talking for about fifteen minutes, and then Shayla put down her stack of schedules, wiped her upper lip, and asked if she could go to the restroom.

"Of course. Here's a pass."

"I'll be right back," Shayla said, rushing from the room.

This was not the first time Sally suspected something was physically wrong with Shayla. This time, when Shayla returned from the restroom, Sally was determined to find out.

* * *

Before Shayla could return to the office, the fire alarm sounded. It couldn't be a scheduled fire drill. This was too early in the school year, and, besides, Sally would have been involved in the planning. No, this had to be a real fire alarm, so Sally went into action clearing the offices and surrounding classrooms and hallways, closing doors, and following the lines of students into the field behind the building.

The day was overcast, and heavy clouds hovered overhead. What had seemed like Indian summer that morning had apparently been whisked away by a brisk wind, a sure sign of fall, but now there was a faint, but distinctive smell of smoke in the air. The students, like animals sensitive to smells, became restless, moving further away from the building. High-pitched chatter punctuated the scene.

Sally looked about for Shayla. If she had used the closest girls' restroom, she should have exited through the same door. She should have joined Sally and the other office personnel by now. The wailing of fire engines filled the air, horns blasting as the responders flew through intersections.

Sally moved through the crowded field looking for Shayla, maintaining a calm exterior, while anxiety bubbled in her stomach.

A few plump raindrops fell onto her head and body, dotting her clothes with spots. Rain would only make it more difficult to keep the students out of the building.

Failing to find Shayla, she would have to go back into the building. A dozen scenarios flickered through Sally's mind, none of them good. Typically, fire drills lasted six to ten minutes. This one had already lasted fifteen, and still there was no signal to return to the building.

Sally pretended to perform a routine fire drill activity as she retraced her steps toward the building. She felt like running, but knew that would prompt pandemonium. As she approached the building, she was forming a plan in her head. She would check the bathroom first, then look for a fireman to help her find Shayla.

When she opened the door, the acrid smell of smoke assaulted her nostrils. It was strong, and it was coming from the hallway outside of the principal's office. She willed herself to ignore the odor, to keep herself from running back out of the building to safety. She had to find Shayla first.

The girls' bathroom was only down the end of the math hallway, near her own office complex. Sally sprinted now that she was out of sight of the crowds. She flung open the bathroom door, still cool to the touch, and rushed in, calling Shayla's name. Hearing no response, she went down the line of stalls, checking each one, but finding them empty. Now she was beginning to panic, and she knew that would not serve anyone well.

She ran out of the bathroom and toward the smoke. She had to alert the firemen that there might be a student in harm's way. The smoke had thickened in just the few seconds she had spent in the girls' room. It was spreading into the hallways now, and Sally knew she should exit the building—but she couldn't. She darted into the hallway, holding her palm over her nose and mouth, as if that would protect her.

She could see movement ahead through the smoke. Firemen in heavy black uniforms and helmets, two of them, were dragging what looked like a body toward the auditorium entrance. "Please don't let it be Shayla," she repeated in her head. The dense smoke was invading her nose and throat and lungs now, causing her to choke. She couldn't go any further into the hallway, so she turned around and ran the length of the building. She turned a corner and then another, racing for the auditorium, like a heroine in a familiar maze.

When she rounded the final corner, she met a dark cloud of steamy, wet soot, almost opaque. She screamed for help, hoping someone would hear her through the mess. It was hard to breathe, and her coughing increased. It was obvious that firehoses had been unleashed into the hallway, creating a sodden mess, but she still couldn't see. She could, however, hear, and what she heard was a male voice shouting, "Stand back. Whoever you are, stay in place."

Sally stood, rooted to the slick, mucky floor. Her eyes burned, and tears ran down her face. A huddle of firemen surrounded a large object on the floor. Sally wiped her eyes to try to see through the darkness what it was, but without moving closer, she couldn't tell. Suddenly the huddle opened up, and she could see it was an inert body, lying on its back.

The only light in the hallway came from the lanterns on the fire hats, and these made cylindrical lines that bounced and intersected as the firemen performed their duties, oblivious to their spectator. A glimmer caught Sally's eye, as one of the helmet-lanterns caught and reflected a pinpoint of golden light off of the body in the hallway.

Oh, no! Sally's stomach leapt into her throat, and she screamed with all the force she could muster when she realized what the lantern had illuminated. The shining object was a familiar solid gold cuff link.

* * *

Sally lost consciousness for a moment, whether from lack of oxygen or from shock, but when she recovered, she saw the black face of a fireman squatting next to her, gazing into her eyes, and shaking her gently. "Are you all right, miss?" he asked.

Her eyes darted around, taking in the ruined walls and messy floor. Then she remembered. Sitting up quickly, she cried, "Stoker! What's happened to Stoker? And, and… Shayla. One of my students was in the building."

The fireman helped Sally sit up. He held a bottle of water for her to sip. The smoke was clearing, but the hallway was still dank and smelly. Looking around, Sally could see the fire's path of destruction, ragged holes in walls and debris littering the area like putrid confetti. "Is this Stoker here on the floor?" she almost yelled.

The fireman nodded. "'Fraid so, miss."

"Is he—is he—d-dead?"

The fireman's eyes watered, whether from smoke or sadness. "We've got a faint pulse, so we're taking him in to the hospital. Police and paramedics should arrive any minute."

Sally wailed Stoker's name. She grabbed the fireman's arm to balance herself as she rose to her feet, then pulled away to rush over to her mentor. "I want to see him," she cried.

The fireman held her back. "Not now. Everyone has a job to do right now, miss. Don't you have a job?"

The fireman's words unlocked the professional part of Sally's brain. She mumbled, "Assistant principal. Office over there, by Door 23." In an instant she remembered. "The fire drill! Everyone's still outside? And Shayla? I've got to find Shayla."

"Is it a Black girl you're looking for?"

Sally nodded. "Pretty, medium build, long hair."

"Is that her?" The fireman pointed to the exterior auditorium doors. There was just enough light coming in through the glass to make it transparent from this side. On the outside of the auditorium Sally could see the back of a female figure, sitting on the curb, hunched over and sobbing. Someone was sitting next to the person, trying to comfort her.

Sally ran to the doors and threw them open. She ran to face the crying figure. "Shayla," she cried. "Thank God you're okay!"

Chapter Eighteen

SALLY MUST HAVE BEEN IN shock. After making sure Shayla was okay, she stood, sucking in air as if she had been holding her breath underwater for an hour. No matter how many deep breaths she took, she just couldn't get enough.

Meanwhile, the entire student body stood behind her in a light rain, their colorful garments dotting the landscape like a Monet painting. With a jolt, Sally realized someone would have to manage this crisis. Leaving Shayla at the curb, she strode toward the crowd in the field, gripping the two-way radio in her hand. Why was it silent? It seemed like hours since the fire alarm had sounded.

She fiddled with the radio buttons, and it came to life with a blast. She must have inadvertently turned it off when she and Shayla were working on the schedule, and never turned it back on. She quickly called Welburton's number, 02.

One beep, and then she heard Wally's voice. "Go ahead, Pearce. What's your location?"

"South side of the building, outside auditorium."

"We're going to bring everyone back into the building in just a minute. I'm testing to see if the PA system works. And I've called for buses."

Welburton's authoritative tone washed over her, bringing a momentary sense of relief.

"I could use your help. There's a lot to do in a little bit of time." He sounded frazzled, but in control.

"What about S-Stoker?"

"No word from the hospital yet. Other worries now. Be sure to keep your radio on."

His voice caused Sally to spring into action, the sense of responsibility flowing through her veins and ligaments and nerves. "I'll get everyone on this side of the building to go around to the east entrance. We need to keep people out of the south hallway." For an instant, the image of Stoker's inert body on the floor outside of his office flashed before her, but she willed it away. *I'll think about it later. Right now there are a lot of people who need me.*

She jogged toward the now-restless and wet masses of people in the parking lot and athletic field. As efficiently as a robot, she created a message pyramid, enlisting people to lead others to the east entrance and back to their classrooms until further notice. Fortunately, there were no classrooms in the main office wing.

The raindrops had morphed into drizzles, enough to act as a pesky annoyance, but the sweet smell of wet grass permeated the air, rejuvenating Sally's lungs. It felt good to be moving, to have a purpose.

* * *

After watching the last of the buses depart from the north side of the campus, Sally gazed up at the sun, breaking through gray strata, and she turned to go back into the building. Her eye caught a figure huddled on the concrete ledge near the door.

As she approached, she could make out the shape as that of a young girl, but she thought all of the students had left by now. In a few more steps she realized the girl was Shayla, and she raced toward her.

"Shayla," she called out.

Shayla uncurled from a near-fetal position and jumped up. "Mrs. Pearce, I was waiting for you."

Sally stared at her student aide with deep concern. Shayla's hair was a mess, and her face was smeared with soot and tear-tracks. She looked pale and frightened, as if she had traveled to hell and back, and she smelled like something rancid. Sally embraced her, rocked her gently from side to side. "Shayla, are you hurt?"

Shayla disengaged from the hug and shook her head. "I'm okay."

"You are obviously not okay. Were you hurt by the fire? I was searching all over for you."

Shayla took a deep breath. "I was sick in the bathroom when the alarm sounded. By the time I came out into the hall, everyone was gone, and I smelled smoke."

"Well, you made it out, and now we'll get you cleaned up and good as new."

Shayla shook her head again and fresh tears spilled from her eyes. Her lips quivered, and she hugged herself. "I—I can't."

"You can't what? Shayla, you need to tell me what's going on." Sally put her arm around Shayla's shoulder and led her gently into the building. She unlocked the door of the first classroom. The two sat down in the darkened classroom, facing each other. "You can tell me, Shayla. Whatever it is, you can tell me."

Shayla put her head down on the desk and uttered a sob, then lifted her head to meet Sally's eyes. "It's what I saw when I was running out of the building. I was heading for the auditorium exit, passing the hallway of the principal's office."

She saw Stoker lying on the floor, thought Sally. *That's what has her so traumatized.*

"What did you see?"

Shayla was now shaking all over, as if shock waves had taken over her bone marrow. "It was before the firemen got there. I saw s-someone on the floor, not moving."

"Yes," Sally prompted. "And?"

"And I saw someone standing, too. Standing with a gun."

"A gun?" Sally was shocked by the introduction of a gun into the picture. She thought Stoker had been overcome by smoke inhalation. "Did you recognize the person with the gun?" she asked, her mind speeding with horrible possibilities.

"I can't tell you. I can't tell anyone." Shayla stood and looked at the door, as if contemplating flight.

"Please sit down, Shayla. You know you can trust me. Tell me who you saw."

"I'm p-pregnant," Shayla blurted. "I feel sick, and I haven't told anybody that either."

Sally understood the *non sequitur*. Whoever it was Shayla had seen with a gun, she felt compelled to keep it secret, so much so that she gave up a lesser secret instead. "Okay, honey, I understand now. I see why you've been running to the bathroom, why you had to go today. Let's get you cleaned up and you can catch your breath." Sally motioned for Shayla to get up, and she put her arm around the girl's shoulders. Calling the police to interview Shayla would have to wait for at least a few minutes.

Calmer, at last, Shayla wiped her face and began walking toward Sally's office. Unfortunately, Sally's anxiety was just beginning.

Chapter Nineteen

THE RAIN HAD STOPPED, AND dusk was approaching. It made for a gray but peaceful tableau. As Shayla and Sally walked to Sally's office, her two-way radio beeped. She nodded at Shayla and took the call from Welburton. "Sally, can you get over to my office ASAP? Supe is on the way over and she wants to see both of us." Without waiting for an answer, he clicked off.

Shayla smoothed her blouse and jeans. "Mrs. Pearce, I know you have a lot to do. Go on ahead."

Sally faced her office worker and gripped her by the shoulders. "I won't leave you right now, with all you've been through."

"It's okay. You've got more people than me to take care of. I'm just gonna go home and take a shower and a nap."

"But, Shayla, I can't let you leave without giving a statement to the police. If you saw someone with a gun, the police will need to interview you."

Shayla's eyes flew open like runaway window shades, and her voice cracked, "The police? Ohhhh, noooo!" She wrested herself away from Sally's light grip and started to run, her long legs sprinting.

Sally started to take off after her, but age and high heels created a distinct disadvantage, and Shayla had disappeared around a corner before Sally gave up. It was against Sally's better judgment to let Shayla leave the premises, but she was at a loss as to how to stop her. Besides, it was true—she had probably spent too much time away from the action already. She made a mental note to call Shayla's house later.

On her way to Welburton's office, she thought she glimpsed that unpleasant Mr. Johnson, the social studies teacher, coming out of the men's restroom. "Mr. Johnson?" she called into the darkened hallway.

Maybe it was just my imagination. Sally's sense of unreality was probably getting the better of her.

She opened the door to Welburton's office, where firemen were just leaving, their faces grimy, and their overalls and coats reeking of a thick burn smell, imprinted on Sally's brain, perhaps permanently. Phone lines rang incessantly, the noise similar to that of angry hornets.

"Don't bother with the phones," cried a woman in high-heeled pumps, glasses, and long, corn-rowed hair. She waltzed in behind Sally. The superintendent, Rowena Blank, shook hands with Wally, and hugged Sally, seemingly nonplussed by their disheveled and odorous appearances. "You've been through a lot," she said.

Everyone sat at the round conference table. Suddenly depleted, Sally put her head in her hands. There was just too much to comprehend at once.

"First of all, thank you for your efficient handling of a very difficult crisis this afternoon. You cleared the building and managed the fire and its aftermath as well as could be expected. There was the potential for much danger, damage and injury, even death, and apparently no one, that is, no one except for Mr. Stoker, was hurt."

Sally couldn't accept the superintendent's bloodless approach. "How is M-Mr. Stoker?" she asked. Her mind revisited the sight of his body, supine on the granite floor, covered with a tarp, so only his cuff link showed.

Rowena shook her head. "DOA at Memorial Hospital, I'm afraid." She patted Sally's forearm, as if to console. "I know you and Stoker had a special bond. He's the one who hired you as his assistant, and he thought the world of you."

Sally burst into tears at this stark confirmation of her worst fears. Dr. Blank turned to Wally and said, "I'm appointing you Acting Principal until we can post the position. It's going to be stressful, and the school is going to be crawling with police. Even though Stoker was new to this community, he had his supporters, and they are going to give you a hard time. I trust you'll have the fortitude and good judgment to ride it out."

Sally could tell Welburton was suppressing a smile—awkward, considering the circumstances. He probably felt like jumping and punching the air, finally to be principal of Lincoln High School. "I'm up to the challenge," he said. "You won't regret this."

The superintendent turned to Sally and said, "Since Welburton will be taking over Stoker's role, you will have many more responsibilities. I'll try to get someone in to help before the change of semesters, but right now stability is going to be very important, and you two are the ones the faculty, students and parents are going to feel most comfortable with. Do you think you can handle discipline, curriculum *and* scheduling for the next couple of months?"

"I-I'll try my best," Sally said. She thought of how Stoker had plucked her out of a dozen applicants, how he had mentored her these past few weeks. "Thankfully, the scheduling is almost complete, so I can turn my attention to the other demands."

"You are both going to have your hands full for a while," the superintendent went on. "The news media is outside. You are not to speak with them, except to politely refer them to me at central office. I will be the only spokesperson, and I will tell them the least I can get away with. You will need to implement a full-blown crisis plan." She pulled red folders from her briefcase and handed one to each. "Starting tomorrow morning, you will have the social workers, school psychologist, and counselors leading back-to-back grief sessions throughout the school day, so students who are grieving, shocked, traumatized, or just distracted, can come for professional help. We will send out a robo-call to all parents announcing the unfortunate demise of Mr. Stoker, extending our sympathies to his family, and stating that school will be in session at regular time tomorrow, under the supervision of Acting Principal Welburton. The main office hallway will be roped off." Dr. Blank uncrossed her legs and picked up her briefcase, as if preparing to leave. "Any questions?"

Sally's mind flashed to the iconic picture of Lyndon Johnson's swearing-in as President after the Kennedy assassination. She felt as stunned as Jackie Kennedy looked in that photograph. She looked down at her clothes, smudged with soot and grime, too. Next she thought of Stoker, dressed so formally, even to the cuff links. "What about Stoker?" she blurted. "I mean, has someone contacted his wife? Do we know anything about arrangements?"

"I went with the fire chief to the Stoker home just before coming here. Rebekah is understandably distraught. I think it will take some time before she gets around to thinking about arrangements. It's a pity. They just moved here." The superintendent opened her briefcase and removed her car keys.

The new Lincoln High Acting Principal stood, reaching across the table to shake hands with the person who had just promoted him. Somehow he looked taller to Sally at that moment, though her mind was still on Stoker.

"Dr. Blank, maybe this is not my business, but I just can't help thinking about poor Mr. Stoker. Can you tell me how he died? Was it smoke inhalation? Was he burned to death? Why wasn't he able to get out of the building like the rest of us?"

Rowena took a deep breath and exhaled with a whoosh. "I think we'd better all sit down again," she advised, "and you might as well know this now. The police are in the main hallway, securing the crime scene. Stoker wasn't killed by the fire at all. Stoker was shot."

* * *

After Dr. Blank dropped the bomb that Stoker had been shot, it was as if the world had gone silent. At some point even the phones had stopped ringing. Sally broke the quiet with a string of questions, the answers to which were, "At this time we don't know." Finally, the superintendent cut off the meeting. "I'll leave you to do your work. Otherwise, you'll be all night getting ready for school tomorrow. When the police get around to questioning you, remember, keep it simple."

When she departed, the two building administrators looked at each other with a collegiality born of new challenges. Sally approached the new principal with arms outstretched. "Guess congratulations are in order, Principal Welburton. I don't feel much like celebrating, but you know you'll have my support."

He accepted the brief hug and nodded. "I'll need it. Helluva way to become principal, eh? It's going to take a lot of oars in the water to get this canoe moving again." Wally paced around the office. "We have so much to do, I hardly know where to start."

"My grandmother used to say, 'The secret of getting ahead is getting started.'" She grabbed a legal pad and started making a two-column list of tasks and doers. "Okay, do you want to meet with maintenance, or shall I?"

Chapter Twenty

WITHIN FIFTEEN MINUTES THE TWO weary administrators had generated a prioritized list of twenty tasks. Sally grabbed her copy and left for her own office to start in on them. As she passed by Door 23, it flew open, and in rushed her harried and worried-looking husband. "Ron!" Sally gasped. "Oh, Ron." She rushed into his arms, smelling the vestiges of shaving cream and fabric softener. The steely resolve that had kept her from breaking down evaporated.

"I heard about the fire on the *Five O'clock News*. I've been calling and calling."

"We haven't answered phones. Sorry, I should've called you. I'm not thinking clearly." Sally clung to her husband as if he were a life raft in the middle of Lake Michigan. In a few minutes she was able to take a full breath. She pulled back and looked him in the face. "Oh, Ron. Stoker is d-dead." With that another surge of grief rose up within her, bringing on fresh tears.

"Mr. Stoker is dead? I didn't hear *that* on the news."

"Dr. Blank is stalling, wants to notify the school community first. I saw Stoker on the floor outside the main office." Sally swallowed the bile that had risen into her throat. "He was covered with a tarp, but I saw his cuff link. It was him."

"Let's go into your office," Ron said, guiding her by the shoulders. "You need to sit down, get some water."

Sally was grateful not to be alone. She'd never get anything done if she couldn't rein in her emotions and stay focused. What would her martial arts trainer have suggested? As she unlocked the door to her office, Sally noticed how dark the interior seemed. "What time is it?"

"Almost six thirty. You must be exhausted."

"I'm tired," Sally admitted. "There's so much to do before tomorrow, though." She pointed to the list of tasks. "And the police are in the building. They'll probably be all over us soon."

"Police?"

"Yeah, evidently Stoker was sh-shot." With that, Sally collapsed into her executive chair and put her head on her desk for a moment.

"Listen, Sally. You've got to pick up your head and listen carefully." Ron's voice had that lawyerly quality she had heard so often when he was talking on the phone to clients. It had the desired effect, too.

"What?" She searched in her desk drawer for a tissue, but her posture was straight, and her breathing controlled.

"When the police come, let me do the talking."

* * *

Sally and Ron tackled the list of tasks together. They laid out an alternative schedule for the next day, shortening each class period to create extra time for students to spend in homeroom, where they could talk about the fire and the death of the principal. Next, they developed a list of talking points for the extended homeroom, and a set of directions for homeroom teachers. Not every teacher would be comfortable leading such a potentially emotional discussion. Since Sally knew the faculty well, she selected teachers to pair with counselors during that period. The cardinal rule, as stated in the crisis management plan, was to make sure the needs of the students were met. Any student who seemed to be experiencing undue fear or grief would be sent to the social worker or school psychologist. After school, the faculty would meet for a briefing and adult counseling session of their own.

"That's done," Sally said, letting competence take over where shock and grief had left off. "Now let's work on how we are going to handle the parents—"

Before they could address this next item, the office door opened, and two young Black men, dressed in slacks, long-sleeved shirts, and ties, jostled each other to enter the room first. Tall-and-Skinny pushed Short-and-Stocky aside with an elbow.

"Hey, what's your rush?"

"It's almost seven. Sorry if I put a wrinkle in your pocket. Sheesh!"

Sally and Ron exchanged glances before Sally took over. "May I help you?"

Tall-and-Skinny looked back at the letters on the door. "Sorry to interrupt, Ms. Pearce." He showed his badge. "Detectives Phillips and Morris here." He pointed to his partner, who also showed a badge. "We're investigating the death of Principal Stoker."

Sally pushed her bangs out of her eyes and grunted. "Oh, is it true Mr. Stoker was shot?"

Ron reached over to touch his wife on the arm.

"I mean, that's what the superintendent said."

Officer Phillips showed his teeth in what might suffice as a smile. "Looks that way. Body's been taken to the morgue. Officers've been taping off the area and collecting information."

"We just want to ask you a few questions," Officer Morris intervened.

Phillips shot him a look.

"Excuse me for interrupting," Ron said. "I'm Mrs. Pearce's husband. Also an attorney." He pulled a business card from a vinyl case in his jacket pocket and handed it to Phillips. "Can you tell me the nature of the questions you wish to ask my wife?"

Morris flinched, and Phillips took over. "Just routine questions. You know, what was her relationship to the deceased, did she know of anyone who might have had it in for him."

Sally watched the surreal interchange as if it were a midnight movie. This couldn't be happening.

Ron moved between the officers and Sally. "I'm sorry, detectives, but my wife has had a great shock today. She is tired and upset, and we were just about to leave for home. I suggest you find Superintendent Blank if you want answers to your questions this evening." He turned to Sally and said, "C'mon, honey. Grab your purse and let's call it a day."

Morris looked at Phillips as if to say, "Are you gonna let this guy get away with this?"

But Detective Phillips straightened his posture and patted his holstered gun. "Very well, sir. We'll head over to district office, but we'll be back first thing tomorrow morning." His dark eyes burned into Sally's light ones. "You get yourself a good night's sleep, Ms. Pearce. Tomorrow's another day."

Chapter Twenty-one

AFTER A MOSTLY SLEEPLESS NIGHT, Acting Principal Welburton picked at the scrambled eggs and sausage his wife June had prepared for him before they both ran off to work. Their usual breakfast was coffee and a granola bar, and truthfully, Wally would have preferred that. The spicy sausage smell was somewhat nauseating. Or maybe it was just a bad case of nerves.

"It's funny," he said, taking a swallow of steaming java. "I've dreamed of being Lincoln's principal for as long as I can remember, but I never thought someone would have to die for me to get it."

"You really should eat your breakfast before rushing off." June was shoveling bites into her own mouth, her eye on the clock. "You're going to need your strength."

Wally stabbed at his eggs and took a bite. His mind was on the school day ahead: the roped-off area outside the main office, the police, grieving and curious kids and parents, a jittery faculty. No one had talked about how to handle fires and murders in administrative classes. Aside from the crisis management plan, he was going to have to wing it.

"You, too," he replied. "The kids in *your* class might be talking about it. Their sisters and brothers may be Lincoln students." Wally glanced at his wife before taking his half-full plate to the sink and dumping its contents in the disposal. "This crisis will affect the entire community, one way or another." He set his dirty dish in the sink and lifted his briefcase from the counter.

"Just be careful, if you know what I mean." June brushed her husband's cheek with her lips as he passed by.

"What *do* you mean?" Wally said, one foot out the door.

"Well, if someone is out to get principals at that school, you could be next."

Wally hesitated for a moment, thinking. He'd never felt threatened at Lincoln before, but then again, he'd never been its principal. Still, he didn't want to start his first day in fear, and he didn't want June to be fearful, either. "Don't worry. After twenty-two years, I've got a lot of friends there."

"Yeah, but you've also seen what happens to friendships when you move up the chain. Just watch your back." June carried her empty plate to the sink and loaded both plates in the dishwasher. "I don't want to get a phone call like poor Mrs. Stoker."

June's words reverberated inside Wally's head, giving him a slight headache. He noticed the pale skin on his hand as he started the car and reminded himself that he was a white man in a Black environment. Friends or not, he would have a treacherous path ahead.

* * *

En route to Lincoln, Wally mentally added to the list of tasks he and Sally had made the night before. Something would have to be done about secretaries. Stoker's secretary, Glenda, had the title, Principal's Secretary. While he and Myrna had been together for many years, the secretaries' union would require him to switch. He'd have to move from one office to another, too, once the fire damage had been cleaned up.

More immediately, he was going to have to get this day started, so homeroom teachers could implement the crisis plan. He had drafted a short speech last night before he left his office, but now he realized that the public address system was inside Stoker's office— momentarily off limits. Maybe he could get the school's police liaison to let him into the closet behind the front office area.

The image of Stoker's covered body lying in the main office hallway flashed before his eyes. Police officers had been working the area when he left the night before. He'd paused to ask if they needed anything, but they'd hardly looked up. He knew today he'd be smothered by police, journalists, maybe even school attorneys.

He tightened his tie at the red light and glanced at his face in the rear view mirror. So much had changed in the past eighteen hours, but aside from the purplish wells underscoring his hazel eyes from lack of sleep, Welburton decided he looked the part of a high school principal: conservative, sober, trustworthy.

He pulled into his regular parking place, the one marked, "Assistant Principal," and added another item to his list of changes. In fact, he threw his gear shift into reverse, backed out, and pulled into the adjacent space, marked, "Principal." It felt fine, finally, to be in the place where he deserved to be. He grabbed his briefcase, buttoning his sport jacket with one hand as he emerged from the car.

He hadn't walked more than ten steps before he was greeted from behind by Norma Dunn, whose parking place was several slots beyond his. Skittering on high heels, she called his name, and was he imagining it, or was she cupping his buttocks in her hand?

"I hear congratulations are in order, Principal Welburton," she trilled. "It couldn't happen to a more deserving person, in my opinion. But then, you know I have always been your biggest fan." Norma's curly eyelashes rose and fell with each word.

"Listen," he replied, "I appreciate your good wishes, but we have a lot of work to do here today. I hope I can count on you to help with getting the faculty on board with the crisis management plan." He was careful not to touch her.

"Of course, sugar," Norma purred. "You know you can count on me for anything. And I mean *anything*." With that, Norma walked ahead, providing Wally with an excellent view of her shapely rear end. She let herself into the building and let the door close behind her with a clang.

Wally remembered how Norma had pursued Mr. Morgan for years, fueling rumors of a more-than-professional relationship. He wondered whether he was going to have to add another item to his list of changes. He definitely did not want to get involved with the faculty association president.

* * *

Wally had expected to get to his office early, so he could organize the day's activities and make sure the crisis plan was in place. What he hadn't counted on was being preempted by the police. As he put the key into the lock on his office door, he noticed it had already been unlocked, and the lights were on inside. June's warning flashed through his mind as he turned the doorknob and eased the door open.

"G'morning, Principal," came a voice from the inner office. "Hope you don't mind we made ourselves comfortable." A tall, wiry guy stood in the space behind Wally's desk.

"Oh, Phillips, it's you," Wally said, relieved to recognize the uninvited visitor.

"And me, too." The pudgy detective, Morris, held out his hand.

Wally shook hands with both men. One of them was wearing too much cologne. "Glad to see our police department is giving us top priority this morning. How did you get into the office?"

"We have our ways," Phillips replied. "Hope you don't mind. We just have a few questions, and we wanted to catch you before things got too busy."

"No problem," Wally said. He looked around for evidence that the detectives had gone through his desk or file cabinet, but everything looked normal. He dumped his briefcase on the conference table and walked around the desk to his executive chair. Sitting, facing Phillips and Morris, he leaned back and flicked his tie.

Morris started. "It's no secret that you competed with Stoker for the principalship." He paused for what seemed to be a minute or more.

Wally waited for the question, and when none came, he said, "Okay."

Phillips broke in. "So how resentful were you when Stoker got the job, him bein' an outsider an' all?"

Wally didn't like the phrasing of the question. "I won't lie. I wanted the job, but that's how it goes in school administration. Sometimes you're up, sometimes you're down."

Morris said, "But how'd y'feel about Stoker? As a boss, I mean?"

Until now, it hadn't occurred to Wally that he might be a suspect in Stoker's death. His stomach lurched. "We had a good relationship. Sure, he had a different style, not what we've been used to, but a good guy, meant well." Was he saying too much? Not enough?

"Different style? How d'ya mean?" Morris asked.

Wally's armpits felt damp, and he tugged at his tie. Phillips was holding a pen and notepad, ready to record his response. "I just mean, meant… Stoker brings, brought… different ideas, different expertise. He came from a school in Tennessee where he had a lot of success."

Phillips asked, "Had Stoker done anything since the start of school that might've upset anyone? Hurt anyone?"

Wally thought of the first day of school when Stoker got Gottschalk all riled up, the way Stoker had handled the threat against Coach Donovan. There were probably half a dozen or more people who had complained about Stoker to him. "Not really. Not any more than usual for a principal at the start of the semester. It's a tough job, setting expectations for discipline, and all."

Morris leaned forward, gut spilling over waistband. "Speaking of discipline, any ideas about how somebody might've brought a gun into the school?"

Wally considered before answering. "Thought about that all night. Getting a gun into the building is not so difficult. We don't have metal detectors at the entrances, you know. But keeping it hidden all day, not having someone tip us off, that is surprising. And upsetting."

"You'll be happy to know we did a locker search with dogs overnight. If a recently-shot firearm was in the building, we would've found it." Phillips closed his notebook. "We're going to need your cooperation, Welburton. Killing the principal, setting the building on fire, these are heinous crimes. We're going to be poking around here a lot in the next coupla days. We've got to catch the scumbag who did this."

Wally straightened up in his chair and aligned his tie with the buttons of his shirt. "So you think the fire was arson? You think the fire was connected to the murder?"

"We don't have answers yet, only questions." Phillips stood, his posture so erect, he could be a tree trunk or a steeple. "But you'll be seein' us around."

Wally strove to keep his composure even. "I'll let the superintendent know. All that we ask is that you do your best to remain discreet, gentlemen. After all, this is a school—filled with innocent kids—and we've got to think of their education."

"Oh, and by the way," Morris said, fixing Wally with a steady gaze. "When was the last time you saw Stoker alive?"

Wally flinched, despite himself. "Me? I-I guess it must have been during the last lunch period. We were both monitoring the kids in the cafeteria. That period ends at 1:52."

Morris replied, "And the fire alarm went off at 2:45. Apparently a lot happened in those fifty-three minutes, but don't worry. We'll find out."

A shiver climbed up Wally's spine. It was going to be hard for anyone to stay focused on education today, especially Wally.

Chapter Twenty-two

LIKE WELBURTON, SALLY HADN'T SLEPT much. She'd kept thinking of Stoker, how he'd made her feel at her interview when he'd hired her, on the several occasions after school when they'd chatted about their backgrounds and philosophies. It seemed as if they had known each other much longer than a few months.

Stoker had seen beyond Sally's white face, her lack of administrative experience. He told her she was one in a million, because she had both intellect and compassion, the two most important qualities of a stellar administrator. "I've got big plans for you," he had said on more than one occasion. Now she would never know what those plans were, and already she was missing Stoker's determination, his style, his focus on the kids.

Also like Welburton, she had dashed off to work, and now she sat in the parking lot in her "Assistant Principal" spot, watching the early bird staff members arriving and gathering in the fall morning. Coach Donovan was bear-hugging a co-worker, and others were coming toward the pair to huddle up in the parking lot.

Sally bit her lip to hold back the surge of feelings rising inside. If only she could turn back the clock, reverse the outcome of yesterday's tragedy. She made a mental note to make sure the flag was raised to half-staff today.

The clean fall breeze whisked through the parking lot, the new sunshine dappling through tree branches onto the pavement. It would have been lovely, had it not been for the smell of cinders and bits of black dust, grim souvenirs.

As she strode past Donovan and his group, she heard a voice.

"Mrs. Pearce?"

She turned to face Ben Gottschalk. Never one of Sally's favorites, the calculus teacher reached out to touch her shoulder with a bony finger. "Mrs. Pearce, what can you tell us about Mr. Stoker's death? We're hearing so many rumors."

"Good morning, Mr. Gottschalk," Sally replied. "I don't have any more information at this point than what's already been shared through last night's telephone tree. Our main focus today has got to be the students." She smoothed the skirt of her olive-colored suit and pulled the matching jacket over her hips. "Now if you'll excuse me."

As she walked past the men, she heard someone mumble, "I'll just *bet* she doesn't know anything. It didn't take her long to go administrative on us."

She wanted to go back and argue, resume her place on the faculty roster, just be one of the teachers, but she had crossed a line and there would never be any going back. She held her head high and thought of Stoker. She would do her utmost to make him proud of having chosen her, even if he wouldn't be here to see her.

* * *

Sally took an unsatisfying deep breath after peering into the main office hallway where the staff mailboxes and message board were. In addition to the acrid-smelling ravages of the fire, there were sawhorses and large black plastic tarps blocking off the area. All of these were decorated with bright yellow ribbons of plastic that said, "CRIME SCENE DO NOT CROSS." It looked like a macabre gift package.

Along the side of the next hallway, near the auditorium entrance, the three administrative secretaries, Glenda, Myrna, and Pat, were already passing out packets of information to teachers. Included were the day's schedule, the curriculum for the special homeroom, the pertinent information from the crisis plan, and suggestions for handling whatever fallout might occur from the previous day's fire and death of the principal. The teachers, usually boisterous and energetic in their morning greetings to one another, today drifted in with somber faces and quiet demeanors.

As she watched the procession of teachers entering the building, a strange sense of the surreal overcame her. It was as if her body were floating in time and space, and the past, present, and future were disconnected from one another. Something nagged at her, too, something or someone she needed to remember.

Shrugging her shoulders, she willed her legs into action. There were too many practical concerns this morning, starting with meeting the counselors and social workers before homeroom. She would make the formal announcement of Stoker's death, and she should probably touch base with Wally, as well. Stoker's voice echoed in her brain, "From those to whom much is given, much is required."

* * *

One of the requirements of the crisis plan was for all staff members to stand at their doors as students passed to their next classes. Having a full and consistent physical presence of staff in the hallways would give students a sense of security, and it would give teachers a chance to address issues or concerns as they saw them happening throughout the day.

So after the extended homeroom, Sally was in the hallway near the Lincoln statue, near where Tyrone Nesbitt slammed his locker shut, a grimace on his face, and a dark look in his eyes. Everyone knew Tyrone from his exceptional skills on the football team, but Sally had taught him English in his freshman year, and he was also Shayla's boyfriend. Tyrone didn't look his usual debonair self, but he had been attacked on the practice field just last week, had his jaw broken. He was probably pushing it to come back to school so soon.

Tyrone almost bumped into Sally on his way to Mr. Gottschalk's class. He caught himself just before the impact. "Sorry, Mrs. Pearce," he said through clenched teeth. "My bad."

"No, *my* bad," Sally replied. "How are you feeling, Tyrone?" She put her arm around the athlete's back in an overture of concern, expecting perhaps a hug in return. What she didn't expect was for Tyrone to cave into her arm, almost doubling over, as if in pain.

"Oh, man. Mrs. Pearce, can I t-talk to you for a few minutes? In p-private?" His voice, muffled by the way he was holding his jaw together, shook.

"Sure. Let's go to my office." Sally led the way, avoiding the dreaded main office hallway. "And I'll give you a pass to class, afterwards."

She and Tyrone sat in the two chairs she and Shayla had occupied just yesterday. It seemed like a decade ago. Sally pulled two tissues from the cardboard box on her desk and handed them to Tyrone, though he wasn't crying or needing to blow his nose.

Tyrone began in a subdued voice. "Y-you know I got hurt. I-I was in the hospital last week." He crumpled the unused tissues in one hand. "Mr. Stoker came to see me there."

"That doesn't surprise me," Sally said. "Mr. Stoker thought a lot of you. He told me so."

"He was a g-good man," Tyrone said, pain in his voice coming either from his emotions or from the physical ailment. "He r-really cares—cared about us." He put his forehead in his cupped hands and swallowed.

The sting of incipient tears made way for Sally's own expression of grief. "This is a big loss for all of us." She wondered whether Tyrone had deeper feelings about Stoker than he was expressing. "Maybe you'd like to write down your feelings, maybe send a card to Mrs. Stoker? I'm sure the family would appreciate that."

"Yeah, maybe."

She patted Tyrone on the shoulder blade. "You know there's a grief center in the multipurpose room. Would you like to go there instead of class?"

Tyrone wiped his face, a symbolic gesture, since there were no real tears. "Nah, I just wanted to talk to you about Mr. Stoker. But there's one more thing—have you seen Shayla today?"

Shayla. Sally had been so preoccupied with administrative tasks on this difficult day. She had meant to follow up on Shayla, but hadn't. "She should be here sixth period." She consulted the clock and glanced at the printout of the day's schedule. "At two-twelve."

"Okay, but I ain't seen her all day. She hangs out at my locker before school and in between classes. We share. But she ain't been there at all today."

"That's odd. Maybe she got to school late, or maybe she's absent. I'll check on her and see." Sally remembered Shayla's dash for the bathroom the day before, followed by the confidence she had shared about being pregnant. "Are you ready to go to class now? You can check back with me after school, and I should have seen or talked to Shayla by then."

Tyrone wiped his face again. He stood and tossed the crumpled tissues into the wastebasket across the room, his eyes lighting up when they hit the target. "Thanks, Ms. Pearce. You're still my favorite teacher, ya know."

Sally smiled at the compliment and offered a hug in return. But as she comforted Tyrone, her thoughts were elsewhere. If Shayla wasn't at school today, where was she? And who was it Shayla had seen with a gun?

Chapter Twenty-three

AS USUAL, WALLY SPENT THE four student lunch periods roaming through the cafeteria, trying to head off trouble before it could get a foothold and escalate into something bigger. But this was the first time he did so as principal. It was all he could do to contain his excitement. Several times he caught himself rocking on his heels, as if he were enjoying the music at a celebratory dance. He admonished himself. If some parent called Dr. Blank to say the new principal was dancing in the cafeteria the day after the old principal was killed, it wouldn't look good at all.

It didn't make it any easier when, one by one, the faculty members supervising the cafeteria came by to congratulate him, all smiles and hearty claps on the back. He could hardly do his job for all the interruptions, but, hey, he'd waited a long time for this day, and he was going to enjoy it.

He cringed, though, when Mr. Johnson, the social studies guy with the New York accent, came over.

"I'm so pleased for you, Mr. Welburton," Johnson said, the odor of a recently eaten sausage sandwich filling the space between them. "Now maybe we can have an orderly school environment."

Wally tilted his face backward to avoid the air pollution. "Didn't you think we had an orderly environment before? After all, I was in charge of discipline."

"Yes, but Mr. Stoker, ah, it's not nice to speak ill of the dead, but—"

Out of the corner of his eye, Wally noticed Melody Singer, the new social studies teacher. She was squatting at the corner of a table, deep in conversation with a student.

"Thanks for the good wishes, Johnson," Wally replied. "Now let's get these kids to clean up the tables and take back their trays." He moved away from Johnson and toward the curly-haired Ms. Singer. When he reached the table, he just stood there, waiting for the conference with the student to end.

Noticing the new principal hovering, Melody stood and smiled. "Can I help you, Mr. Welburton?"

"I don't want to interrupt your conversation. I just wanted to say hello. You are one of our shining stars, you know." Wally leaned across Ms. Singer to ask the student, "Isn't Ms. Singer one of the best teachers ever?"

The student stared at Wally, brow furrowed. "I guess so," she replied.

Wally turned back to Ms. Singer, his lips widening into what he hoped was an endearing smile. "I want you to know that you can come to me any time, if you need assistance with your students. You will always have my support."

"I appreciate that," Ms. Singer said. She looked at her watch and said, "If you'll please excuse me, we only have three minutes left, and I need to finish talking to Tanisha here."

"Of course, of course," Wally said, and moved on.

"Hey, you," Wally called into the corner to a group of juniors huddled together around the center of the rectangular table. "What's goin' on over there?"

"Nothin', man," one of the students replied, as the rest moved swiftly to hide something from view.

Wally caught a glimpse of a shiny penny as it rolled from someone's hands onto the table. "You better not let me see any pitching penny games. That's a three-day suspension for gambling."

One of the kids muttered, "Sheesh," under his breath, while the others replied, "Yes, sir."

Wally turned toward the opposite side of the room, where Coach Donovan was talking to the team's quarterback. As he approached, the player excused himself and walked away.

"What was that all about?" Wally asked the coach.

"Just talking to Tyrone about when the doctor will release him to play again. You know he has a broken jaw."

"We need him on the field ASAP, don't we?"

"Yes, but we can't risk having him re-injure. Stoker saw the doctor when he visited Tyrone at the hospital, and the doc said he shouldn't play as long as the wire is in place."

"Stoker? When did Stoker go to the hospital?"

"I guess the day after the incident. Not sure." Donovan jingled the change in his pocket before saying, "Listen, Wally. I think we should call off practice for this afternoon. The kids are having a hard day, and I don't think it's right to make them stay."

"You don't think it's best to keep things going as much as normal? Keep the kids in their routine?"

Donovan's eyes narrowed, as if he were seeing a stranger, instead of his old buddy. "C'mon, now. We've just had a fire and a murder. Let's give the kids some catch-up time, don't you think?"

Wally said, "Uh, yeah. I guess you're right. But make it clear that tomorrow everything goes back to normal." He swatted Donovan on the arm and went back to monitoring the students. He didn't feel much different from when he was assistant principal, after all.

Chapter Twenty-four

BEFORE SALLY COULD CHECK ON Shayla, there was a knock on her office door, and when she looked up from her computer, she saw Phillips and Morris, the two police detectives from the previous night. Her stomach flipped. She wished she could transport Ron back to her office to protect her from their inquiries.

"Mind if we come in?" one of them asked in a cheerier-than-necessary voice. Without waiting for her reply, they stepped into her office and sat in the two guest chairs opposite her desk.

Sally's gaze traveled from one to the other before she said, "Won't you sit down?"

Phillips, the tall and skinny one, grinned, his teeth reminding Sally of a jack o'lantern. "Didn't mean to be presumptuous, Ms. Pearce. You knew we were coming back today."

Morris just looked down, as if reading something fascinating on his lap.

"What can I do for you?" Sally asked, hoping whatever it was, she could handle it.

"Can we shut the door?" Phillips began. He jumped up before receiving Sally's answer. He closed the door and began twisting the wand to close the mini-blinds covering the glass windows to the outer office.

Still standing at her desk, Sally felt a trickle of sweat forming at the back of her neck, though the air conditioning was working just fine. "Gentlemen, with all due respect, school is in session, and it's a difficult day. We are understaffed. I have a million things I need to be doing."

110

"We won't be long," Phillips said. "We just have a few routine questions, and we'll let you get back to your work." He exchanged glances with Morris, who sat up straighter and pulled a notepad from his jacket pocket.

Sally sat, resigned to listening to the detectives. As much as she'd like to avoid their questions, her duties as assistant principal required her to cooperate, despite her husband's warning. The sooner she started, the sooner she could get back to looking for Shayla. The perspiration ran down her spine, but her face remained impassive.

Phillips began. "Ms. Pearce, what was your relationship with Mr. Stoker?"

Dozens of things ran through Sally's mind, but which ones would be pertinent in this horrible situation? "He was my principal. He hired me as his assistant principal. I will always be grateful to him for that."

"We know Stoker just started working here, but can you give us your opinion about his work? Was he competent? Was he liked by the school community?"

Sally squirmed a little, wondering how to answer. Her loyalty to Stoker battled with her natural inclination to tell the truth. But what *was* the truth? She was beginning to see that the life of an administrator was full of complexities, sometimes including subterfuge, obfuscation, sabotage, and lies. Someone in this school community had likely killed Stoker. Like him or not, he didn't deserve that. She resolved at that moment to be as helpful as she could to the police. It was the least she could do to repay Stoker for his faith in her.

She said, "In my opinion, gentlemen, Mr. Stoker was a real leader. He brought a wealth of knowledge and training in how to promote academic success. He was student-oriented, and he modeled his beliefs every day. I learned a lot from him. His death is a huge loss to Lincoln High."

Morris gave a snort as he shifted his bulk from one side to the other. He apparently was having trouble keeping up with typing her answers.

Phillips leaned forward. "Were you aware of any threats, any animosities toward Mr. Stoker either from inside or outside of the school?"

Each question chipped away at that bedrock of security, perhaps illusory, that allowed Sally to work at Lincoln High School. If Stoker could provoke sufficient anger to lead to his violent death on campus, how safe was she? She picked at a fingernail, lost in thought.

"Mrs. Pearce?"

"Uh, I'm sorry. What was the question?"

Phillips exchanged glances with Morris, then repeated his question.

Sally had the distinct impression that she was failing an exam, and the wetness down her back increased. "No specific threats or animosities that I know of. Just the usual competitions and turf battles that every principal faces."

"Turf battles?"

"Yes. People who wanted to be principal and didn't get it. People who curry favor with the new principal in hopes of getting attention or prestige. The school is full of people with their own agendas."

Morris uttered a grunt that sounded like, "Uh-huh," as his fingers recorded Sally's responses. "Maybe police politics are similar to school politics."

Phillips persisted. "People with their own agendas. That's exactly what we are looking for, Mrs. Pearce. I want you to consider anyone you know who might have had a conflict with Mr. Stoker—whether it's another administrator, teacher, staff member, parent or student— and I want you to share your thoughts with us." He pulled a business card from a case in his back pocket. "Call me day or night. Okay?"

Sally thought of telling Phillips about Shayla's comment, about her having seen someone with a gun. But until she talked to Shayla, until she had more information, it might do more harm than good. She decided to wait. She could always call Phillips, day or night. She put Phillips' card in her pencil drawer, where she could find it quickly. "Okay."

"The sooner we apprehend the person who killed Mr. Stoker, the safer the school will be." Phillips nodded to Morris, who covered his notepad and put it away in his jacket. "And now, we will leave you to your school duties. We appreciate your time."

Relieved that the interview was almost over, Sally stood, exhaling a bit too loudly in the process.

"We are, however, going to interview a few more people, and after school we are going to examine the crime scene area in the main office. We would like to have you join us around four o'clock. I'm sure the search will turn up some items that you can identify and explain."

Glancing at the clock, Sally counted the minutes until four o'clock, just under three hours. She hoped that would give her enough time to get around to all of the classrooms. It was important for the students and staff to see some stability, some normalcy. If they saw her looking unafraid and in control, they might feel the same way.

She wrote "Main office, 4 pm," on her desk calendar, as if she might forget. As the detectives shook her hand and filed out of the office, she re-opened the blinds. The top thing on *her* agenda was to talk to Shayla.

Chapter Twenty-five

FIVE MINUTES BEFORE THE DISMISSAL bell, a Midwestern-accented voice burst into the classrooms through the public address system. "May I please have your attention, faculty and students? This is Principal Welburton. First, I want to thank the teachers, counselors, deans, social workers, and the entire faculty and student body for maintaining a positive academic environment today, despite the difficult circumstances here at Lincoln High School. Today you have all been Warriors.

"Anyone in need of assistance in the coming days and weeks, know this faculty stands ready to help. Just let your teacher or counselor know.

"Additionally, there will be no after-school activities today. No athletics, no club meetings, no late buses. We anticipate returning to normal after-school activities beginning tomorrow. Faculty, once students are dismissed and the building cleared, there will be a meeting in the auditorium. Have a good evening, and remember, at Lincoln High School we are all winning Warriors."

Tyrone shifted positions at his desk in Mr. Johnson's economics class. His jaw was killing him. He couldn't remember football practice ever being cancelled, but he wouldn't have been able to play anyway. It had been a strange day without Mr. Stoker around. Funny how much he'd missed him, considering he'd just met him a few weeks ago. Most of all, Tyrone was antsy about Shayla. He hoped Mrs. Pearce would come through with some news. When the bell rang, he'd run to Mrs. Pearce's office to see if she'd heard anything.

"Hey, Nesbitt," Mr. Johnson called, peering over his half-glasses.

114

"Sit up straight. Your brain can't work when you're bent over like an old man."

Tyrone shot a sideways glance at the student on his left, as if to say, "Do you believe this guy, getting on my case?" Then he straightened his spine and shoulders and lifted his head. He looked straight ahead, avoiding eye contact with Mr. Johnson. He knew better than to argue with the man. He was already failing the class.

A group of students in the back of the room began a conversation about Mr. Stoker. Tyrone heard bits and pieces. "Awesome principal," "Really liked us kids," "Feel bad for his family." And then, "Who would want to harm him?"

Mr. Johnson raised himself a few inches from the stool at his podium in the front center of the room and pointed his index finger at the group of talkers. "Young men. Young ladies. Class is not over. Please conduct yourselves accordingly." He sat back down.

Before they could respond, the dismissal bell rang, and the students pushed their way out of the classroom with the vigor of ball carriers toward the goal line. Tyrone hung back, protecting his jaw from accidental prodding or bumping.

As he moved past Mr. Johnson, Tyrone looked away, but the annoying man reached out an arm to halt his progress. "Listen here, Nesbitt. I, ah, want to have a word with you."

Tyrone stopped walking and turned slowly to face his teacher.

"I, ah, need you to make up two tests and three papers. School has been in session only two weeks, and I'm afraid you are dreadfully behind already."

Tyrone measured his words, not only because of the throbbing in his jaw, but because irritation was boiling into full-fledged anger. "How can I get caught up then?" he spat between clenched teeth. "I'm going to have practice every day after school." He touched his jaw. "Even if I don't play, I have to go."

"Don't you think academics are more important than football?" The teacher stood with arms crossed, a bulwark of self-importance. "Failing this class could make you ineligible."

"Seems like you don't care. Why don't you *help* me instead of threatening me?" Tyrone started to strike the teacher's arms and push

115

him away, three-piece suit and all, but at the last second he held back. He muttered, "Man, do I miss Mr. Stoker."

Johnson took a step back and raised an eyebrow. "Stoker? What does *he* have to do with it? I never saw anything so great about Stoker, anyway."

"Listen, Mr. Johnson. I don't mean any disrespect, you unnerstand." Tyrone touched his jaw. "Mr. Stoker was a great man. He really cared about us kids. He *inspired* us. He wouldn't put it all on us. He would say, 'What can we, as a school, do to help you be successful?'"

Johnson gazed at the toes of his polished black wingtips. He appeared to be gathering thoughts for a rejoinder, but before he uttered a word, Tyrone brushed past him.

"I gotta go now, or I'll miss the bus. No late buses today, remember?"

* * *

Tyrone flew down the steps from the third to first floor, hoping to catch Mrs. Pearce before she left her office for the faculty meeting in the auditorium. He cursed Mr. Johnson for having kept him after class, and for what? He was still failing econ, and no plan in sight. Right now, all he wanted was his sweet Shayla. When he saw her he was going to wrap her in his arms and never let go.

The halls were empty of students already, no sounds but the soft plodding of his own gym shoes on the granite stairs and floors. Funny how the building didn't seem like a school without kids in it.

As he approached the auditorium hallway, his ears picked up subdued sounds of many voices. The teachers' meeting was probably getting underway. Now near the main office, the burned-dust smell of the fire's remains assaulted Tyrone's nostrils. The hallway was roped off with yellow tape and plastic tarps, with only a tiny pathway open to foot traffic. Tyrone re-routed himself. Getting too close to the crime scene might cause him to vomit, or at the very least, cry. Instead, he took the long way to Mrs. Pearce's office, around the Lincoln statue hallway and past Mr. Welburton's office.

As he turned the final corner, he passed darkened classrooms with closed doors. Running had made his jaw ache like a fresh wound. He slowed as he approached Mrs. Pearce's office, but before he got there, he saw *that* door closed, as well, and the lights out. *Damn that Mr. Johnson!*

Tyrone did an about-face and stumbled toward the north exit, where the buses would be. Tired and hurting, he decided to take Shayla's bus instead of his own. He'd go to her house and find out for himself why she wasn't at school.

Just as he reached the door, though, he saw the last bus, the one to Shayla's neighborhood, pull off. Feeling thoroughly defeated, Tyrone pushed the exit bar and trudged down the concrete steps. Apparently the Lincoln Warriors' quarterback would be walking home.

Chapter Twenty-six

THE AUDITORIUM STAGE WAS LITTERED with the bare frames of the set for the fall play, hammered out by stagecraft students earlier that day, and the smell of sawdust permeated the air. Wally stood at the podium, speaking into the microphone, his body backed by what appeared to be a huge throne. How appropriate, thought Sally, as she looked at her watch for the umpteenth time.

It was almost four, and she had promised the detectives she would meet them at Stoker's office. As much as she dreaded the task ahead, she found herself tapping her foot, wishing the meeting to be over. Stoker hadn't believed in long meetings. Apparently Wally had a different style. Sally tried to concentrate on what he said, but all she could make out was, "Unfortunately, *this*," and, "Unfortunately, *that*." She felt pretty sure if she were principal, she wouldn't be keeping all these teachers here so late on what had been a very stressful day for everyone.

Just before leaving her office for the meeting, Sally had tried calling Shayla's house. The phone had rung and rung. She'd tried in vain to locate a work phone number for Shayla's mom, but dropped everything when she realized how late it was.

She peered at the faculty and staff in the seats around her. Every face bore a serious expression. The absence of side conversations and grumblings also made a statement about the mood at Lincoln High School. Finally, Wally wound up his comments, only to introduce the school psychologist and two social workers. It looked like there might be another half hour of agenda.

Sally looked at her watch again. One minute past four, and she had to leave. She rose from her seat in the darkened auditorium and walked bent over, so as not to block the view of the teachers sitting behind her. She scooted out of her row and rushed up the aisle on the balls of her feet, trying to keep her heels from clattering on the marble floor. On her way out, she noticed Mr. Gottschalk and Ms. Dunn sitting together in the back row. Gottschalk stared at Sally while leaning to whisper in Ms. Dunn's ear, but Norma continued to look straight ahead.

It was only about fifty feet from the auditorium to the principal's office, and Sally could see Phillips and Morris pushing around the yellow crime scene tape. Sally tried, but failed, to ignore the dark stains on the floor by the door. The stench of burned drywall caused her to gag, and she wondered whether she would be able to do this.

"Here, put this on," Phillips said, handing a drugstore mask to Sally, another to Morris, then putting one on his own face. "We won't be here long, but it's best not to breathe fumes while we're here."

Sally donned her mask, placing the elastic string past her ears and bisecting her pageboy hairdo in the middle of the back. By this time, Morris had unlocked the door, and the trio stepped gingerly through the threshold. The waiting room and the mail room were a mucky mess. Remnants of upholstered furniture and debris from fire and water created an eerie tableau of chaos. It would take time to restore these rooms to usable spaces.

Morris unlocked the inner door leading to Stoker's office, then held his arm out to usher Sally and Phillips ahead of him. There was no electricity, and the light from the south side windows was already growing dim. Nothing could have prepared Sally, though, for what she saw inside.

Stoker's conference table and guest chairs were strewn about, as if tossed by an angry giant. The solid oak executive desk, which must have weighed a couple hundred pounds, lay tilted on its side. The professional library bookshelves along one wall remained intact, as if mocking the destruction in the rest of the room.

"No fire damage in this room?" Sally asked, her throat tight and her nose stinging, despite the mask.

"No, just smoke, and water from the sprinkler system," Phillips replied. "The fire was set out in the hallway."

"But what happened to the furniture?"

"Obviously, a struggle. We think someone confronted Stoker, fought with him in here. Not sure about the timeline. Thought you might have some ideas."

Sally shook her head.

Phillips pulled plastic gloves out of his pants pocket and handed a pair to Sally and Morris before putting them on. "Not sure if the guys are finished fingerprinting yet, but the room has been photographed."

He stepped around the principal's desk. "Morris, can you give me a hand?"

The two detectives righted the heavy desk, while Sally stood fixed, as if her feet had become cement blocks. Morris pulled open a drawer. Phillips peered into the drawer, then opened several more. "How 'bout helping us go through these papers and things? Maybe you can tell what's significant and what's not."

Morris righted the executive chair and said, "Let's use this to stack everything on, okay?" As he and Phillips alternated taking things out of the drawers and heaping them onto the chair, a thousand thoughts flowed through Sally's mind. How would the contents of *her* drawers look to others under similar circumstances? How had Stoker filled his desk drawers with so much in just a few short weeks? How would she be able to tell if one item were more significant than another?

Most of the things being piled up for her review were benign—a district telephone directory, a calendar, a curriculum guide, a stack of student passes. The second and third drawers were emptied, and Sally still could see nothing of interest. The fourth drawer, though, was filled with envelopes neatly stacked and rubber-banded, curled at the corners. It appeared that these were items from Mr. Stoker's mail that he had deemed important enough to save.

"These might be relevant. Might take me awhile to go through them. I feel strange reading Mr. Stoker's private mail, though." She opened the first envelope in the first stack and saw a copy of the principal's contract.

"We've already gotten permission from Dr. Blank. She said you would be the person in the school Stoker trusted most."

Heat flushed Sally's face and neck from the compliment, though she didn't relish the task ahead. She was already having a difficult time handling her grief, and going through Stoker's papers might open the floodgates. She patted the stack of envelopes, as if they were an extension of Stoker himself, as if touching his personal items might bring him back. "I'll give it my best shot."

By now it was becoming dark in the office, and the masks and gloves contributed to the uncomfortable mugginess. Morris pulled the items out of the bottom drawer and set them on the chair. The first was a box of chocolate candy. Opening the box, he said, "Expensive candy, none eaten. Any idea about this?"

Sally shook her head. "Sometimes I keep food in my desk in case I'm hungry, but that looks more like a gift."

Morris placed the box in an evidence bag and set it aside. He lifted a six-inch stack of papers from the bottom drawer and passed it to Sally. "Looks like this is everything." In his haste, and hers, the bottommost item slipped through her fingers and fell on the floor. Sally bent to retrieve the unusual envelope, the size of a greeting card, and lavender in color. It had been ripped open, unlike the others, and instead of a formal address, the single word, *Stoker*, was scrawled across the front.

Sally had an idea who might have sent that one to Mr. Stoker, as her mind revisited the "Seven-Up" signal Stoker had devised so she could witness his meeting with Ms. Dunn. By now, she was hot and tired and filled with emotions, so when Morris said, "Looks like that's all there is," she stuffed the envelope out of sight and carried the last batch of envelopes against her chest.

"Can we go now?" Sally asked. "Can I take these home with me and go through them tonight?" She rubbed her eyes and patted at the perspiration on her forehead under her bangs.

"I don't have a problem with that, as long as you are careful," Morris replied. "You?" he asked Phillips.

"No-o," Phillips replied. "Just be sure to bring it all back tomorrow morning, and be careful. Here's another pair of gloves to wear

121

when you handle the documents. Any one piece may turn out to be evidence."

The detectives helped Sally carry the documents to her office, where she loaded them into her briefcase, and then they escorted her to her car. As she drove away from Lincoln High School, she couldn't help thinking there might be a figurative bomb in her back seat, and that she might very well be the one to detonate it.

Chapter Twenty-seven

FIRST THING NEXT MORNING, WELBURTON summoned Sally into his office. "Sorry to take you away from your office, but you need to see this," he said, holding out a note printed on a half sheet of notebook paper.

Sally sat down on one of the conference chairs to read it.

YOU MAY BE PRINCIPLE, BUT YOU AIN'T IN CHARGE. LINCOLN IS DEVILS TURF.

Instead of a signature, there was a pitchfork scrawled under the word, "turf."

"Do you think this is authentic? Did it really come from the Black Devils?" Sally asked.

Wally sat opposite her and leaned back, flipping his tie with a casualness that belied the anxiety germinating in his gut. "It's entirely possible. Wannabes don't usually act this bold."

"But—why? Why would the Devils send such a thing to you? Why now?" Sally said. "Unless—"

"Unless they were trying to make a political statement after the fire and Stoker's death, staking claim to the school." Wally's grim smile seemed to put an exclamation point on his opinion.

"Aren't they always claiming the school is their turf? It's got to be more than that." Sally's eyebrows formed a shallow "V". "Maybe they don't like it that a white principal has succeeded a Black one."

Wally's eye twitched. "Why would that matter, Sally? Do I need to start being afraid to lead a Black school after all these years here? And what about you? Are you afraid?"

Sighing, Sally handed back the note. "It's just a possible explanation. You know as well as I do that some Blacks resent it that white people have positions of authority, make the 'big salaries.' The students also test us all the time, trying to gauge whether we are here for the right reasons. And the gangs—"

"The gangs are hoodlums, pure and simple. They respect no one in authority, Black *or* white. They exist to make money, and the way they do it is by staking out territory. They want money, and they want power."

Sally's eyes met Welburton's, and she blurted in a hoarse whisper, "Enough to kill the principal and set fire to the school?" Her hands flew to her mouth. "I honestly hadn't considered that Stoker's murder might have been gang-related. It seemed to me that all the students loved him."

Wally rose and walked around his desk to place an arm around Sally's shoulders. He thought he could detect a slight quiver as she leaned her head against him for a second, then pulled away and also stood. "Look," he said, "we've dealt with the Black Devils for as long as they've been in existence. They've got their ways, and we've got ours. Ordinarily, I wouldn't give much credence to a note like this, but remember, school's only been in session for a couple of weeks, and we've already had two gang-related incidents. They like to do things in threes. Also in sixes."

Sally began pacing in the area around the conference table. "Refresh my memory, what were the other two incidents?"

"That's right. You were still involved in scheduling issues. There was a threat against Coach Donovan. Then an attack on the team's quarterback."

"Oh, Tyrone. I know about that. His girlfriend Shayla works in my office sixth period." Sally's hand returned to her mouth. "Do you think those two events are linked?"

Wally rocked on his heels before answering. School discipline was his forte, and a little piece of him was enjoying being an expert, despite the dismal circumstances. "Well, we know who was responsible for threatening the coach. It was Claude Davis. He—"

"Claude Davis?" Sally interrupted. "That's my office worker's brother!" Sally paled and retook her seat. Wally wondered whether she would faint.

"You okay?" he asked. When she nodded, he went on. "He's a known BD. We went for expulsion, but Stoker wanted to handle it his way. He made some suspension deal with Davis, who apologized and promised not to do it again.

"As for the assault and battery on Tyrone Nesbitt, it's still an open case. No witnesses except for Nesbitt himself, and he either didn't see the guy, or he's not talking. Still, it reeks of gang."

"So w-where are we?" Pointing to the note lying on Wally's desk, she asked, "You think the Black Devils are responsible for all of it, even the f-fire, and S-Stoker?" She gulped air. "I-I just never thought of gangs as doing something that heinous. Really and truly, they are just kids."

"Big mistake to underestimate what gangbangers will do. It's precisely because they're kids that they are dangerous. They think they're invincible, and they're easy to manipulate. Gang leaders can take control of their minds and bodies, and force them to do some very bad things."

Sally nodded. "So what are you going to do now?"

Wally sat, picked up the note, leaned back in his chair. "I'm going to turn it over to the police immediately. Let them investigate. I just wanted to give you a heads-up, since I know you're working with them, too. Besides, you and I need to stick together. This job's hard enough for ten administrators, but there's just the two of us now. You can trust me, and I can trust you. As for the rest of the people around here—I don't trust any of them."

* * *

Sally returned to her office, her mind writhing with evil thoughts like that of the snaky-headed Medusa. The idea that Stoker might have been killed by a gang-banger echoed in her mind like the tolling of a bell that she couldn't unring. And Claude Davis—could he really be so different from his twin, Shayla?

She woke up her computer to access Claude's attendance record.

There it was in neon green letters, "Suspended." Claude had been out of school since the second day, and he was still out. There was no way she could track his whereabouts.

She tried to call the Davis household again, letting the phone ring and ring. Remembering Shayla's admission that she had seen someone with a gun, she felt a cold chill like she had when Wally had mentioned Claude's name. If Shayla didn't show up again today, and if she couldn't get an answer on the phone, she might have to drive to her house after school.

Wally's warning not to underestimate the nefarious actions of the gangs rankled, too, but there was a part of her that believed that Shayla, and by extension her family, was good and decent.

And then she thought about Wally's final comment, the one about sticking together, trusting each other. The note Wally had showed her certainly pointed to the Devils, but it could have been written by anyone. At this point, Sally wasn't even sure she could trust Wally.

Chapter Twenty-eight

ONE OF SALLY'S FAVORITE PARTS of being an administrator was walking the halls during passing periods. Most people regarded it as "fluff time," but Sally used it with purpose. She liked to feel the pulse of the building as she observed both students and teachers. In her few weeks as an assistant principal, she had discovered something not taught in administration classes. She could influence school climate simply by spreading good cheer during passing periods.

And at no time had Lincoln High School needed a boost in school climate more than now. So between homeroom and first period, Sally made it a point to interact positively with everyone she met in the hallways. There were just two minutes left before the tardy bell when she bumped into Tyrone, who was slamming his locker shut with excessive force.

"Tyrone, I'm sooo glad to run into you. Have you spoken with Shayla?"

"No, ma'am," Tyrone replied, rubbing his right jaw. "I was hoping *you* had. I've been calling and calling, but no answer."

"Where's your first period class?" Sally asked.

Tyrone pointed toward the second floor.

"C'mon, I'll walk you to class." Sally sprinted up the stairs, heels tapping on the marble, to keep up with the agile football player. "What time do you get off from practice this afternoon?"

"Five-thirty, why?"

"If I can't make contact with Shayla by then, maybe I'll drive over to her house. Want to go with me?"

* * *

Detectives Phillips and Morris were waiting for Sally when she returned from walking the halls. Today their eyebrows were knitted, and the corners of their mouths turned downward. They were mumbling to each other as she entered the office.

"Good morning, gentlemen," Sally chirped, as though all was right in the little world the three of them occupied.

Both stood, but Morris' show of chivalry was marred by his knocking over of a philodendron plant, scattering soil all over the carpet. "Sorry, sorry," he said, bending over to sweep the mess into his palm and pour it back into the flower pot.

Unperturbed, Phillips addressed Sally in a serious tone. "Did you have time to review the documents from the principal's desk?"

"Yes, I did," Sally replied, glancing at the philodendron she had been nurturing for weeks. "I've made a list of documents and notated those that may hold relevance in your investigation. I should tell you, though, that I don't think there's much here." She handed a copy of her list to the detective.

Items Retrieved from R.J. Stoker's Desk, September 18:
Principal's contract, current
Registration form for upcoming professional development workshop
Receipt for purchases of books for professional library
Letter of recommendation for newly hired school nurse
Absentee lists from last week
Daily announcements from last week
Evaluation calendar*
Notes from formative walk-through evaluations*
Notes of congratulation on new position at Lincoln
Receipt for dry cleaning
Anonymous note asking Stoker to meet on third floor*

Phillips looked the list over, pursing his lips as he read.
"Here are the original documents," Sally said, handing the stack

over. "I'll be glad to explain any of them to you."

"Hmm," Phillips said, "names of teachers on this evaluation calendar?"

"Those are the ones Mr. Stoker was set to evaluate this semester. That next set of papers shows what he'd already observed in their classrooms. As I said, nothing stands out, but you can see which teachers he thought highly of and which ones he didn't."

"We're going to want to interview those teachers, see what they thought of their new principal." Phillips handed the list to Morris. "What about this anonymous note?"

Sally pointed to the stack of documents. "It's that last envelope on the bottom. The lavender one." Initially, Sally had thought to omit the note from her list, but Ron had convinced her of the importance of including everything.

Phillips pulled the envelope from the bottom of the stack and opened it. As he read the invitation to meet on the third floor, his eyes flared. "Any idea who might have sent this?"

Sally looked at the floor, then took a deep breath. "I really can't say with any authority. There's no handwriting to recognize or other identifying facts, but—"

Morris interrupted. "Your impressions are important, ma'am."

"Well, I think it might have come from Ms. Dunn. Her classroom and office are on the third floor. She—"

Phillips eyed Sally's face. "Any reason she might have sent something like this to Mr. Stoker?"

Sally fidgeted. "I—I can't really say." She wanted to cooperate with the police, but accusing someone without evidence would be stepping too far out on an unsteady precipice. At that moment, Sally remembered the other anonymous note, the one sent to Wally. "Have you two seen the note sent to Mr. Welburton?"

Morris answered. "The one supposedly from the Black Devils? Yeah, we seen it just before we came here."

"What's your opinion on that?" Phillips asked.

Sally's mind wandered to Shayla's having seen someone with a gun. If he knew, Ron would probably push her to share that with the detectives, too, but until she could find Shayla, Sally judged the comment as dubious, possibly a hallucination.

"Mrs. Pearce?"

"Oh, sorry. I'm as unsure about that as I am about *this* note. It's going to take more than a couple of anonymous notes to figure out who killed Mr. Stoker."

"I know *that's* right," Phillips agreed. "What I really wish is that we could find the murder weapon."

Chapter Twenty-nine

SALLY HAD SPENT A BUSY day at Lincoln, where things seemed slowly to be calming down into a new normal, except that neither Claude nor Shayla had appeared in any of their classes. Sally was reviewing the eligibility list to see which students would be unable to participate in clubs or sports that week. She wasn't surprised to see grades adversely affected as a result of all the stress in the school. She sighed, thinking it would be a challenge to reverse the trend.

Tyrone tapped on the frame of her door. He was suited up for football practice, even though Sally knew he hadn't yet been cleared to play. The coach would most likely have him walk through the plays.

"Oh, hi, Tyrone, I was just thinking about you. Looks like you're having some trouble in Mr. Johnson's class?"

"Yes, ma'am," he said, through clenched teeth, still protecting his jaw. "Also in Mr. Gottschalk's. I'm working on that. Hopefully I can get those grades up before my doc clears me to play again—maybe next week."

"Wasn't Mr. Stoker setting up tutoring for members of the team?" Stoker had explained to Sally how important it was to provide extra help for these young men with scholarship potential. It might make or break their chances for rising above their circumstances.

"Yes, ma'am. I met with Ms. Woods during zero period yesterday and today."

"That's great, Tyrone. Keep up the good work, and it will pay off." Sally made a mental note to check with Aretha Woods to see how the tutoring was going.

131

"Ms. Pearce, did you still want to go by Shayla's after practice today?" Tyrone picked at a spot on his uniform. The bleakness in his eyes revealed his worry. Sally couldn't help thinking how much more he would worry if he knew about the pregnancy.

"Absolutely. Come on back as soon as Coach Donovan lets you go, and we'll go together. I'll take you home afterwards." A flicker of a smile on Tyrone's face reminded Sally of how little it took to make a difference in a student's life. Whether or not they found Shayla, taking action to find her would make both of them feel better.

* * *

The sun was beginning to bleed into the horizon when Sally and Tyrone headed out of the faculty parking lot in Sally's Audi toward Shayla's house. Much as she wanted to go there, Sally wouldn't have felt as comfortable going by herself, despite her black belt in kickboxing. She had traded her competition garb for a pin-striped business suit.

The neighborhoods surrounding the school were modest, but well-maintained, but as they drove west along the main thoroughfare, the homes and businesses grew more and more dilapidated. People were out walking or waiting for the bus, some congregating in groups. Sally tried to see the landscape through the eyes of Shayla or Tyrone, kids for whom this environment was normal, instead of something one drove through on the way to someplace better.

She glanced at Tyrone, whose head was resting against the passenger window. His eyes were closed, and he rubbed his jaw. Just before they drew up to Shayla's house, a run-down wood-frame structure with corrugated metal on one side, Tyrone opened his eyes.

He pointed to the dark and forlorn-looking house. Weeds were growing everywhere, even around the wooden steps to the porch. It had been weeks since anyone had paid attention to the yard, such as it was. "Looks like nobody's home. Don't know what I was expecting." His fists balled up on his lap.

"It's not like Shayla to have unexcused absences from school," Sally agreed. "If she were here, surely she would have at least answered the phone when we called." She parked the car in a gravel path next to the house, and cut off the engine. "Shall we see if anyone's there?"

The two of them climbed out of the car and trudged past a dogwood tree, up the three steps to a tiny porch. A bucket with a mop and a faint smell of mold stood next to a broom, and a thin brown blanket had been thrown over the porch railing. Sally pushed the doorbell button, but Tyrone said, "That don't work. Not for a long time."

He knocked on the door, banged on it, hard. "Anybody home?" he called, keeping up the knocking. He kicked the bottom of the door for good measure. There was no response.

Sally looked around. The air was getting cooler and darker, and she felt a chill. There was no point in staying outside an empty house. She dug into her purse, looking for a pen and notepad. She thought to leave a note in the mailbox for Ms. Davis.

A scrawny cat, lolling on a branch of the dogwood, screeched, and Sally almost dropped her purse. Regaining her equilibrium, she scribbled a message and her phone number on a Post-it note, then pressed it onto the inside of the rusted mailbox, where a couple of thin circulars lay, curled up.

Meanwhile, Tyrone had jumped down the three steps and started looking around the perimeter of the tiny house. His feet made crunching sounds on the gravel, as he jumped to get eye level with the windows. "Can't see nothing inside. Too dark," he muttered, disappointment evident in his voice.

As he returned to the front, a nearby streetlight came on, bathing the front of the house. An old woman opened her door across the street and peered at the lighted porch of the Davis house, making Sally feel exposed. She was ready to leave, but Tyrone called out.

"Hey, what's this? Something shiny here, under the steps." He bent over, peering into the cavernous hole under the worn wooden steps. "Ms. Pearce, c'mere." He pointed into the dark space.

Sally joined him at the base of the first stair and looked where he pointed. What she saw caused her to gasp and cover her mouth. Shoved under the frame of the little staircase, inside the darkened hole, was a .45 caliber handgun.

Chapter Thirty

WHILE SALLY WAS WAITING FOR Tyrone to finish with practice, two Lincoln teachers were meeting on the third floor with Norma Dunn. "Mr. Gottschalk, Mr. Johnson, I've called you here to discuss the grievance you initiated against the administrative evaluation practices." Perched on the corner of her teacher's desk, she crossed one leg over the other, heedless of the patch of thigh exposed.

The gentlemen apparently were paying attention, as they set down their grade books and took seats in nearby student desks and stared at the faculty association president. Noticing the direction of their gazes, Norma scooted a little, pulling her skirt down a fraction of an inch. She clearly enjoyed the attention, though.

"Ahem, gentlemen." She smiled like a poker player raking in the winnings. "Basically the question is, do you want to go forward with the grievance, now that Stoker is no longer the principal?"

Gottschalk leaned forward, scratching his head and messing his comb-over. "What's the protocol here? Never filed a grievance before. Hope I never have to again."

Norma uncrossed her legs. "There isn't a protocol to match our exact situation. We've never had a principal die in office, at least that I'm aware of. I spoke with Mr. Stoker about the grievance, which is the first step. He indicated he wouldn't change the way he was conducting evaluations. The next step would be to file a formal grievance with the superintendent's office. That is, if you want to proceed."

Mr. Johnson unbuttoned his vest and leaned back in the student desk. A whiff of menthol floated in the air. "Can't we just wait to see how Welburton behaves as principal?"

"You can," Norma explained, "but it would mean closing out this particular grievance. There are specific timelines we must observe, and time is running out on this one. You should also realize that the grievance is not personal. In other words, it was initiated against the administration as a whole, not against Stoker. Technically, that means it included Welburton and Pearce, as well as Stoker."

"But Mr. Stoker is the one who was showing favoritism to the younger teachers, the one who was siding with students all the time. He was turning this school on its ear."

"Let me put in my two cents' worth," Gottschalk said. "Wally Welburton has always been a good guy, supportive of teachers. I'm betting he'll go back to the old ways in no time. We'll be restored to our former authority, and before long Lincoln will forget it even had a Stoker trying to change things. I say, drop the grievance."

"Do you agree, Mr. Johnson?"

Johnson nodded. "I'm not such a Welburton fan, and heaven knows, I think Pearce is a complete waste of time and position—her scheduling practices are abominable—but, we can always file another grievance at a later date. You can pull the trigger on shutting this one down."

Norma winced at the unfortunate metaphor. "As you wish, gentlemen. Meanwhile, let's maintain our highest standards of professional teaching practice in our classrooms. That way no one can say we aren't doing our best to earn our salaries and benefits." She stood as if to dismiss the class of two.

Mr. Gottschalk gathered his grade book and empty coffee mug, signaled a salute to Ms. Dunn and Mr. Johnson, and lumbered out of the room. Mr. Johnson lingered, busying himself with flipping through a stack of test papers inside his grade book.

Trying to block out his mentholated scent, Norma walked around to her desk and sat. She unlocked the desk and opened the bottom drawer, where her purse and scarf sat. She opened her purse and took out her sunglasses, hoping Mr. Johnson would take the hint and leave. Something about his hanging around was giving her the willies.

"Ah, Ms. Dunn," Johnson said. "I thought we could have a word in private." Johnson leaned back and rubbed his thighs with both hands.

"What is it?" Norma asked, as she rubbed the lenses of her sunglasses with the corner of the scarf. "It's getting late, and I have another appointment."

"I sincerely doubt you have another appointment." He picked at a fingernail. "Don't you want to be alone with me?"

Not wanting to show her distaste for the social studies teacher, and especially not wanting to show fear, she replied, "That depends, Mr. Johnson. What is it you want?"

Johnson twirled a pen on the desk, a cat playing with a mouse. "Well, to start with, you're a fine-looking woman, intelligent and competent."

Norma interrupted. "Just stop right there. I'm not going to fall for any flimflam flattery from you or any other teacher in this building."

"I just thought," he said, staring into her eyes, "we are two single Black people with good careers and a lot in common. I thought we might go out to dinner sometime, have a little fun."

Norma cringed inside at the thought of having dinner with this supercilious windbag. She was much more comfortable being the aggressor in a relationship, but she would never want to get involved with someone like this New York transplant. "Thank you for the offer, Mr. Johnson, but I try never to mix work and pleasure." She removed her car keys from her purse and stood.

"You might want to sit back down, *Ms. Dunn*," Johnson replied, a harsh tone flavoring his words. "I might not be native to the Midwest, and I've only been at Lincoln High School for eight years, but I'm not a fool."

"Whatever do you mean?" Norma asked, her eyes narrowing. She sat down.

"You're a pretty little package, and you apparently enjoy running the faculty association, too. It's just that you also have a pretty little reputation for cozying up to administrators. So that not-mixing-work-with-pleasure line just don't play with me."

Inside a tiny flame of concern ignited, but Norma kept it turned down low. "Okay, Mr. Johnson. I don't want to go out with you because you're not my type." She stood again. "Let's go."

"Not so fast. I just want to ask you one more question." He twirled the pen, even faster. "You see, the day of the fire, when Stoker was killed, I had taken a diuretic. Instead of evacuating the building, I went to the bathroom, and I remained in the building for quite a while."

Norma's eyebrows rose slightly, but the flame intensified. "So what's your question?"

"What were you doing in the main office hallway long after everyone had evacuated? What were you doing standing near Stoker's dead body?"

Chapter Thirty-one

FIRST THING THE NEXT DAY the detectives made a visit to Wally's office. They were carrying steaming cups of coffee from a local diner and even brought an extra for the new principal. Perhaps they thought a little generosity would yield some information.

Wally wasn't in a generous mood, however. The task of running a large urban high school was a lot harder than he had anticipated, and exhaustion made his eyes dry and his mouth tense. He'd give anything to be rid of these guys, snooping around the building and in and out of his office all the time.

"What can I do for you today?" Wally asked, as he took the lid off of his Styrofoam cup and inhaled the fumes. Maybe he should be nice to the detectives, after all.

"More like what we can do for you," Phillips replied, taking a chair without being invited.

"You have news?" Wally's voice was more hopeful than he felt.

"Some news. The autopsy's back. Some questions answered, but others to ask." Phillips blew on his coffee, then took a sip.

Morris took out his notepad, causing Wally to flinch. So this meeting would be more of the same.

Phillips continued, "Evidently Mr. Stoker fought hard against his attacker. He had a number of defensive injuries, along with a broken jaw and multiple contusions on his arms, legs, and trunk. Death was caused by a gunshot wound to his head, fired at close range. Fire and smoke damage apparently were incidental."

Wally clutched his coffee cup and looked down. He couldn't think of anything to say.

"Pretty brutal way to die, a man in his prime, a leader—don't you agree?" Phillips stared at Wally, forcing a response.

Wally straightened his posture. "What? Oh, yes. Quite brutal." He picked up the end of his tie and laid it back down on his middle. "Wait. Did you say Stoker had a broken jaw?" A light flickered in Wally's greenish eyes.

Phillips nodded, staring at Wally's substantial biceps, not for the first time. Wally squirmed.

"Which jaw was it?" Wally asked, before taking another sip.

"Left, I believe."

"Well, that's curious," Wally said, leaning back and fingering his tie.

"You mean because of the broken jaw on the football field two weeks ago?" Phillips asked. "Our officer told us about that."

Wally shifted his position and leaned forward, suddenly animated. "But don't you see? The same person might have done both crimes. It was also the left jaw of our quarterback."

"Easy, easy," Morris warned from the side chair, where he was taking notes.

Phillips added, "We don't want to jump to conclusions. That's what he's trying to say."

Unmollified, Wally continued, "No, don't you see? We think the guy who hit Tyrone might be a Black Devil. It all fits with the note. Both crimes were gang-related!"

"Unless—" Phillips began.

"Unless what? I've got a sneaking suspicion Claude Davis might have been involved with the attack on Tyrone. He confessed to threatening the coach a few days earlier, and he's still on suspension for that."

"Wait a minute. Was Davis on suspension the day of the killing?"

"Yeah, so what?"

"Well, doesn't suspension mean he would be banned from the building?"

"Yeah, but that doesn't mean he didn't sneak in, do the deed, and sneak out again." Wally stood and began pacing. "Don't you see? The Black Devils threatened the football coach, then the quarterback, then the principal. Now they're sending threatening notes to me."

"Cool your jets, Principal Welburton," Phillips replied. "We need evidence, man. Not sayin' we *don't* have a Black Devils hit here, but if you can help us get some solid evidence, we'd feel a whole lot better." Phillips took a long swallow of coffee, leaning his head back to capture the last drop.

"Okay," Wally said, sitting down again. "What do you need?"

"Forensic evidence, fingerprints, blood, hair or skin, footprints, something we can match up to the person and the crime scene. You do investigations here at the school. You know what we're looking for." Phillips nodded at Morris, and they both rose from their seats.

Wally wanted to rail at the detectives. What in the hell were the police doing for two days in the main office hallway, cordoned off with yellow tape? If they hadn't found any hard evidence there, how did they expect him to find anything?

What he said instead was, "Will do. Thanks for stopping by, gentlemen. And thanks for the coffee."

* * *

As they stepped out into the hallway, Morris patted the Lincoln statue, a habit he'd had since his own high school days in this building. He grinned at Phillips. "Methinks he doth protest too much. He almost ignited when you told him about the broken jaw."

"Yeah, I noticed. Good thing he doesn't know about the weapon."

"Hah, you mean that ballistics matched the gun to the bullet in Stoker's head?"

"Yes, but also that the gun was hidden under the steps at Claude Davis' house. We owe a lot to Mrs. Pearce for finding that bit of forensic evidence."

"Ol' Wally would have a field day with that, for sure. I have to admit. Looks like Davis might be our man."

"Don't be so sure, Morris. There were only a few partial fingerprints on the weapon, besides those of Pearce and Nesbitt, and Davis is nowhere to be found. Just like the note, anyone could make it look like Davis is the perp. Anyone, that is, who knows what's been going on with Davis at Lincoln High School. I'm not prepared to rule anyone out—even our friend Wally Welburton."

Chapter Thirty-two

TYRONE COULDN'T BELIEVE HIS EYES when he found a three-by-six-inch box that had arrived in the mail the next day. Postmarked from Hayneville, Alabama, addressed in Shayla's handwriting, the package had been sitting in his mailbox when he came in after practice. Alabama! What was Shayla doing in Alabama?

He clutched the package to his chest, hoping its contents would answer the many questions plaguing him. He unlocked the door and darted to the kitchen table, where Gran had left a thick slice of carrot cake, his favorite, wrapped in plastic, for his evening snack. He ignored the sweet, spicy smell. All he could think of at the moment was opening the package from Shayla.

He ripped at the tape, then picked up a table knife. As he hacked at the edges, he noticed there was no return address. Finally, the wrapping came off, and he opened the box. What he found was an irregularly shaped wad of bubble wrap, held together by a rubber band. His fingers shook as he opened the layers. He gasped when he saw what was at the core—his senior ring.

Tyrone searched through the bubble wrap, the box, the brown paper outer wrap, looking for a letter, a note, anything to explain this mystery—nothing. Why would Shayla return his ring? Was this her way of breaking up with him? Or was she telling him she was okay, somewhere in Alabama?

Tyrone slid the ring onto his finger. It fit perfectly, just as it had that first day, before he gave it to Shayla to wear on a chain around her neck. He paced around the tiny house, trying to remember a connection between the Davises and Alabama. The last time he had been at Shayla's he'd seen a pile of mail sitting on the counter. Had any of the envelopes been from Alabama? Had Mrs. Davis ever mentioned family in Alabama? He strained to remember.

Even if he could make a connection, there were a thousand other questions pounding in his blood. Why would Shayla, and most likely her mother and brother, pick up and leave so suddenly? It was their senior year, for heaven's sake. They had looked forward to this year for a long time, anticipating the fun they would have at homecoming, prom, and graduation. The school year had just started, and already it was totally fucked up.

So many bad things had happened in the past two weeks—Shayla, Mr. Stoker, his jaw. Bitter tears stung his eyes, and he was glad no one was here to see the strong quarterback cry. Suddenly he remembered the evening he was attacked after practice. He hadn't breathed a word about who had attacked him. He'd been carrying the equipment off the field, on his way to meet Shayla by the cafeteria. She'd had something important to tell him, but what was it?

Maybe she had known she would be leaving town. Maybe she hadn't wanted to give him the bad news after he'd been hurt, when she was sitting with him in the hospital. Afterwards, it seemed there had been no time at all before the principal was killed and Shayla had disappeared. Tyrone felt like punching something.

Now he was left wearing his own ring, trying to heal his jaw and bring up his grades, and with a gnawing in his gut that spoke of more than physical hunger. He wished Mr. Stoker could be here to help him handle all this.

These were the times Tyrone missed having a dad in his life, or even a mom. He loved his Gran more than anything, but sometimes a guy just needed a different kind of emotional support. With Shayla he had felt connected, important, manly. He needed her, and she needed him. If that wasn't true love, he didn't know what was.

Well, at least Shayla had been thinking about him, had reached out to communicate. At least she was alive. Tyrone didn't know what it all meant, but he was hatching a plan. Tomorrow he would go to Mrs. Pearce's office and tell her about the package. She cared about Shayla, and she seemed to know high school kids pretty well. Maybe she would know what to do next.

Chapter Thirty-three

ONE THING WALLY BELIEVED IN as an administrator was supporting teachers. It was one of the reasons he had been so popular with the faculty over the years. The teachers knew in a conflict between teacher and student, Wally would always align himself with the teacher. This default position had caused a bit of friction with students and parents from time to time, but Wally was proud that the school had a reputation in the community for being "tough on discipline." Otherwise, it may have been nearly impossible to hire such a dedicated faculty.

Of course, some times were easier than others to support teachers. Today was a perfect example. Before homeroom this morning, Coach Donovan had sidled up to Wally in the hallway.

"Hey, Wally, how's it going?" the coach said, slapping his friend on the back.

"Isn't it a little early in the morning to be chewing gum?" Wally retorted, a running joke between them that had started after hours at a bar years ago.

Donovan grinned. A glob of slippery pink showed between his molars on the right side. "Listen," he said, lowering his voice, "Can you do me a favor? Our quarterback, Tyrone Nesbitt, has been cleared by his doctor to play next Friday. Only problem, he's flagging econ with that new guy, Johnson. The kid's been tutored. He's studying his butt off, but he still can't make headway with Johnson. Any way you could talk to the guy?"

"Okay, sure," Wally replied. "But at the end of the day, the teachers control the grades. You know that."

"Well, Stoker arranged for the tutor. He was going to—"

"Not you, too? I'm gonna throttle the next person who tells me what Mr. Stoker was going to do." Wally's face grew hot, and he bit his lower lip. "You of all people. You should be the last person praising Stoker, after the way he treated the kid who threatened your life."

"Okay, okay. Calm down. I just want to play my quarterback. The guy's got scholarship potential, too."

* * *

During lunch duty, Wally had a chance to talk to Mr. Johnson, who was vigorously monitoring the return of trays and clean up. If the econ teacher had been holding his nose to block out the cafeteria smells, he couldn't have looked unhappier. Wally tapped him on the shoulder of his business suit and pulled him over. "Can I ask you something?"

"Of course, Mr. Welburton. What is it?"

Wally leaned closer, aiming for privacy, but catching a too-strong whiff of Johnson's menthol aftershave. "Can you tell me off the top of your head whether Tyrone Nesbitt is passing econ?"

"May I ask why?" A tiny sniff punctuated the question.

"The kid's had a rocky start to the new school year, and I hear he's been tutored. I'm hoping to see him play football on Saturday."

Johnson pulled away and stared at Wally. "I hope you're not asking me to pass him without merit. Are you?" Not waiting for an answer, he went on. "Because if you are, that truly disappoints me. Does no administrator in this school support its teachers?"

Wounded, Wally replied, "As principal of this school, I can assure you that we support our teachers. You've been here long enough to know that."

"Well, you can't prove it by me. First, Mrs. Pearce loads my classes with too many students. How can I be expected to manage so many problems, so many papers to grade? Then Mr. Stoker harasses me with his repeated walk-through visits, his comments about my teaching methods. Now you—"

"Now I, Mr. Johnson, am merely asking a question." Wally was becoming concerned about the man's emotional reaction in the midst of the cafeteria hubbub. It wouldn't do to have this conversation overheard.

"Let me ask *you* a question. How do you expect me to give wholesale passes to students who don't study, don't do homework, and don't even bring their materials to class? Mr. Stoker told me to motivate them. I don't see anything in my contract, nor was there anything in my preparation to become a teacher, about motivating students. I don't consider that my job."

Sorry that he had begun this conversation in the first place, and noticing the imminent end of the lunch period, Wally adopted a conciliatory tone. "All I asked about is one student, Tyrone Nesbitt. He seems like a sincere enough young man. Are you saying he's lazy?"

Johnson took a deep breath. "Well, ah, naturally, I was talking about my students in general. Tyrone—Tyrone is not the worst of the bunch, and I will admit he has been doing a little better this past week."

"Could you see your way to reevaluating his grades, then? I hear the kid's been studying extra hard for your class."

Mr. Johnson thought for a few seconds before plunging on. "I will take another look at my grade book, and if he has improved enough, I will remove his name from the ineligibility report."

Wally nodded and smiled.

"However," Johnson continued, "I ask that you do something for me, as well."

The smile evaporated from Wally's face. "What's that?"

Mr. Johnson whispered into Wally's ear just as the bell rang to end the lunch period. The teacher dashed off to class, leaving Wally with a deepening frown. Why does everything have to be so damned complicated?

Chapter Thirty-four

BEFORE SCHOOL THE NEXT MORNING, Sally found Melody Singer, the young social studies teacher, sitting in the hallway outside her office door. Usually Melody's springy golden curls and her gleaming smile gave Sally a sense that the quality of teaching and learning at Lincoln High was healthy and strong. Today, though, Melody dabbed at her red-rimmed eyes with a tissue, and her expression was anything but joyful.

Sally helped the young teacher up and offered a warm smile. "I'm glad to see you this morning, but I'm sorry you're so upset. Come on into the inner sanctum and tell me how I can help."

Melody plopped down into a chair and slumped over. She covered her face with her hands, and her shoulders shook with silent sobs. She looked as though talking would be impossible.

Sally closed the door and adjusted the blinds for privacy. She sat down next to Melody and patted her on the arm. "Now, now. Tell me what's going on."

Melody exhaled and dabbed her eyes. "I—I don't know where to start." She shifted in the chair and sat up straighter. "You know, my classroom is next to Mr. Johnson's, the econ teacher."

Sally cringed inwardly. She knew whatever was coming couldn't be good, but she nodded.

Melody's sobs had turned into soft hiccups. "Ever since day one, Mr. Johnson has been on my case, *hic*. He says he can't teach for all the noise coming from, *hic*, my classroom." Melody paused to take a deep breath and wipe her forehead. "The thing is, my classes *aren't* noisy. The kids are just engaged. I use a lot of auditory and tactile-

148

kinesthetic activities to promote brain activity. He just doesn't get it."

Sally smiled. "I've seen you teaching. Your students are on-task and involved. That's how they learn best."

"Yeah." Melody nodded. "Explain that to Mr. Grumpy. He complained about me to Mr. Stoker, and Mr. Stoker defended me, so for a few days things were peaceful. But now, Mr. S-Stoker's dead, and Ol' Grump-face has gone to Mr. Welburton about me."

"I'm sure Mr. Welburton won't take sides against you. He knows you're a good teacher."

"That's just it. Mr. Welburton called me in and read me the riot act. He reminded me I'm untenured. He told me he's going to keep a close watch on me this year, and if I don't improve, he'll recommend termination. Ohhhh… what am I going to do? I don't know any other way to teach."

"This just doesn't sound right. Did Mr. Welburton say those exact words?"

Melody squared her shoulders and looked Sally in the eye. "Mrs. Pearce, I am not exaggerating. It's even worse than that."

Sally felt a lump forming in her gut, as she braced herself for what would come next. "Tell me."

"When I was leaving Mr. Welburton's office, I was very upset. I was thinking about my students, how upset they were going to be if I started boring them to death every day like Mr. Johnson does with his kids. I was almost to the door when Mr. Welburton touched me."

"What do you mean, touched you? How? Where?" Sally whispered.

"He grabbed my rear end and pinched it. It shocked me so much I just stood there, and then, as if he realized how he had hurt me, he touched me there again, this time patting me. I jumped away from him, and he said, 'I'm sorry if I hurt you. I only meant to show you how beautiful you are and how much you tempt me.'"

Sally kept her voice even, although she felt like screaming. Hadn't things been bad enough with a new job, a murder, a missing student, and possible gang threats? If this story were true, Sally's fellow administrator could be facing a scandal. Besides being married, Wally was the principal now. He'd be a fool to mess with a faculty member, especially one so young and vulnerable. "Melody, I want you to tell me exactly what you said and did after that."

"That's just it," Melody whined, fresh tears spilling from both eyes. "I didn't say anything. I didn't know what to say. I was afraid if I argued with him, I might l-lose my j-job. I started to walk out the door, and he said, 'Don't say a word to anyone about this. It's our little secret. Just the first of many little secrets.'"

Sally stood and walked around her desk, sitting in her executive chair. She pulled a legal pad and pen from a desk drawer and handed it to Melody. "You did the right thing by coming to me. We can't have this kind of thing going on in our school. I know you're upset, but you need to put this in writing, all of it, all of the words and actions. Once you commit it all to paper, I will handle it from there."

As Melody began a frantic scribbling on the legal pad, Sally began planning her next steps. At the very least, she would ask to move Melody from Wally's evaluation list to hers. She might also switch Melody's classroom to the first floor to get her away from Mr. Johnson. The more she thought about it, the angrier she was.

She would have to take these charges seriously, but Wally was entitled to explain things from his point of view, too. The dance they would engage in would have many complicated steps, and before the music ended, one or both administrators may have to leave the floor.

Chapter Thirty-five

DETECTIVES PHILLIPS AND MORRIS RETURNED to the principal's office, but Wally's secretary, Myrna, stopped them at her desk, just inside the door. "He's out doing classroom observations this morning. Can I help you with anything?"

Phillips looked around the plump assistant to assure himself of Welburton's absence. "Yes, ma'am," he replied, "we want to talk to him about fingerprints." He couldn't help noticing the half-eaten donut on the desk and a tiny twitch in the corner of Myrna's mouth.

"Fingerprints?"

"Do you know whether the school district has ever fingerprinted the staff?" Phillips pressed his thumb on the ledge of Myrna's desk and rolled it from one side to the other.

"N-no, I don't think so. If the state or the district required fingerprints, I think I would know it." Myrna frowned. "Mr. Welburton should be back in about an hour, though, if you want to come back."

Was it Phillips' imagination, or was there a quaver in her voice? Some people were naturally tense whenever speaking with a cop, but what would this lady have to fear?

Phillips straightened the pleats in his rumpled pants. "Actually, we have some business to do with Mrs. Pearce, so if your boss comes in before we get back, he can reach us over there."

Myrna reached for her message pad and scribbled. When she finished, she ripped off the sheet and impaled it on the metal spindle on the corner of her desk. "I'll give him the message," she said, and managed a lopsided smile.

The detectives arrived at Sally's office just as she did. She had just completed a teacher evaluation of her own. Her brain was churning with thoughts of how she might handle Mr. Gottschalk's observation report. The teacher showed so many deficiencies in just that one class period. It would require a lot of diplomacy to address them.

Phillips and Morris nodded at Pat, Sally's secretary, and Morris stepped ahead of Sally to open the door to her inner office for her, his too-strong after shave overwhelming her. Sally rolled her eyes at Pat on her way in. She plopped her evaluation notebook down on her desk and took a seat, motioning for the detectives to do the same.

Dispensing with preliminaries, Phillips said, "We stopped by the principal's office first. We're looking for fingerprints."

Confused, Sally asked, "Fingerprints? At the crime site, you mean?" She pointed in the direction of the main office.

"No, sorry," Phillips replied. "I mean fingerprints of administrators and staff members in the school. We have some prints we're trying to match up."

Morris jumped in. "Remember we printed you last week when you turned in the gun? Well, we need more, faculty mostly, but we need to exclude the Nesbitt kid's prints. Can't do that without his guardian."

"I thought police have access to all kinds of fingerprint banks through the FBI and CIA and places like that. At least that's how they do it in mystery books I read."

Phillips smiled. "We do. But unless a person has had previous run-ins with the law, or unless his place of work has submitted fingerprints for some reason, there would be no fingerprints on file for him. And our prints fall into that category."

Sally shivered. "On the gun?" She couldn't help thinking of Shayla and wondering whom she had seen with a gun. Actually, she had been thinking about Shayla non-stop, ever since Tyrone had barged into the office the day before to show her the senior ring mailed from Alabama. She needed to tell the detectives about Shayla soon. The phrase "obstruction of justice" had been swimming around in her cerebral cortex for days.

Phillips intruded on her thoughts. "Yes, prints on the gun and from the crime scene as well."

Sally's mind was racing. To her knowledge there was no bank of fingerprints for faculty. She herself had never been fingerprinted until last week when she handed over the .45 caliber pistol to Morris at the police station. "Surely you aren't thinking of fingerprinting all three hundred faculty and staff members?" She couldn't imagine what a stir that would cause. The school year was already disrupted enough.

"No," Phillips responded, "that would be expensive and time-consuming, besides creating a lot of unnecessary chaos. We thought we'd start with the new principal, the people on the evaluation list, the woman you think wrote the anonymous letter, any disgruntled students."

"And anyone else you think might have had a beef with Stoker," Morris added.

Sally thought again about what Shayla had witnessed. She pictured the girl, constantly touching Tyrone's ring on its chain. It must have taken a lot of resolve for her to part with it. Poor Tyrone, he was so bewildered and worried. Sally felt as if she had swallowed a stone, and it was sitting, unmovable, in her gut.

"All right, gentlemen," she said with a deep sigh. "We have something to talk about. There is something I think you should know."

Chapter Thirty-six

"**Y**OU'VE GOT TO DO SOMETHING," Ms. Dunn urged Wally. "The man is a frigging time bomb." The students and faculty monitors had all vacated the cafeteria after the final lunch period, so, except for a few cafeteria workers bustling about, clattering trays, Norma and Wally were alone. "Mr. Johnson is a menace to the school."

"Weren't you just defending him when he was complaining about Stoker? I heard you went so far as to file a grievance on his behalf." Wally moved past, as he straightened up tables after the final lunch period. Not his job, but he had a lot of nervous energy whenever Norma Dunn came around. He wished she'd leave.

Norma placed her vermillion-manicured hand on his forearm, pressing harder than necessary to get his attention. "I know, I know," she replied, "that was before I realized how truly crazy the man is. He and Mr. Gottschalk convinced me Stoker was harassing them, and I bought it. But now Mr. Johnson is harassing *me*. I can't turn around in this building without finding him peeping at me around a corner, grinning like the cat who wants to pounce on the canary."

Wally turned to face Norma. Didn't she realize that was what she was doing to him? "I know that can be aggravating," he said. "But have you told him his attentions are not welcome?"

"Come on, Wally. Of course I did. Do you think I'm an idiot?" Norma pulled her tight skirt down, wiggling her hips in the process. "Look, I know I can be a flirt at times, but I swear to you, I have never, ever flirted with that guy."

Wally didn't mention that there wasn't a guy on two legs and

154

breathing that Norma Dunn hadn't flirted with. Instead, he said, "Just what do you expect me to do? I can't fire the guy because he looked at you cross-eyed." He patted his tie in place, then thought for a moment.

"I'll tell you what," he said, "between you and me?"

Norma gazed into Wally's silver-green eyes and nodded.

"Johnson's been a pain in the ass since day one, complaining, and giving bad grades. Kids say he doesn't teach. Parents have been calling in, too." Wally looked around to make sure this conversation wasn't being overheard. "Why don't you do this? If he bothers you again, just tell him you have an in with me, and you're going to make sure I put him on remediation due to his failure rates."

Norma blinked, as if she could hardly believe it. "You mean, really? You mean I have an in with you? Oh, Wally." She threw herself into Wally for a hug, almost knocking him over. "Thank you, thank you. How can I ever repay you?"

Wally stepped back and fixed his tie and jacket. "No need to repay me, Ms. Dunn," he said, turning on his heel. "Now let's get back to work, shall we?"

* * *

Wally's two-way radio beeped, just as he was leaving the cafeteria. He pushed the button. "Go ahead."

"Pearce here. Can you stop by my office?"

"Be there in a minute. Ten-four." Wally clicked off and quickened his pace. He had a lot to do today, and he didn't need to be sidetracked one more time by another woman with an agenda. On the other hand, Sally didn't bother him that often, and as the only other administrator in the building, he needed to keep her on his side.

"What's up?" he asked as he breezed into her inner office, ignoring Pat.

Sally motioned to close the door.

Whatever it was, Wally was beginning to feel acid burning in his gut, a fireball. He sat.

"Phillips and Morris were here earlier," she began.

"What's going on?" He leaned back and placed his hands behind his head.

"They have the gun that killed Stoker, a .45 caliber pistol."

That *was* news, but Wally kept his face impassive. "Really? Where was it found?"

Sally replied, "Outside of the house of two of our students, Claude and Shayla Davis." She examined a cuticle. "It could've been planted there by anyone, though."

"Okay." Wally gestured with his hand as if to say, "Tell me more."

"The serial number on the gun traced it back to a big gang theft last year in the city."

Wally let out air, easing the spin of the acid ball a bit. "Fits with the anonymous note and the other things. I'll be so glad to get this over and done with. It's a major disruption to the school."

"Not so fast. The detectives want to fingerprint various people on the faculty and student body, including you. They have a list, and they want to do it immediately."

"Why don't they just fingerprint the Davises?"

"Because the Davises are nowhere to be found. Claude, Shayla, even the mom. The kids haven't been in school since Stoker's murder."

Wally looked at his lap for a few moments, then jerked his head up and made eye contact with Sally. "So is that it? Is that why you paged me?"

"Uh, no, not entirely. There's something else I want to talk to you about." Sally glanced around for possible eavesdroppers. "I've had a visit from Melody Singer."

Wally's right eyebrow lifted an inch. "Melody? What did she want?"

"She wan-ted," Sally stuttered, "to tell me about your in-ap-pro-pri-ate attentions to her." It was Sally's turn to break eye contact. "This is very hard for me to discuss with you, Wally, but I'm willing to hear your side of the story."

Wally's face flushed three shades darker than the rose-colored upholstery. "I haven't made any inappropriate—"

"Are you saying you never threatened her job or touched her rear end?"

The fiery ball began to gather force again. "Oh, come on, Sally. She's exaggerating. I might have reminded her of her untenured status, but I do that with every untenured teacher. And if I touched her butt, it was an accident. Maybe she just brushed past my hand or something."

Sally stood and began to pace. "Okay. I can't make you admit it, but your denial is pretty flimsy, and Melody's report was clear and detailed. If you want to go fishing from the company pier, I can't stop you. All I can say is you have a lot to lose if this goes any further."

Wally rose to his full height and straightened his tie and jacket. He said, "I'll remind you that I am the boss around here, not you. I've got a lot of work to do now. Tell the detectives we'll work with them to get the fingerprints they want. See you later."

Sally's ears reverberated with the slamming of two doors.

* * *

When Wally returned to his office, he found a message to call Detective Phillips. It was marked urgent. The sigh he uttered was so loud, it caused Myrna to jump and give him a strange look.

"Uh, it's nothing. I just wish this police business would get finished, so we can get back to being a high school." He took the pink slip of paper into his inner office and threw it onto his desk. He took off his sport jacket and hung it on the hook on the back of the door. He sat down in his executive chair and swiveled.

His gaze moved from one framed photo to another on the wall, pictures of him with other important people. Mr. Morgan stood next to him in so many of the shots, reminding Wally that he had always been second in command, never first. There had never been a photo of him standing next to Stoker, and now there never would be.

Damn that Melody Singer! And damn those detectives, the gangbangers, Sally Pearce, and everyone who was interfering with his enjoyment of being principal. After waiting all these years to get the job, he deserved better. He picked up a pencil from his desk and stabbed it into the pink phone memo. Then he picked up the phone to return Phillips' call.

Chapter Thirty-seven

DETECTIVE MORRIS, SALLY, TYRONE, AND Tyrone's Gran stood around the perimeter of the conference table in Sally's office. Morris was setting up the materials for inking Tyrone's thumb and first two fingers on both hands. The ink had a pungent, not unpleasant smell. No one spoke, although Tyrone made eye contact with Sally and Gran, alternately.

Tyrone knew he was innocent of any wrongdoing, but the act of being fingerprinted by the police was enough to cause him to itch in places that couldn't be scratched. Too many Black kids before him had been accused, convicted, and punished for crimes they never committed. Tyrone had grown up with this background music, so he felt a certain panic yawning and stretching inside of him, almost, but not yet quite awake.

As if he were a mind reader, the detective said, "Nothing to be 'fraid of, son. You aren't a suspect, but we know your prints are on the gun, and we have to exclude 'em." He looked at Gran and nodded. "Thankful your grandmother could make it, too, since you're a minor. Now, just give me your right thumb." Morris pressed the thumb gently onto the ink pad, then onto the template, rolling it from side to side to pick up all of the whorls. He repeated the action for the other thumb and four fingers, mumbling encouragement like, "Good job," "That's fine now," and "Almost done," as they went along.

When they were finished, Morris closed the lid on the ink pad and handed a moist towelette to Tyrone. "Let's sit down for a minute, if you don't mind," he said, pointing to the chairs on either side of him at the table.

Tyrone wanted to bolt, but Gran caught his eye and pointed her head toward the chair. He sat.

The detective asked Gran, "Do we have the mailed package here?"

The woman nodded. She pointed to the plastic bag on the table in front of her, then pushed it over to Morris. Tyrone winced at the thought of having police touch it, this piece of Shayla that belonged to him alone. He knew he had to give it up, and they would probably ruin it with fingerprint testing and other techniques. He wanted to grab it and run far, far away, but he caught the stern look in his grandmother's eye and remained still.

Morris examined the package wrappings through the plastic bag. "You did a nice job of bagging this for us." When he had looked at everything, he addressed Tyrone. "Is this the only communication you've had from Shayla since the day of Mr. Stoker's death?"

"Yes, sir."

"Is there anything that came in the package that's not here now, a letter? A note?"

"No, sir. Just my ring." He pointed to the ring on his left hand. "Shayla was wearing it on a chain around her neck. I don't know why she sent it back." His jaw was starting to ache again.

"Do you know why they might have gone to Alabama? Who they might be stayin' with?"

Tyrone had considered these questions hundreds of times, and the only thing he could come up with was something having to do with Claude. Shayla's brother had been scary for a long time, and Tyrone had never wanted to have anything to do with him. That day on the football field, when Claude had cut him and broken his jaw, had cemented Tyrone's knowledge that Claude was a gang member. As angry as he was about his injuries, he felt a measure of gratitude to Claude for sparing his life. He hadn't breathed a word about his attacker, and he wouldn't now.

"No, sir. I don't have any idea. All I know is I sure do miss her." He touched his ring, and an image of Shayla's long black hair, her toned arms, her musical laugh, floated before his face.

Morris took a deep breath and exhaled. "Okay, young man. I 'ppreciate your cooperation. Can I count on you to let me know if you hear any more from Shayla or any member of her family?" He removed a business card from his pocket and slid it over to Tyrone.

"Yessir. I will." Tyrone took the card and put it in his own pocket. It felt weird, talking about Shayla with this stranger.

Gran, who had observed all this in silence, said, "Detective, I'd like a card, too. Mr. Stoker was a decent, God-fearing man. Whoever took his life needs to be brought to justice. If I can help, I will."

Chapter Thirty-eight

WHILE MORRIS WAS TAKING FINGERPRINT samples in Sally Pearce's office, Phillips was investigating the Davis family, particularly Claude Davis. What he'd found out so far was standard fare: Mother—Monique Davis, age 36, works security job at IBM downtown, night shift, LKA 12587 Dogwood Avenue (rental), no criminal record, no public aid.

Son—Claude J. Davis, age 18, senior at Abraham Lincoln High School, LKA same, no criminal record, no public aid.

Daughter—Shayla M. Davis, age 18, senior at Abraham Lincoln High School, LKA same.

No father on birth certificates or lease.

He'd put in a call to the chief of police in Hayneville, Alabama, Bert Thompson. If it weren't almost eight hundred miles away, Phillips would have driven there himself to look around.

Thompson was cooperative enough. When Phillips told him about the investigation of the murder of the high school principal, he got real quiet for a second, then said, "Sorry about that. We'll help you find the scumbag however we can." That was one thing about cops. They had a brotherhood based on, "Your Crime is My Crime." Most of the time it worked better than the opposing brotherhood of thieves and murderers.

"I'd like you to assist me with locating the Davis family." Phillips wrapped the telephone cord around his fist. "We want to question the son, Claude J. Davis. I'll send you particulars. The daughter goes with one of the students at the school. She sent him a package, postmarked there. Best guess—they're staying with relatives."

161

"Send me what you've got, and I'm on it," Thompson replied.

Ten minutes later, Phillips' dedicated line rang. When he picked it up, Principal Welburton was on the other end.

"Returning your call," Wally said, after exchanging terse preliminaries. He leaned back in his chair and toyed with his tie. "You said it was urgent."

"Ah, yes. We've, ah, we've found the murder weapon, and we need your help."

"I heard it from Ms. Pearce. You found it at the Davis house?"

"Right. So what I need from you is any and all records: discipline, grade, attendance, health, you name it, for Claude Davis."

"You could get those through the registrar," Wally said, a coolness in his tone of voice.

"Yes, I know, but the registrar can't tell me what I want to know most. I understand you were involved in a matter between Davis and the football coach, a matter in which you and Mr. Stoker disagreed."

"News gets around fast." Wally hated having others know his business. "How did you know about that incident?"

"We have our ways." Phillips waited to let that sink in before asking, "Would you be available for a video interview here at the station? We want to get on record the exact facts of what happened when Davis threatened the coach."

"Video? When did you guys start doing that?"

"Someone donated a camcorder to the station last year. It's turned out to be very effective. So when can you come in?"

It didn't escape Wally's notice that the detective had said "when" and not "if." He sighed again, glancing at his desk calendar. "It'll have to be after school. This school has already had more than its share of interruptions."

"Fine. See you at four thirty this afternoon. And bring those documents on Claude Davis, please. Oh, and one more thing. Have you been fingerprinted yet?"

"Not yet. I'll go over to Ms. Pearce's office before I come to the station this afternoon." Wally sighed and hung up the phone, feeling less like a principal and more like a toady.

Chapter Thirty-nine

ARRIVING AT THE POLICE STATION a few minutes after five o'clock, Wally came under the scrutiny of the rotund desk clerk, who had been a Lincoln parent a few years before. Her son had been suspended for plagiarism, and she had launched a counter-attack on the dean and Wally, both. Now her wicked grin spoke volumes, as it added to Wally's discomfiture at being away from his own turf.

"Well, well, if it ain't *Mr.* Welburton, right in this here po-lice station," she cackled. "Sit yosself down, and I'll tell Detective Phillips you here."

Not wanting to engage in any conversation whatsoever with the woman—Ms. Coleman, if he remembered correctly—Wally found a seat in the stuffy waiting room. The institutional furniture and drab green color of the walls were faintly depressing. Somebody had left a section of the newspaper on the chair next to him, so he busied himself with scanning the morning's local reports. He was glad to see nothing about Lincoln High School.

A door opened about ten feet away, and Detective Phillips strode in, wearing his usual slacks and sport jacket. "How ya doin'?" the detective asked, extending his hand in greeting. "Thanks for coming over this evening. Appreciate your cooperation."

Wally felt like asking, "What choice did I have?" but he just shook the man's hand. "Sorry I'm late. Hard to get away from the building these days."

"C'mon back to our 'video room.' We got you set up here." He ushered Wally into a closet-sized room, dingy, despite smelling like lemon disinfectant. Probably hadn't been used for a while. A

163

rectangular table and six wooden chairs took up most of the space. A video screen on a tripod had been set up at one end, probably as a backdrop. A foot-long black Canon camcorder sat on the table's other end. Walking into the room, Wally shrugged off the feeling of a chicken walking into a slaughterhouse.

"You mind if I bring in Officer Smith to film the interview?" Phillips busied himself with arranging chairs and plugging in the camcorder. "I still haven't got the hang of this new technology."

"Sure. No problem." Still standing, Wally eyed the hot seat in front of the screen.

After a few minutes, Phillips, Welburton, and Smith were all in their places, ready to roll. Phillips introduced the interview with the date, time, and names and titles of those present. He had Wally clarify that he was being interviewed and videotaped by his own free will. Just before launching into his questions, he read the Miranda warnings.

"Wait a minute," Wally almost yelled. "Why are you warning me of my right to remain silent? Am I under arrest?" He slammed both hands on the tabletop and stood as if to go. "What kind of stunt are you trying to pull?"

Phillips grabbed Wally by the arm. "Take it easy, man. You aren't under arrest. I'm just going to ask you routine questions about school business related to this investigation. That's all."

"Then why the warnings?"

"SOP. We do it with every video we make. Otherwise, we can't use it as evidence down the line if things change."

"If I become a suspect, you mean?" Wally wasn't going to fall for this bullshit. They must think he was an idiot. "The deal's off. No video." He made as if to flee the claustrophobic room.

"Hold on a minute. I'd think again before you stroll right out of here. I'll concede the video, if you want, but if you don't answer our questions, you'll be interfering with the murder investigation. You don't want to be an uncooperative witness, do you?"

Feeling trapped, Wally plopped down. He could postpone everything by insisting on an attorney. He thought of calling Sally to get the number for her husband Ron. He just needed a few minutes to think.

"You want some water, coffee, pop?" Phillips asked, suddenly Mr. Hospitality. He nodded his head toward the door, motioning for Smith to play gofer.

Seeing a way to buy time, Wally said, "Okay. Coffee. Black." As Smith left the room, Wally mulled over his options. He could call a lawyer, a step he was hoping not to have to make. He could nix the video and give an interview. He could just walk out and let them come after him with a subpoena. None of these appealed to him, but if he were clever, he might be able to get more than he'd give in an interview. He needed to know more about what the police had in the way of evidence, and if he played this right, he just might be able to find out.

* * *

The coffee was surprisingly fragrant and rich-tasting considering the location and time of day. Someone must have made a fresh pot. Wally drained the cup and straightened the polyester tie at his collar. "Okay, Phillips, we'll do the interview now. No video, just you and me."

"And a tape recorder? I can't take notes and ask questions at the same time."

"Fair enough."

Phillips dashed out to get a tape recorder, returning in under a minute and plugging it into the socket in the wall. "I still need to Mirandize, though, just in case."

Wally waved his hand in dismissal. Somehow a tape recorder didn't seem as dangerous as a video, or maybe he was wearing down. "Go ahead, and I reserve the right to stop at any time, regardless of the question. Let's get this show on the road."

After the general preliminary questions, Phillips narrowed the focus to the school incident with Claude Davis. He referred to the stack of records Wally had brought in with him. "I see here this student had a serious infraction just this school year involving the threatening of a faculty member?"

"Yeah, he admitted to putting a note on Coach Donovan's car. A copy of the actual note is in the file."

The detective flipped the pages until he saw the words: **Black Devils hate honky coaches. Stop coaching, or die!!!** "Do you believe Claude is a member of the Black Devils gang?"

"There's no reason *not* to believe it. He's not the kind of kid who'd come up with something like this on his own."

Phillips leaned forward. "Had he ever played on the football team? Had a class or conflict with the coach? Anything where he'd be motivated to threaten him?"

"Not that I'm aware of."

"No previous problems with white faculty members?"

"Nope. That's why it smacks of gang." Wally loosened his tie and leaned back. "These grown-up gangbangers use the young ones to create havoc in public places as a sort of initiation task. It tests the courage of the kids and results in a show of force. It starts a cycle of fear and intimidation. Why am I telling you this? You know."

Phillips nodded. "So what happened when the note was discovered?"

"The havoc got started. Donovan's popular with the kids. He was blown away. We caught Davis, drew up expulsion papers—b-but Stoker had other ideas." Wally stopped himself from commenting on Stoker's naiveté.

"Mr. Stoker didn't want to go for expulsion?"

"No, Stoker sided with the kid for some reason. Thought he could teach him a lesson a different way. He even offered the kid a job working in the main office. I hated—" Wally caught himself. It wouldn't do to say he hated anything about Stoker at this point in time.

"You hated, what?"

"I hated to see anyone expelled, too." Wally looked at the floor and mumbled.

"Was Davis punished at all for threatening the coach?"

"Yeah, he had a ten-day suspension. Not a great way to start off the school year, but a good sight better than being expelled, especially in your senior year."

"Was Donovan satisfied with the outcome of the case?"

"Not really. Like most of the staff, Donovan likes tight discipline, the way Mr. Morgan and I ran the school. Donovan's here late every day, working with the team, and he worried about having the kid on campus where he might actually carry out his threat." Wally considered whether the police had Donovan on a list of suspects, his motivation to kill Stoker resulting from the mishandling of this incident. "Listen, you're not suspecting Donovan of anything, are you? Donovan's a good guy. He doesn't have a violent bone in his body—except for the normal kind you see on a football field, that is."

"Let's get back to Davis," Phillips said, ignoring Wally's question. "Any prior problems? Anything with weapons, battery, arson?"

"You can look at his record. He was suspended a number of times in years past, but never for anything that serious—mostly skipping class, insubordination, a couple of fights."

"Has he been back on campus since this episode?"

"Not to my knowledge. Suspension's over. He should be back and cracking the books to earn his credits, but when I pulled his attendance records for you, I noticed he's still out." Maybe Wally should have been paying more attention to Davis. He'd been too busy since becoming principal. "You guys looking for him?"

Phillips ignored the question and asked one of his own. "Any other gang stuff going on you want to tell me about?"

Wally sat up straighter. He'd felt more comfortable when the topic was Claude Davis. "We have incidents every day. You know how it is. Some are overtly gang-related, some not."

"Let me be more specific. I'm asking for your opinion as an expert in the administration of the school. Do you think the fire and the murder of Stoker were gang-related?"

Wally fiddled with his tie and tucked in his shirt a bit more. "I didn't think so—at first. But later, I—well, I got that note—telling me whose turf the school was. Maybe the whole thing was a gang hit."

"Is there any reason you can think of why the BDs would want Stoker out of the way?"

"I've wondered about that. Stoker was student-friendly from the first day. Not a hard ass like Mr. Morgan and me. You'd think they'd have it in for the ones who worked to put them away. All I can think is they didn't like having a kinder, gentler high school. They'd rather have the familiar roles and patterns. That, plus the attention that comes from claiming responsibility for the crime."

Phillips leaned back in his chair, stretching his arms out. "Okay, let's say the gangs had nothing to do with it. Is there anyone on the faculty who might have had it in for Stoker?"

Wally folded his hands together and took a breath. He knew who the person was who benefitted most from Stoker's death. "I'm not sure where you're going with that question. Wasn't the weapon linked to a gang theft?"

"It could've fallen into the hands of anyone after that. Answer the question, please."

"Stoker was so new. He didn't have time to make many friends, or enemies. I'd say there were a few people who didn't care for him. Gottschalk, the calculus teacher, challenged him at the first faculty meeting. Stoker put him in his place immediately, so I guess there was some resentment there."

"Any others?"

"There's an oddball teaching economics, a guy from New York, Johnson's his name. He and Gottschalk joined forces to file a grievance." He thought about Norma Dunn's complaint about Johnson's stalking her. "Probably a tempest in a teapot, but those are the only two I can think of."

"Let's get back to Claude Davis," Phillips said. "Can you think of anywhere he might be if he's not at school?"

An odd question, Wally thought. Had Davis skipped town? "You might ask Ms. Pearce about that. I think his sister works in her office."

A knock at the door interrupted the questioning, and Officer Smith stuck his head inside. "Phone call for you from Alabama. He said it's important."

Phillips punched the "Stop" button on the tape recorder and stood. "Thanks for coming in, Welburton. I 'ppreciate your time. I gotta take this call."

Relieved as he was to have completed the interview, Wally was left with a new puzzle. What would a detective in the Midwest think was so important in Alabama?

Chapter Forty

SALLY WAS PACKING UP THE enrollment reports, data to be compiled for the state report the following day. With all of the commotion surrounding the fingerprinting in her office, she hadn't had a minute to work on them during the school day. Her stomach growled, reminding her she hadn't eaten anything since breakfast. Maybe she and Ron could grab a quick bite out, and then he could help her with the statistical report. It had to be accurate, because Lincoln would be accountable for the test scores for the exact numbers of students identified by class.

After dinner and the enrollment report, maybe Ron could give her a foot massage, and...

"Hey, Ms. Pearce."

Sally looked up from stuffing the printouts into her briefcase. Tyrone was leaning on the door frame, still dressed in his football attire, a folded piece of paper clutched in his hand. A half-smile appeared for a second, but didn't do much to lighten the misery in his eyes. A pang of pity stabbed her heart.

"Was that a little smile I saw on your face? Is your jaw feeling better?" She set her briefcase down and opened her arms.

The quarterback moved in for a quick hug. "Thanks," he said. "Okay if I sit down?"

Sally's stomach gurgled again, but she couldn't brush off this kid. He had been through so much.

He sat and rubbed his jaw with one hand, while the other gripped the paper. "Actually, the jaw's better. Doc says I can play on Friday night."

"That's terrific news. Think you'll be eligible, grade-wise?"

"That, too. Now if Shayla were here, I'd be totally slammin'." No smile this time. "I wanted to talk to you about this," he said, as he unfolded the paper and handed it over.

Sally's stomach clenched with a foreboding that had nothing to do with hunger. On the half sheet of notebook paper was the all-too-familiar lettering:

WHERE'D THEY GO? GIVE UP CUCKOO OR GIVE UP THE GIRL FOR GOOD.

Sally turned the note over, but that was it, nothing on the back. "Where did you get this?"

"It was in my gym locker when I came in from practice just now. We don't have locks on those, y'know."

"How would anyone know that it was *your* locker?" Sally hugged herself, chilled. "Who is Cuckoo? Who do you think put this there? How did they get into the locker room? When—"

"Hold up, Ms. Pearce," Tyrone said, the half-smile returning for a moment. "That's a lot of questions." He touched his jaw. "Cuckoo is Claude, Shayla's brother. That's his street name. My guess is some gangbanger put the note there, maybe even somebody on the team for all I know. Whoever it was, it wasn't anyone important, just a kid ordered to do a task."

She should call Wally. He was in charge of discipline and far more experienced in these matters. She glanced at the clock: 6:18, and Wally usually left before six. "We have to call your Gran," she said finally.

"Please, no," Tyrone replied. "She'll get all worried. She's been through enough with my jaw, and me bein' so down about Shayla. I don't want to give her more reason to fret."

She put a hand on Tyrone's arm. "This note constitutes a threat, Tyrone. Gran is your guardian; she needs to know. She needs to be on board in the interest of your safety." Sally picked up the receiver and pushed the phone base to Tyrone, so he could punch in the number.

The phone rang eight, nine, ten times, but no one answered and no machine came on to take a message. Sally said, "Tell you what, I'll drive you home. Maybe she'll be there by the time we get there, and I'll talk with her in person. If she's not there, I'll trust you to tell her about the note and that I'll be calling later tonight."

"Also," Sally went on, "we need to make a copy of this note and preserve the original for the police. It could be evidence. It might have fingerprints." She glanced at her conference table where fingerprint smudges from the day's activity remained as grisly souvenirs.

By now, hunger had taken up residence in Sally's gut and was making itself at home. Sally pulled a stick of spearmint gum out of a pocket in her purse, offering it to Tyrone first.

He shook his head. "My jaw, remember?"

Sally peeled the wrapper and folded the gum into a neat little square before popping it into her mouth. The fresh spearmint flavor burst in her mouth. This would have to do for a while.

"Let me go change out of these clothes, then. I'll be right back." Tyrone took off before Sally could admonish him to be careful in the locker room.

She took the few minutes to call Wally and Detective Phillips about the note. Neither answered, but she left voicemails for both.

It was forty minutes later when they drove up to Tyrone's house. Yellow stripes of light flowed from behind the blinds in the front window. "Gran's at home now," Tyrone said. "You wanna come in?"

Sally unfastened her seat belt and grabbed her purse and briefcase. She hoped this would be a brief visit, for everyone's sake. Before Tyrone could use his key, the front door opened, and his grandmother stood in the opening, a dark form backed by warm light.

"Look who's here," Gran said, a note of wonder in her voice. "I was just talking about you with Detective Phillips at the police station."

Tyrone threw a questioning look at Sally. Entering the house, he bent to kiss his grandmother's forehead.

"May I come in?" Sally asked. "Tyrone and I have something to share with you."

"Of course, come right in. Sit down, and make yourself comfortable." Gran ushered Sally into the single room, where the aroma of fresh cornbread almost knocked Sally over. "Thank you for bringing Tyrone home. I thought he'd be taking the activity bus after practice." She reached up to rub the top of Tyrone's head as he sat next to Sally at the little table.

After Sally explained the reason for her visit, and Tyrone showed his Gran the copy of the note he'd found in his locker, Sally mentioned the need to report it to the detectives. "It may or may not be pertinent to the investigation into Stoker's murder, but until we know, we need to treat it as evidence. I'm also concerned by the content of the note. I want to make sure Tyrone, Shayla, and Claude are protected as much as possible. I want to discuss this with Principal Welburton in terms of placing extra security around football practice and any other areas where Tyrone might be vulnerable."

Gran hugged Sally. "I 'ppreciate everything you're doing for my boy here, Ms. Pearce. I don't know what I'd do if you weren't there at school to watch out for him and all our young people. These are mighty trying times with all that's happened to Tyrone and Mr. Stoker. I'm just 'bout ready to move outta here and go someplace where nobody knows us. That's what I'm guessing the Davises did."

Sally tried to ignore the mouth-watering smell coming from the oven. She gathered her belongings, but then remembered. "Did you say you had been at the police station, Ms. Nesbitt?"

"Um, yes, I did." Gran looked away into the kitchen and muttered, "Excuse me," as she left to put on oven mitts and check on the cornbread. When she opened the oven door to test for doneness, the delectable smell rushed through the room. "Looks done," she said, pulling the pan from the oven rack and setting it on the stovetop. "Would you like a piece?"

Sally grinned like a child at Christmas. "I'd *love* it."

Gran made space in the refrigerator, so she could set the pan of cornbread there to speed-cool. She made a show of taking out the butter and three small paper plates. "Hope you like my cornbread. Recipe's been in the family for generations."

"I'm sure I will. If it tastes as good as it smells, I'll be transported to heaven."

Tyrone fidgeted with the copy of the note on the table, then rolled the salt shaker between his palms. "Gran, what were you doing at the police station?"

Gran shuffled back to the table and sat down. When she spoke, her words came out slowly. "W-well," she said, "you know Miss Minnie who lives across from the Davises?"

Tyrone shook his head.

"Well, she goes to our church, and she knows who *you* are. She's been telling me for a long time 'bout your comings and goings over there."

Tyrone's face reddened, but he remained silent.

Gran went on, looking into Tyrone's face, as if Sally weren't in the room at all. "She told me she saw you over there two days ago, looking around. She said you were with a lady in a suit and heels. She thought it might have been a white lady." With that, Gran turned to look at Sally. "Might that be you, Ms. Pearce?"

Sally remembered the old lady across the street who had opened her door just before they found the gun. "Yes, that was the day Tyrone and I went to see why no one was answering the phone. The police know all about it."

"Yes, I know." Gran pulled the pan of cornbread out of the refrigerator and laid her palm on top. "Just cool enough to cut a coupla pieces." She took up a serrated knife and sawed through the honey-colored crust. She lifted three perfectly equal squares, one at a time, and put them on the plates. Next she cut them in half horizontally and put generous pats of butter between the still-warm halves. She handed the first one to Sally, the second to Tyrone.

Sally was ready to put her face into the plate and gobble the cornbread whole, but she waited until Gran said Grace and nodded at her. Then the light, buttery bite of sunshine exploded in Sally's mouth, and the warm nourishment soothed her from the inside out.

When they had finished the first three pieces, Gran said, "I'll pack you up a piece to take home." She set about buttering another square and nesting it between two paper plates. "Tyrone, you'll have to wait till dinner to get some more."

Tyrone picked a cornbread crumb from the corner of his mouth and popped it inside. "So what else did Miss Minnie have to say about me?"

Gran's forehead wrinkled as she examined Tyrone's face, then Sally's. "Everything ain't all about you, Baby. Miss Minnie was being interviewed by the police, and she asked me to go with her to the station. They was going to videotape her, and she was nervous. I remembered how nice Detective Phillips was, giving me his card and all, so I said yes."

Sally gathered her belongings. "That was very nice of you, Ms. Nesbitt. I hope Miss Minnie's interview was a help to the police."

"I think it was. The detective seemed especially interested when she told him she saw the same lady two other times by herself, once before and once after seeing her with Tyrone." She handed the still-warm package to Sally. "She said the 'bright' lady seemed mighty preoccupied with something in or around the porch steps."

This time, both Tyrone and Gran fixed their gazes on Sally's face, which had crumpled in bewilderment. In stereo-like unison, they said, "Ms. Pearce, was that you?"

Chapter Forty-one

BERT THOMPSON PRIDED HIMSELF ON being efficient and speedy, especially when it came to solving cases. He didn't have more than one murder every four or five years in Hayneville, Alabama, so when called upon to help with an investigation in a big city in the Midwest, he put everything else on the back burner and started looking for Claude Davis. With only 874 residents to keep track of, he didn't expect much difficulty in flushing out the newcomers.

He started at the Lowndes County Courthouse, looking at real estate rolls under the name of "Davis." One Davis family lived on Tuskeena Street, but they were white. Going to the churches would probably be a better route, and if he had to guess, the Greater Mt. Olive AME Zion Church, the largest Black church in town, would be a great place to start. Shirley Holt prayed there, and Thompson knew her from his high school days, when she'd crossed the color line to work in the school cafeteria.

Thompson looked up Ms. Holt's address in the slender phone directory and decided to pay her a visit. As he passed the NO OUTLET sign at the head of the narrow street, he wondered how this visit would be received by the elderly woman. He hoped she wouldn't be alarmed by having a cop car in her driveway and a police chief in her living room.

He rang the doorbell and waited on the shadeless stoop. Peeling white paint showed through the patched mesh of the screen door. He brushed the perspiration from his forehead. More than a minute passed, and he could hear no sounds from within. He decided to leave. Maybe calling on the phone would be better. As he turned to go, the door creaked open. Behind it stood a thin woman with skin the color of strong, hot tea, and hair tied up in a pink-and-white kerchief. Large black eyes looked past him at the police car, then rested on his face, before she broke into a smile.

"Why, Hubert Thompson, is that you?" she cackled, as she pushed the screen door open. "Come on in, boy. I haven't seen you in a dog's age, my chicken-fried-steak kid." She stood aside and made room for him to enter.

Thompson removed his hat and crossed the threshold, inhaling the coolness and the clean piney smell. "Thank you, ma'am. I won't keep you long."

"Just you come on in and don't worry about keepin' me. Now that I'm retired, I don't get many visitors." She smiled, showing pink gums and teeth larger than he remembered. "Sit on down," she said, pointing to a persimmon-colored sofa topped with crocheted back and arm covers. "Can I offer you some lemonade, or some sweet tea? It's mighty hot out there already."

"No, thank you, ma'am," Thompson replied. "I appreciate the offer, though." He sat on the sofa, as directed. "Fact is, I'm working on a case with another police department up north, and I thought of you and wondered if you might be able to help me."

"Well, I didn't 'spect this was a social call," Ms. Holt replied. "Still, it's nice you remembered me after all these years. And you being chief of police, at that." She adjusted the folds of her pink housecoat and folded her hands in her lap. "What can I do for you?"

Thompson grinned as if Ms. Holt had just placed two portions on his plate, instead of one. "There's a family from up north, mother, daughter, and son. Seems they're stayin' in Hayneville. My colleague asked me to help locate them."

A frown replaced the pleasant expression on Ms. Holt's face. "What for? Is they in trouble?"

"I believe the police want to question them about something that happened before they left town. If the shoe was on the other foot, if I was looking for someone who went up there, I sure would appreciate having them help me." Thompson reached in his pocket and pulled out copies of the yearbook photos of Claude and Shayla Davis. "This is what the kids look like. Have you seen them anywhere, in church maybe?"

Ms. Holt stared into space, as if she had suddenly become deaf, dumb, and blind. Obviously she didn't want to look at the pictures, didn't want to get involved. It wasn't surprising. In fact, it was typical for people to protect their own, especially when their own belonged to a different ethnic group than the inquiring police officer's

Thompson continued to hold out the pictures, though, as he maintained eye contact. He nodded as if to say, "Go ahead. It's okay." After an uncomfortable minute, the stand-off ended, and Ms. Holt took the papers. She pulled a pair of half-glasses from the pocket of her housecoat and put them on. Squinting first at Shayla's, then at Claude's picture, she began moving her lips, though no sound came out.

The chief gave her time, hoping that the moving lips indicated recognition. Finally, he could wait no longer. "Ms. Holt," he said, tapping his foot on the floor with nervous energy, "Have you seen either of these young people?"

The woman blinked rapidly, and Thompson noticed a single tear escaping from her eye and migrating down her cheek. Eventually it fell onto the housecoat, replaced by a successor.

"Ms. Holt, do you know these people?"

Nodding slowly, Ms. Holt handed the photos back to Thompson. "Y-yes, Chief Thompson, I know these young people." She walked over to the window and gazed out. "These is the grandchildren of my sister. They're my kin." She looked back at Thompson with a steady gaze. "I just hope to God they aren't in any trouble."

Chapter Forty-two

AT THE SAME TIME THAT Thompson was locating the Davises in Alabama, Melody Singer stood in her Lincoln High classroom, implementing a lesson based on the Salem witchcraft trials. Her eleventh graders sat in a circular arrangement as they enacted a Socratic seminar. Three open-ended questions were written on the blackboard in colored chalk:

1. Would you denounce your beliefs in order to save your life? Why or why not?
2. Why have people succumbed to hate and fear during crucial times in history?
3. What could we do as a people to combat mass hysteria?

So far the discussion had been lively, but orderly. Melody walked around the outside of the circle, occasionally tapping the shoulder of a participant or leaning over a desk to look at a student's notes. Group norms called for snapping of fingers to show agreement, thumbs down to show disagreement. So far there had been a lot of snapping, but very few thumbs.

Melody smiled, pleased by the quality of the responses, as well as the high level of student engagement. These were the reasons she had gone into teaching in the first place. As the class period went on, the students became more and more animated. She wished Mr. Stoker were here to observe. He would've loved it when Angel said, "I couldn't live with myself if I had to live a lie. That would be as good as saying the persecutors were right." *Snap, snap, snap* filled the room. Melody thought about her own predicament with Mr. Johnson's complaining about her teaching methods and Mr. Welburton's insinuating her job was in his grabby hands. Perhaps Angel's statement applied to her, as well.

Jeremy commented, "I think the 'willed ignorance' of those people in Salem who stood by without doing anything to stop the witchcraft trials was just like the people in Germany who remained silent when Jews were persecuted during World War II."

Fired with passion, Simon threw his arm into the air with such force he caused his rickety wooden desk to topple with a crash. There was a split-second of silence, then pandemonium, as teacher and other students sought to make sure Simon was okay.

Dazed, and likely starting to bruise, Simon extricated himself from the desk. "I'm okay—really, I'm okay."

Again silence ruled, so the knock at the door seemed like a pounding. Thirty pairs of eyes turned toward the sound. The tall, slim frame of the teacher from next door filled the doorway, and a murderous look filled his face. "Ms. Singah," he said, like a fire-breathing dragon, "please, this is an institution of learning, not a barnyard."

Angel looked around at her classmates. "Is that man calling us all animals?"

Jeremy stood and clenched his fists, as if preparing to attack the teacher. "Why're you always coming over here, complaining? Why don't you teach your own classes and leave us alone? I know kids in your classes who say they ain't learning *nothing*."

"Yeah," Angel almost shouted. "We are *learning* in this class. We are thinking and learning, and loving it."

Melody stepped in and said, "Class, Mr. Johnson probably heard Simon's desk fall and came over to see if we needed assistance." She looked at Johnson as if to confirm, but he was staring at his fingernails. "Thank you for your concern, Mr. Johnson, but you can see that Simon is quite okay."

Johnson backed out of the doorway without another word. The class roared in laughter, and a few students bumped fists, as if a huge victory had been won.

Melody, sensing a teachable moment, said in a carefully modulated voice, "Class, let's not become a hysterical mob, or we will fall prey to the same pattern we've just condemned in others."

* * *

At the end of the school day, after all the students had cleared the building, Mr. Johnson appeared at the doorway again. It was the first time Melody had ever seen the man without his suit jacket. His vest was unbuttoned, his tie loosened. Melody steeled herself for another confrontation.

"May I come in?"

"Sure." She took a sip of water from the plastic bottle on her desk. "Want to sit down?" She pointed to the pod of student desks closest to her own, and he eased himself into one of the four desks.

Johnson gazed at the three Socratic questions, still on the blackboard. "Interesting lesson you had today." He removed his glasses and fixed her with a myopic stare. "In fact, you even taught me something."

Melody couldn't believe her ears. "You taught me something, too, Mr. Johnson."

"I've been so fixated on your youth, your use of non-traditional teaching methods, your popularity with the administration and the students. Perhaps it was just the green-eyed monster rearing its head. What I should have been doing was figuring out *why* your teaching was so effective, and mine, alas, was not." He leaned back and crossed one long leg over the opposite knee. "I blamed you for my lack of success, and that was wrong. I hope you'll accept my apology."

"Of course I do." Melody fiddled with the pages of her grade book, wondering about his sincerity. "You know, I'm happy to share my lesson plans with you. Even though we don't teach the same subjects, we're both social studies teachers, and these methods are very adaptable."

"That's very kind of you. I probably don't deserve it." He examined the shine on his wingtips.

"Don't be ridiculous, Mr. Johnson. Do you want to know what lesson I learned from you today? I learned how easily misunderstandings can turn to prejudice and intolerance, and how vigilant we, as teachers, have to be to reverse that tide before it becomes a tsunami."

Johnson rose and straightened the four desks. "You are pretty wise for your years, Ms. Singer. Why don't you call me Derrick?"

"Okay, Derrick, and you can call me Melody."

"Melody? That has quite a nice ring to it." Johnson stood and straightened the suspenders beneath his open vest. He offered his hand to Melody, who gave it a firm shake. "I look forward to learning about your teaching methods." He turned toward the door and muttered, "I suppose I will have to rescind my request of Mr. Welburton."

"What was that?" Melody called after him.

"Oh, nothing," Derrick mumbled. "Sometimes old men tend to talk to themselves."

Chapter Forty-three

JUST BEFORE LUNCH THE NEXT morning, Sally was sitting in the back of the chemistry lab, scripting the lesson for a teacher evaluation. As part of her summer preparation for the assistant principal job, she had learned how to conduct formative evaluations for instructional improvement. One of the keys was to take thorough, objectively-stated notes, describing with precision as much of the lesson as possible, including everything the teacher and students were saying and doing.

Sally had developed a personal shorthand system for scripting. Her pen was flying and her mind was focused on both the copper-acetone experiment and the reactions of the students as they observed it. She had drawn a rudimentary map of the classroom, and now she was marking each station with a symbol, indicating how engaged the students appeared to be at that station. Whenever a student asked a question or made a comment, she recorded that in note form, as well.

"A catalyst is used to cause a chemical reaction, yet at the end of the experiment, the catalyst remains unchanged," the teacher explained. "First I will illustrate the concept with this bit of copper foil, a blowtorch, and a cup full of acetone. Afterwards, you will conduct an experiment of your own using a catalyst."

Sally scripted what the teacher said and watched the faces of the students as the teacher held the copper foil with pliers and heated it with the torch. When the S-shaped foil was red hot, he lowered the foil into the acetone.

"Turn off the lights, Cameron," the teacher instructed.

With the lights off, everyone in the room could see the bright, glowing form of the copper foil inside the acetone. The foil, but not the pliers or the acetone, illuminated the classroom with an orange-pink shine, a mini fiery sun inside of the glass.

"Cool," one of the students said.

"No, hot," said another, and the students giggled. Most of the students, however, seemed too fixated on the glowing metal to speak.

After a few minutes, the glow subsided, and the teacher pulled the foil from the glass. He asked Cameron to turn the lights back on. "What do you notice now that the experiment is over, class?"

One girl's hand shot up high and fast. "The copper foil looks exactly the same as it did before the experiment."

"That's exactly right, Darneisha, and that's what a catalyst is: it causes the reaction, but is unchanged by it." The teacher went on, "The bell for lunch is about to ring, and when we return, you will conduct a catalytic experiment of your own."

Sally captured all of this in words and symbols on her legal pad, and when the lunch bell sounded, she remained seated, watching as students departed. What she was thinking was how like a catalyst Mr. Stoker had been in this school. His brief principalship had brought a big paradigm shift to Lincoln High. Everyone was adjusting to a new way of doing business, a new way of treating students and parents. Some had really liked it, and some, obviously, had not, but in her view, the school had glowed with promise. Now she feared it would slip back into the old ways, and Stoker's efforts would be forgotten. She would always think of Stoker, though, as a hero, someone who provided unchanging advocacy for student success.

* * *

Sally was eager to return to her office. She had a list of tasks a mile long, and she was famished. Skipping breakfast had been expedient, but not smart. Fortunately, a tuna salad sandwich, pickle, carrot sticks, and a Granny Smith waited in her mini-fridge.

"Not so fast," Pat said, as Sally breezed past her to unlock the inner office. "I think you'll want to return this call before you do anything else." She held a pink message slip between two fingers.

Sally glanced at Pat's neat handwriting. "Pls call Detective Morris, in re: Claude and Shayla Davis." Sally almost dropped the note in excitement. "News about Shayla?" she asked. "Did he say what, specifically, it was?"

Pat shook her head. "No, but I could tell from his voice, he considered it to be good news."

Sally unlocked her door, juggling keys, evaluation notebook, and pink message slip. She dashed to her phone and keyed in Morris' number. Her hunger pangs were all but forgotten.

The detective answered on the first ring.

"You have news about the Davis kids?" Sally asked.

"Yes, I do, but before we get to that, I need to ask you a question."

"Okay, go ahead."

"You know that evening when you found the gun at the Davis house, under the steps?"

"Y-yes." Sally remembered what Tyrone's grandmother had said about the neighbor having seen a white woman at the house several times.

"Had you ever been to that house before or after that night?" Morris' tone was neutral.

So there it was. "No, Detective. That was the one and only time I was ever at the Davis house, and Tyrone Nesbitt was with me the entire time. I hope you believe me."

Detective Morris sighed softly. "I do believe you, Mrs. Pearce. You've been more than cooperative with us, but I had to ask. Someone saw a woman who resembled you outside that house. We have to follow up on it."

Sally realized she had been holding her breath. Now she took in a lung full and said, "What about the Davises?"

"Yes, I thought you'd want to know. Your lead helped us get a warrant, and the Nesbitt boy's package helped us find the family. They *were* in Hayneville, Alabama, as we thought, staying with some relatives." Morris paused, and Sally could hear papers shuffling. "Anyway, all three of them are on their way back here, should arrive here at the police station around nine p.m."

"Are they—are they under arrest? Are they in trouble?" Sally

184

hugged herself with her free hand. She wouldn't be able to forgive herself if she had been the cause of Shayla's arrest. She knew the girl couldn't have had anything to do with Mr. Stoker's death. Claude was a different matter. She didn't know enough about him to have an opinion.

"Let's put it this way," Morris replied. "We have some questions for them, and we'll see where we go from there."

"Detective Morris," Sally said, "I'd bet my life that Shayla is completely innocent."

"Don't worry, Mrs. Pearce." Sally thought she could hear a smile in his voice. "Your office aide doesn't need a character witness at this point. Oh, and one more thing. We've identified fingerprints on some of the items from Mr. Stoker's desk. We'd like to talk to you about those."

"You can't tell me now?"

"No, it'll keep until this evening. You are planning to come in?"

"Yes, of course. I want to be there to see Shayla, if nothing else." Sally thought for a second. "What about a lawyer?" Sally asked. "Will the Davises have a lawyer available to them when they arrive tonight?"

"Well, that's not up to me. I don't know too many lawyers who want to spend their Thursday night hanging around the police station, waiting for persons of interest to arrive. Anyway, I thought you'd like to know."

Sally's mind was racing like a car on the Indy 500 track. "Yes, thank you for telling me. Thank you very much." She pushed the button on the base of her desk phone to disconnect the call, still holding the receiver to her ear.

After a minute of reflection, she lifted her finger and listened for the dial tone. She keyed in the number of her husband's cell phone. When he answered, she said, "Honey, do you have any plans for tonight?"

Chapter Forty-four

RIDING IN THE BACK SEAT of the police car, Shayla tried to zone out everything—the sporadic sputtering of the police radio from the front, the monotonous thrumming of the fast-moving car on I-65, even the nearness of her brother's thigh against hers—as they traveled back home. She felt dizzy, nauseated almost to the point of calling out to stop the car, so she could throw up.

They'd been traveling since morning, and they wouldn't arrive at their destination until about ten p.m. Judging by the shadows made by trees and buildings as they whizzed past, it was only mid-afternoon. She had already asked to stop for a restroom twice, and she needed to ask again. Her mother had turned her head from the front seat and given her a questioning stare the last time.

Could it be only eight days since they'd made this trip by train and buses in the other direction? It seemed like a year. Shayla reached inside the collar of her t-shirt, so she could slide the slim metal chain between thumb and forefinger. Even without Tyrone's class ring on the chain, she felt calmed by the sensation of links against skin, the rhythm of her hand movements.

She still hadn't told anyone she was pregnant. Not Tyrone, not Mama, not Claude. Only Mrs. Pearce knew, and Shayla felt pretty sure her secret was safe. Soon she would have to break the news, but right now it seemed like other matters had priority over her internal drama. She knew her mama hadn't slept much since Mr. Stoker was killed and they had left home. The two of them had been sharing a narrow bed at Auntie's house, and the restlessness of each had been multiplied by physical closeness and emotional remoteness. Shayla knew her mother was worried to the bone about Claude. She just couldn't add more to her worry by announcing her pregnancy now.

Shayla focused on her brother's head, bobbing gently in the seat next to her, where he had been handcuffed. He hadn't uttered a word since they'd left. He was only eighteen, still a kid, really, and he was bearing a lot of weight on his shoulders. She knew it was his own fault for getting involved with the gang in the first place and for doing all the other things they'd made him do, but she couldn't help feeling sorry for him. She thought of a quote from a Harry Potter book she'd read: "I don't go looking for trouble. Trouble usually finds me."

Really, a part of Shayla was looking forward to returning home. She missed Tyrone and school and a normal life with an intensity she had never imagined. She wanted to catch up in all her classes and apply for scholarships. She wanted to go to the homecoming dance with the quarterback of the football team. If it had been up to her, she never would have left in the first place.

As the car sped on, she reflected on how the day Mr. Stoker was killed, her life had ceased to be her own. If she hadn't been in the bathroom during the fire alarm, she never would have seen Claude outside of the main office, standing over the principal with a gun, his hands shaking like scrawny branches in a violent windstorm. Horrified, she had screamed and run outside.

She regretted telling Mrs. Pearce what she had seen, even though she was careful not to say whom she had seen, but she knew she would have to tell Mama. Mama was the only other person she could trust. Mama would know what to do.

By the time Shayla had arrived at home that day, she'd heard the water running in the shower. "Claude?" she had called into the peeling veneer of the bathroom door. "Claude, answer me." She'd pounded on the door till it bounced on its hinges, but no one answered. Perhaps a half hour later the sound of running water came to an abrupt halt. "You in there, Claude Davis?" Shayla screamed.

A muffled voice replied, "Yeah, it's me. Stop your hollerin'. I'll be out in a minute." When the door opened, she saw her brother, wrapped in a towel, his clothes thrown into a pile behind him, his face drawn into the deepest, darkest frown she had ever seen. His eyes were swollen and red from tears, and his hands were shaking.

"Oh, Claude," Shayla had cried, throwing herself into his arms, "I saw you. I saw you in the hallway with Mr. Stoker." Her sobs returned with the force of a geyser, and seeing her cry prompted fresh tears from her brother.

"Let's go sit down," Claude had said, reaching for a pair of sweat pants and a plaid shirt on the hook behind the door. "We don't have much time, but we need to talk before Mama gets home." He led his sister to the shabby sofa in the front room. He donned his clothes and went to get a glass of water for Shayla. "Here, drink this." He sat, putting his arm around her trembling shoulders.

"It's not what it looked like," he began, his voice quavering beyond control. "I promise you, Baby Sister. You don't need to worry."

Shayla had started to hyperventilate, so she drew her feet up on the couch, tucked her head between her knees, and wrapped her arms around. She looked like a roly-poly, curled and protected. She'd concentrated on inhaling and exhaling, thinking of the tiny fetus inside of her. Finally, she regained control of her breathing and uncurled, taking a sip of water from the glass Claude had brought.

"Claude," Shayla said, her voice clear, but shaky. "Who else might've seen you there with Mr. Stoker? You say it's not what it looked like, but what it looked like was that you killed our principal."

"I know. I know that's how it looked. I wish I could go back and make it come out different, but I ain't killed the guy. At least I don't think I did." Claude took a sip from the glass he'd brought his sister. "As for who saw me? I have no idea. That whole time is a blank page in my mind. I didn't even know *you* was there."

"What are we gonna tell Mama, Claude? You're in real serious trouble."

Claude had patted his sister's kneecaps. "We just gonna tell her the truth. And she likely gonna tell *us* we got to leave town."

Now, in the police car on the way back home, Shayla had the feeling that the approaching night would wrap her family in darkness and swallow them whole. She would never have a chance to graduate and go to college. She would never see Tyrone again or tell him about the baby. The poor little baby in her belly would never see the light of day.

Chapter Forty-five

THAT SAME DAY AFTER SCHOOL, on the way to the practice field, Coach Donovan stopped by Wally's office to thank him. "I don't know what you did, buddy," he said, clapping Wally on the shoulder, "but I've got my quarterback and all my linemen ready to play on Friday night. How did you get that New York stuffed shirt Johnson to work with my kids?"

Wally held his surprise inside. Whatever the reason for the change in Mr. Johnson's eligibility report, Wally would be glad to take credit for it. "We aim to please," he replied, flipping his tie and patting it in place on his midriff. "By the way, Coach, you haven't seen or heard from Claude Davis lately, have you?"

"No, and I hope I never do. I can't see anything good ever coming from that boy, despite Mr. Stoker's attempt to rehabilitate him." Donovan smacked his glob of bubble gum. "Why? You hear something?"

"Not exactly." Wally thought of the anonymous notes with gang messages. "Davis' suspension is over, but he's not back at school. I guess Stoker's faith in him was misplaced." He stretched his back and winced. "You ask me, Davis is a prime suspect in Stoker's death. He's just crazy enough to kill the man who was trying to help him."

Donovan looked at Wally through scrunched-up eyebrows. "Weren't you the guy who said not to worry about Davis? That he was all talk and no action? You told me not to be afraid of his threat on my life, and now you're saying he may have killed Stoker?" Donovan chomped on his gum, as if he were masticating Davis himself. "Whatsamatter with you, buddy? The new job getting to ya?"

Caught in his own patter, Wally felt seeds of worry sprouting in his gut. He seemed to have lost his cool, confident persona in these stressful days since becoming principal. "I guess you're right, Coach." Changing the subject, he pointed to the disarray in the office, where he had been preparing to move to the newly remodeled principal's office. "I was here till almost midnight last night, packing up, and I'm only about halfway finished." He patted his tie again and said, "Anyway, I'm glad you'll be playing with a full team again. Count on me being there to cheer them on."

As Donovan left, Wally turned his attention to his calendar. It would be another late night tonight with the parent advisory committee meeting. Maybe he could get Sally to start taking over this group, so he could free up a night to have dinner at home once a month. He never really liked working with parents anyway—they were too demanding.

The phone rang, and Myrna put the call on hold, then stood in the doorway to Welburton's inner office. "It's those police detectives again," she said, her voice quavering. "They make me so nervous I could scream."

Wally couldn't understand why two bumbling detectives would have such an effect on someone so steady and reliable as Myrna. He wanted to find out, but he needed to take the call first. He held up a finger toward Myrna, as he punched the flashing button on his desk phone.

"Welburton. How can I help you?"

"Guess you know about Claude Davis," Phillips said.

"What about Davis?"

"We found him in Alabama. Mother and sister, too." It was annoying how Phillips spoke in short sentences and left Wally hanging. It was as if he expected Wally to beg for more.

"How would I know that?" Wally asked.

"Your colleague Mrs. Pearce knows. Thought you two talk on a regular basis."

Wally leaned back in his chair and fingered his tie. It was true, he hadn't spoken to Sally as much since she'd lambasted him about

Melody Singer. Ignoring the dig about his communication with Sally, he asked, "So what about Davis? Is he a suspect?"

"Let's just say he's still a person of interest. We're bringing him back here tonight. Thought you might want to talk to him, yourself. I'm sure you're still investigating things on your end."

"Uh, yeah. Sure, I would," Wally replied, wondering whether Phillips' offer was as generous as it sounded, or whether he had an ulterior motive for getting Wally in to the police station again. "When were you thinking?"

"Around about ten p.m. Tonight."

After Phillips hung up, Wally still held the receiver to his ear. He did have some questions for Davis, but they might not be the same ones the police would be asking.

More immediately, he needed to communicate with his secretary. He walked out into the outer office, which was quiet for the moment. "Myrna, what has got you so nervous with the police?"

Myrna flinched at the question, and when she looked up from her computer, he could see her eyes were full of tears. "I'm afraid I c-can't say," she answered.

Wally put a hand on the older woman's shoulder. "Can't say, or won't say? I would like to know why you are so upset."

Grabbing a couple of tissues, Myrna dabbed at her eyes and blew her nose. She fiddled with her hearing aid, as well. "The r-reason I'm so nervous is 'cause I'm worried about you."

"About me?" Wally was beginning to question whether he had good communication with anyone these days. "What about me?"

Now tears flowed freely down both cheeks, and Myrna tried to mop them up with a tissue. "F-first of all, I c-couldn't stop thinking about Mr. S-Stoker. How I always thought you were the one most at risk of being harmed by the g-gangs."

"You mean because I'm in charge of discipline?"

"Yes, and so many of the bad kids and their parents have it in for you all the time."

"But what about the police upsets you now?" Wally asked.

"I-I j-just think, those detectives… the way they come in here asking questions, making demands… the way they look around for you, as if I'm covering up for you. I think they suspect Mr. Stoker's murderer is you."

Chapter Forty-six

SALLY'S OFFICE SEEMED STUFFY AND still as she unlocked the door and dropped her briefcase on a chair after an afternoon of meetings. She usually treasured this quiet time, after the office staff had left for the day. If the circumstances allowed, it could be the most productive time of day.

Sally's plan was to return phone calls and emails, so she could meet Ron for a late dinner before heading to the police station. The thought of seeing Shayla again cast a rose-colored glow over everything, despite the circumstances. She wondered whether Tyrone knew that Shayla was coming home, but she supposed if he did, he'd be in here jumping out of his skin in anticipation. It wasn't her place to tell him, but if she knew Shayla, it wouldn't be long before Shayla made contact and resumed wearing his senior ring around her neck.

As Sally punched in her four-digit voicemail code, she heard the automated voice reply, "You have forty-two new messages." Sally gasped at the sheer number, the highest she had ever had in one day.

Wally's secretary, Myrna, helped listen to *his* messages and return calls, but she had never enlisted Pat's help, partly because Mr. Stoker had told her it was important for an administrator to stay personally connected with the public.

"After all, these people are the ones paying your salary, and whatever they're calling about, it's vital to them. Don't make the mistake of handing them off to someone else, or you'll lose their support."

Sally had taken Stoker's advice to heart, and she was diligent about returning calls and emails within twenty-four hours. Today it would require a disciplined marathon. She kicked off her pumps, grabbed her memo pad, and started taking notes and phone numbers. It would probably take a half hour just to listen to all the messages.

Parents wanting to change their children's teachers, a complaint about the time of the early lunch period, a couple of bus problems—Sally's pen scribbled notes as quickly as the callers spoke. About halfway through, there was a message from Superintendent Blank. Sally sat a little straighter.

"—Not urgent and no need to call me back today, but just wanted to make you aware. There are a group of parents who want to honor Mr. Stoker's memory. They want to have something in the school—a bench, a wall hanging, a statue, or maybe a scholarship—in tribute to Mr. Stoker. They need someone in the building to sit on their committee and guide their decisions. I think you'd be the most appropriate person, don't you?" A pause, and then, "Let me know your thoughts in the next several days."

Sally jotted, "Dr. B, Stoker tribute." That was nice, honoring Mr. Stoker. Imagine how much he would have been honored if he had served several years at Lincoln. It would be a pleasure to serve on that committee.

Next in the queue was an anonymous voicemail, a raspy-voice, muttering something unintelligible. Sally strained to hear the message, holding a hand to her outside ear, but all she could make out was, "Watch it." She replayed the message several times, trying to discern something more, trying to recognize the voice. If it was a threat, it couldn't have come at a worse time, with Stoker's death hanging over her like an immutable cloud. Still, she fought the possibility that she might be in danger as Assistant Principal of Lincoln High. She loved her job and didn't want to abandon the community she felt privileged to serve. Finally, she put the message on "save." She would think about it later. Now it was getting late, and she needed to move on.

The first sounds of the next message gave Sally a jolt of pleasure. "Mrs. Pearce?" it began, and right away Sally recognized Shayla's sweet voice. "I'm coming back home, Mrs. Pearce, and I need to talk to you. Those things I told you—the things I didn't tell anyone else—I hope you didn't tell anyone. Sorry I missed you, and you can't call me back, but I guess I'll be seeing you soon." Shayla paused to take in a deep breath. "I hope you didn't tell. Bye."

A guilty pang pierced Sally's heart. While she had kept the secret of Shayla's pregnancy, she had likely exposed Shayla to a lot of police scrutiny over her comment that she had seen someone with a gun. Whoever it was, it had been traumatic enough to cause Shayla to sob in hysterics just after the fire and murder. If it had been her brother Claude, it may have been what had driven the family to leave town. The fact that Sally had also been instrumental in finding the murder weapon at Shayla's house raised another welt of conscience. Moreover, she had been the one to tell Phillips about the package Tyrone had received from Alabama. As much as she cared about Shayla, almost as a surrogate daughter, she certainly wasn't doing anything to make the girl's situation more tolerable.

Sally replayed the message, noting the time it had come in: 8:58 a.m. Shayla must have called before she left Alabama. This message she also put on save, although she couldn't explain why. Perhaps it seemed like a gift worth savoring again, coming after so many days of missing the girl and worrying about her. The reunion tonight would be joyous, but tempered by more worries about what lay ahead.

The rest of the voicemails beckoned first. Like an efficient soldier, Sally marched through the drill of making notes and returning calls. She made sure her voice was full of warmth and concern. She was sure Mr. Stoker would have approved.

Chapter Forty-seven

THAT SAME AFTERNOON, MR. JOHNSON, wearing his three-piece suit, stood in front of the microwave oven in the teacher's lounge, warming some homemade split pea soup, when Norma Dunn burst into the room, holding a Lean Cuisine. Something about the old geezer looked different, though Norma couldn't put her finger on what it was.

"Oh, hello, Ms. Dunn," he said. "I'll just be a minute—no, thirty-eight seconds—and then you can have the microwave."

"No rush," she replied. "Aren't you here mighty late this evening?" *Was it a haircut? Dental cleaning? The man looked seriously better than ever before.*

The economics teacher smiled, revealing straight, even teeth. The microwave beeped, and he turned his back. After removing his dinner and stirring it, releasing the aroma of the thick, green broth, he bowed and gestured for Norma to step up to the counter.

His gallantry was not lost on her. Why hadn't she noticed how polite he was? She inserted her chicken with almonds into the oven and set it for three and a half minutes.

Mr. Johnson had taken his soup to the table and begun eating it, a cloth napkin on his lap. He looked like a well-bred aristocrat, out of place in this utilitarian setting. Norma wondered again why he was here so late, and why he hadn't answered her when she'd asked.

Matter of fact, after all of her plans to fend him off, holding Wally's threat in case she had to use it, she hadn't seen as much as Mr. Johnson's shadow since that uncomfortable exchange in her classroom when he'd asked her out. Maybe her efforts to discourage his advances had worked, or maybe, judging by the tingly feeling she got watching him eat so mannerably, they had worked a little too well.

When her meal was ready, she held it by the edges and carried it over to the table, where Mr. Johnson was finishing up. "May I sit with you, Derrick?" she asked, batting her eyelashes.

"As you wish, Ms. Dunn. I am just leaving. I have a meeting to go to."

"The grievance committee meeting? I'm headed that way, too." Maybe they could sit together.

"No, the curriculum meeting. My neighbor, Ms. Singer, suggested I join that group."

Norma was astonished. "Ms. Singer? The young white girl? I thought you hated the way she teaches."

Mr. Johnson flashed a slice of pearly whites at the faculty association president. "That was before. No harm in an old teacher learning some new tricks, now is there?" He gathered his empty bowl and spoon, wiped the table with his napkin, and pushed in his chair. Without as much as making eye contact, he turned on his heel and made for the exit, the creases in his pants and the shine on his shoes leaving a lasting impression on Norma's brain.

Something warm and wet was dripping near the toe of her navy leather pump. The crushed plastic serving dish was embedded in her right hand, and her chicken and almonds were swimming in blood.

Chapter Forty-eight

IT WAS ALREADY DUSK WHEN Sally left the office, but the outside lights hadn't come on yet. Judging by the number of cars in the parking lot, there were still several meetings going on, but there was nobody around. Even the parking lot security guard was nowhere in sight.

With her left arm, Sally was carrying a stack of folders and scheduling printouts, plus her briefcase and handbag, so she was trying not to lose her balance as she stepped toward the car. She wielded the keys to her 1989 Pontiac in her right hand. About two feet from her car, she heard a low whistle, coming from behind some parked cars across the lot. The memory of the voicemail saying, "Watch it," flashed through her mind, and her legs weakened beneath her.

Her first thought was to put down the reports and run over to investigate, probably some kids playing a silly game. Last year she might have done that, but now, facing whoever it was, solo, in the dark, and without security backup was not a good idea. Instead she thrust her car key into the slot, unlocked the car, threw her armload into the passenger seat, and locked herself in. She turned on the ignition and sped out of the parking lot, waiting to fasten her seat belt until she reached a lighted corner. She was surprised to find her heart pounding with fear.

When had she become so jumpy? After she was well away from the school, she chided herself for being such a scaredy-cat. After all, it was the same parking lot she'd used twice a day, every day, for years. Still, with the recent string of upsetting events—the threat on the coach, the assault on Tyrone, the fire, Mr. Stoker's murder, and all of the crazy gang threats coming in—it was a wonder she wasn't terrified to come to work each day.

She didn't want to be afraid. She remembered how she had laughed it off years ago, when some visiting teachers had clutched their purses in the hallways, fearful that something bad might happen to them in this urban school. She hoped she would never become like that. Lincoln was a school like any other, filled with kids who needed to take their places in the world. And she would never feel as needed anywhere else.

As she drove out of the school's neighborhood, she eased up on the accelerator and turned on the radio. Nirvana's "All Apologies" filled the car with emotion and helped Sally regroup. She was looking forward to discussing everything with Ron at dinner, before their meeting at the police station. Her day, it seemed, was just getting started.

* * *

Sally pulled into a parking place at Giuseppe's, an Italian hole-in-the-wall, where she and Ron loved to eat whenever they had something to talk about. The owners gave them a quiet booth in the back, and they served authentic homemade classic Italian dishes to die for. Seeing Ron's car caused the knot in Sally's stomach to loosen.

As she entered the restaurant, she was enveloped by the aromas of garlic and oregano, so comforting she felt tears forming. She hugged Lucia, the owner-chef-hostess, who directed her to her usual booth. The dim overhead light shone directly over Ron's head, spotlighting the grey streaks in his thick head of dark hair and the endearing laugh lines around his mouth. If he weren't already hers, she would do everything she could to win him over. Outside of Lincoln High, he was her world.

Ron stood when Sally approached the table. He opened his arms and enfolded her into them, then kissed her with a passion that seemed new, despite its familiarity. "How's my girl?" he asked, his voice throaty.

They sat, and Sally answered by scooting as close to him as humanly possible. She put her hand on his knee and gave it a squeeze. "Thank you for going with me tonight. We have a lot to talk about before we get to the police station, though."

For the next several minutes, Sally shared her latest concerns about the meeting at the police station, including the voicemail from Shayla. As eager as she was to have Shayla back, she had a lot of trepidation over what would happen to Claude. Even if he survived the police investigation, he would be facing pressure from the gang. She remembered the "Give up Cuckoo" note in Tyrone's gym locker. "You know, I don't know Claude as well as Shayla, but Mr. Stoker had faith in him, enough to give him a job working in the main office, instead of being expelled. I just can't see him turning around and killing the person who was mentoring him."

"If Claude didn't do it, who else might have?"

Sally shivered, a cold hand of fear gripping her throat, and her voice fell to a whisper. "I hate to put this into words, but I've had serious concerns that it might have been Wally. I've known him so long, and trusted him for years, but lately he just doesn't seem like the same person."

Ron put his arm around Sally and gave her a hug. "Could be the pressures of being principal under these circumstances. You know, I'm not happy about your working in that environment, now that all this has happened. You can't leave now, since you are under contract, but when this school year is over, I think you should look for a different school."

Tears formed in Sally's eyes at the prospect of leaving Lincoln. "I can't leave Lincoln. I care so much about everybody there: students, teachers, parents, Pat, counselors, deans, support personnel, custodians. I can't just give them all up and start over somewhere else. Besides, someone needs to carry on Mr. Stoker's mission. He had big plans to transform the school, and I'm the person he entrusted to help."

Ron's lips pressed into a line. "We've got time to talk about this later. I understand your attachment to the school and to Stoker's memory. Right now I want to talk about this meeting at the police station." He scratched his temple, where a few gray hairs glinted in the candlelight. "The main reason I am accompanying you is to protect *you*, Sally. Don't forget, the police asked if you had been to the Davis house before or after the day you found the gun, and your fingerprints are on the gun, too."

"But I'm not a suspect. Detective Phillips told me—"

"I know what he told you, but I don't want you to do any talking, nevertheless. Just please let me do the talking."

"But what about Claude? He's the one who will need your protection the most."

"If Claude and his mother want to engage me as his attorney, I'll speak for him, too, and as little as possible. Mostly I want to find out as much as I can about what the police have on him. There must be something, or they wouldn't have been able to extradite him from Alabama."

Sally started to speak, but stopped when she saw Lucia approaching the booth with steamy platters of food. "Did you order?" she asked Ron.

"Yes, the usual. I told her to skip the wine tonight, since we are technically both on duty." The aromas coming from the *osso bucco*, rice balls, veal marsala, pasta with marinara, and garlic bread merged to create a perfect culinary symphony in Sally's brain, and her taste buds responded in kind.

For a few minutes, talk of murder ceased, and the clink of knives and forks on china took over. It wasn't long, though, before Sally put down her utensils and stared into space. The fear she had felt in the parking lot was intruding into the cozy dinner with her husband.

"What's the matter?" Ron asked, putting down his own fork.

Sally flinched. Telling Ron about the warning voicemail and the whistle in the parking lot was probably not a good idea. He worried enough about her in the Lincoln environment. On the other hand, she might feel safer having him know everything. Maybe he could suggest something to help her cope.

Looking at her watch, Sally said, "We don't really have time to get into it now." She pasted a smile on her face and a lilt into her voice. "I'll save it for when we get home. Meanwhile, do you want to share some cannoli?"

Chapter Forty-nine

IT WAS 9:30 WHEN SALLY and Ron arrived at the police station in Ron's car. They had left Sally's car in the parking lot at Giuseppe's. Sally had called earlier to let the detectives know she'd be bringing her husband along, possibly to represent Claude. Ms. Coleman greeted Sally with a broad showing of peg-like teeth, followed by a bear hug. Sally had taught the woman's son in ninth grade and encouraged him to join the speech team. "Welcome, Ms. Pearce," she said, "and is this the Mr.? I know why you're here. They's just gettin' started in the back room now. You just go on ahead in."

Sally exchanged a glance with Ron. What luck that they were just on time. They hurried toward the closed door at the back of the lobby. The lights were on behind the frosted chicken wire-laced glass, and Sally could barely make out the sounds of voices beyond it. As she opened the door and stepped into the tiny hallway, she recognized Detective Phillips' husky voice.

"—Oh, here comes someone now," he said. His mouth formed a welcoming crescent when he recognized Sally. "Mrs. Pearce, c'mon in and take a seat. And is this Mr. Pearce?" The detective rose to shake hands with Ron, who managed to hold the chair out for his wife at the same time.

Sally's eyes roved from person to person around the table: Phillips, Morris, a white guy in a business suit. Claude was sprawled at the table, his head down on his tattooed arms. Mrs. Davis sat, arms crossed, a weary expression making her look older than her years. Finally, Sally's eyes lit on Shayla. She felt the sting of incipient tears and had to restrain herself from running around the table to give her office worker a hug. In truth, she wasn't sure her hug would be welcome after having divulged so much to the police. The mixture of concern and guilt was creating a toxic soup in her gut. Maybe the fact that she had brought her attorney-husband along would count for penance.

Shayla had been looking down, curly eyelashes grazing her cheeks, chin propped on palms supported by elbows. When Phillips had called Sally's name, Shayla perked up, and a hint of a smile worked at the corners of her mouth.

Phillips continued speaking, seemingly unaware of the nonverbal communication going across the table. "Thank you for coming, Mr. and Mrs. Pearce. I believe you know 'most everyone at the table here, but let's do introductions: Bert Thompson, Chief of Police, Hayneville, Alabama; Mrs. Monique Davis; Claude Davis; Shayla Davis; and, of course, Detective Morris and me. We are also expecting Principal Welburton in about fifteen minutes, but we're going to get started. I know it's late, but we have some important business here." Phillips opened a folder and sorted through a stack of papers.

"Now we all know we are here in the matter of the death of R. J. Stoker, Principal of Lincoln High School, as well as the arson fire there on the day of Mr. Stoker's death." Phillips looked from one to another before continuing. "Since the time of the incident, we have been trying to locate Claude J. Davis." He nodded toward Claude, who, having picked up his head when Phillips began talking, now slid down in his seat.

"We are grateful to our colleague, Bert Thompson, Hayneville Police Chief, not just for his assistance in locating Mr. Davis, but for personally bringing him back to us for questioning." Phillips nodded at Thompson, who returned the favor.

"Now, you may be wondering why we invited Mrs. Pearce and her husband to this meeting—"

At that moment, someone knocked on the door. "Come in," Phillips said, looking annoyed.

"I beg your pardon, Detective," Mrs. Coleman said. She lumbered over to Phillips, a note in her hand, and bent to whisper in his ear.

Phillips' eyes grew larger as he heard the news. He scanned the faces of the people before him, then addressed Detective Morris in a calm tone. "Could you go with Mrs. Coleman right away? Do an I-8 and report back. I'll carry on here."

The fear that Sally had felt earlier crept back into her psyche like a spider, determined to catch her in its web. Whatever was going on, it had to be important to interrupt this meeting with Claude. She just hoped it had nothing to do with Lincoln High School. Under the table, Ron nudged her with his knee, as if to tamp down her emotion.

Phillips scooted his chair back and stood. He paced in a tight circle near his place, one hand holding his chin. There was obviously a snafu of some kind, and the air was charged with tension as thick as smoke in a four-alarm fire. "I'll tell you what we'll do here," Phillips said. "Something's come up, and we need to re-group. I'm going to ask Chief Thompson, Monique, and Shayla to wait out in the lobby, while I interview Claude separately."

Ron Pearce spoke then. "With all due respect, Detective Phillips, I would like to offer my legal services to Mrs. Davis and Claude. Since Claude is now eighteen, it is up to him alone to decide on representation, but as a courtesy, I'd like to get Mrs. Davis' approval. If they agree, I must insist upon being present when you interview my client."

Shayla and her mother exchanged glances, and Shayla mouthed, "Thank you, Jesus."

Mrs. Davis squeezed her son's elbow and said, "I'd be pleased to have you represent Claude, Mr. Pearce. That is, if we can pay you."

Claude nodded. Two vertical lines in his forehead betrayed his mood.

"No worries about paying me," Ron replied. "I would like to have a few minutes with my client, though, before you interview him."

Phillips replied, "Fine. Actually, I need to speak with Mrs. Pearce for a few minutes, alone, as well."

Sally twitched when she heard her name, but Ron straightened and confronted Phillips. "May I ask why?"

"Just routine, Mr. Pearce. Your wife is not a suspect."

"I would prefer to be present when you speak with my wife, and also with Claude." Ron's cheeks flamed.

Sally remembered Ron's admonition against talking to the police, but she had been talking to them all along, and she felt comfortable with the detective. She put her arm through Ron's and addressed Phillips. "May I speak to my husband in private for just a moment?"

Sally led Ron through the chicken-wire door into the hallway, where they were alone. "Honey, it's much more important for you to be with Claude than with me. Claude is a suspect, and he needs your help. Guilty or not, he's probably scared out of his mind, and so are his mother and sister."

Ron started to object, but Sally said, "Please, trust me to handle myself with the detective. I've already talked to him several times without your being present. Please, Ron. Go talk to Claude while I talk to Phillips."

* * *

Phillips ushered Ron and Claude into the "video room," while Chief Thompson spoke with Mrs. Davis and Shayla. Then Phillips hustled Sally into his small office and closed the door.

"I asked you to come here tonight because I need a special favor, something related to the case, but before I tell you that, I need to tell you why Detective Morris left the meeting so suddenly."

Sally felt a cold fist wrap itself around her insides and squeeze. This couldn't be good.

"Apparently there was another shooting at Lincoln High School, this time in the parking lot." Phillips' eyes searched Sally's before he went on.

"Who was shot?" she asked, trembling from her core. The mantra for administrators, "Stay calm, confident, and relaxed," was singing in her head in an absurd parody, as she remembered her own parking lot incident just a few hours before.

"The principal, Mr Welburton. He was getting into his car, and someone shot him from behind."

"Is he going to be okay?" Sally asked. *Please let him be okay.*

"They're taking him to the hospital, but it doesn't look good." He patted Sally's hand.

"Omigod," Sally cried. "It can't be true!" Sally's skin grew cold and prickly, and the floor rushed up to her face, as she collapsed in a heap.

Chapter Fifty

WHEN SALLY CAME TO, SHE was lying on the floor, and Ron was hovering over her, the faint aroma of his aftershave competing with the stale odor of the carpet beneath her. A cold cloth on her forehead informed her that she must have passed out, but why? She strained to recall, and then suddenly she remembered with a gasp. "Wally—Ron, something's happened to Wally. We have to find out how he is."

"Shh, my love. Right now all we have to be concerned with is how *you* are." Ron turned the cloth over, so the cooler side lay against her forehead. "You've had a shock. All this stress is finally getting to you."

"No, really. I've got to get up and see about Wally." Sally sat up on her elbows and looked around. She and Ron were alone in the detective's office. "Help me up," she said, offering both arms to her husband. She brushed herself off, arranged her skirt and tucked in her blouse.

"Sit down a minute and get your bearings," Ron said. "Here's some water." He handed her a paper cup, half-filled. "There's no need to rush."

Like the gust of a harsh wind, it hit Sally that "no need to rush" meant bad news. "Are you saying Wally's dead?" Her eyes searched her husband's, looking for the truth.

"I'm sorry," he muttered, looking down. "I know he was your colleague and friend. According to Phillips, he never really had a chance after being shot in the parking lot."

Sally covered her face with her hands and began to cry. "I—I can't believe it. First Stoker and now Wally. And—and, oh, no!" Sally didn't want to tell Ron about the mysterious voicemail and noises in the parking lot, but the words came rushing out with an uncontrollable force.

The look on Ron's face confirmed her reluctance to tell him. His jaw muscles were working double-time, and his mouth was a line etched in stone.

"I didn't want to worry you. That's why I didn't tell you at dinner. Obviously I wasn't the target—Wally was—since I was in the parking lot, and no one touched me."

Ron wrapped her in a bear hug, and she rested her face on the warmth of his chest. She wished she could stay there forever, but then she remembered Shayla, and Claude, and something else Detective Phillips wanted to tell her.

Sally checked her watch, 10:25. "We'd better get back to doing what we came here for. It's getting late."

* * *

Everyone in the video room looked tired: Ron, Phillips, and especially Claude. Younger by far, he wore the expression of an old man whose outlook on life had passed from pessimism to desolation. His head appeared too big for his neck. His coffee-colored skin took on a greenish cast from the wall color.

In the few minutes he had spent alone with Ron, he had almost lost it. He was grateful to have an attorney through some incredible gift of fate, but the guy scared him all the same.

"Listen up, Claude. These are some serious charges the police want to lay on you. Arson in a school, murder of the principal. You could end up on Death Row."

"—But I didn't do it. I didn't kill Mr. Stoker." His eyes found his attorney's and held.

"Right now I'm not interested in what you did or did not do. If I'm going to represent you, I need for you to clam up. You don't reply to any of the detective's questions, you hear? Not even with facial expressions or body language. The only people to say anything in that room are the detective and me. Got it?"

"Yeah. Are they gonna hold me, man? Are they gonna keep me in this dump?"

"I don't know yet. Depends on what they've got on you, but my guess is yes. They won't want you blowing in the wind while they're building their case. They couldn't have brought you in from Alabama, with the police chief as an escort, no less, if they didn't have something."

"I'll tell you what they have, man. Okay if I talk to *you*?"

"Later. Let's get through tonight. I'll hear your story once we see how deep the shit goes, maybe tomorrow. Meanwhile, let me do the talking."

* * *

While Ron was briefing Claude, Phillips brought Sally a Diet Coke and a package of Lorna Doones. She sipped and took small bites from the vanilla-flavored squares, while the detective looked over his notes.

When he found the page he was looking for, he folded the page open and put a telephone book on top to hold it. "Okay, Ms. Pearce, I hope you're feeling better now. Terrible shock, terrible."

"Much better now," Sally replied, between bites. "You said you needed a favor?"

"Yes, we do." The detective's dental work gleamed at her between his lips. "We have a statement from a Mrs. Minnie Sumpter, who lives across the street from the Davises."

"You mean the lady who saw Tyrone and me the day we found the gun under the porch stairs?"

"The very same one. Well, she says she saw you there two other times, once before and once after that day."

"Well, she is mistaken." Sally clipped the ends of her words, a bit of attitude creeping into her tone. "The only day I was there was the day I went with Tyrone, the day we found the gun."

Phillips pointed to the open page on his desk. "It says here in her statement that you were wearing a navy suit and heels on all three days." He glanced at Sally's attire. "Maybe it's the same suit you have on now."

Sally pulled on the sleeves of her pin-striped jacket, tucking the white frilly cuffs inside. "I may have been wearing this suit the day we found the gun, but I assure you—"

"—I understand. Let me explain the favor." Phillips leaned forward and lowered his voice to a whisper, even though there were only the two of them in his office.

Sally listened intently, and after hearing Phillips' favor, she nodded. After Stoker, and after Wally, she knew what she needed to do.

Chapter Fifty-one

IT WAS PAST MIDNIGHT WHEN Sally and Ron left the police station. Hardly any conversation passed between them. Hardly any traffic was on the road, either.

"Do you want to get your car tonight or tomorrow morning?" Ron asked.

Sally was curled up, as much in a fetal position as she could achieve while wearing a seat belt. Her head rested on the cool glass of the passenger window, and her eyes were closed.

"Sally? Your car?"

"Let's get it tomorrow. I've had it for one night."

Sally couldn't stop thinking about Wally, how much he had always wanted to be principal, and how short-lived his administration was. She kept pushing away the thought of what a narrow escape she might have had in the parking lot. It wouldn't do to dwell on that. The school needed her now more than ever.

In just a few hours she would have to return to her office and take charge of another crisis. This time she wouldn't have Wally to help. Probably Dr. Blank would step in. Sally's eyelids opened and closed, flirting with sleep, and her head lolled, until she jerked it back into place.

"Ron," she said in a voice thickened with exhaustion, "how did the interview with Claude go?"

"You know I can't discuss it with you. Attorney-client privilege."

She straightened her posture. "Oh, crap. I'm not asking for details. Just give me a broad idea. How much trouble is he in?"

Ron yawned and kept his eyes on the road. "Sorry. Can't discuss, and besides, this was only a preliminary interview. Not much asked, not much answered. I'll meet with Claude again tomorrow—rather, later today."

She was too tired for hurt feelings. "Well, at least the time you spent with him and Phillips gave me a chance to talk to Shayla and Mrs. Davis. Shayla's going to come back to school tomorrow—rather, today. I'm so glad she's back, and I know a football quarterback who is going to feel the same way."

* * *

When Sally and Ron walked in the door, they were greeted by their puppy, Archie. Ron took him for a much-needed walk, while Sally started getting ready for bed. Right away, she noticed the blinking of the answering machine. While she hated to open what might be Pandora's box, she felt obligated to listen.

She punched the button, and the first of seven messages blared into the room. "Mrs. Pearce, Dr. Blank. It's 8:15 and I must talk to you. Call me no matter what time tonight." It was close to 1 a.m., but Dr. Blank would expect her to call. Considering the bad news, she probably wouldn't be waking her, either.

Sally stopped the tape and dialed Dr. Blank's number. She was wide awake now. She grabbed a notepad and pen.

Answering on the first ring, Dr. Blank said, "I've been waiting for your call. I tried to get you at school, at home, in your car."

"I'm sorry. I haven't been in my car. I've been at the police station till just now. They told me about Wally. How tragic this is!"

Frost chilled the superintendent's voice. "Police station? Was it personal or business?"

"It was related to the Stoker investigation. I was planning to report to you about it in the morning."

"Yes, well now we have another investigation to deal with. I'll be moving into the principal's office to help with the fallout."

Sally's mind went into action mode. "We need to initiate another crisis plan immediately. If reporters try to interview faculty members, we'll make sure to refer them to you."

"I like your thinking," Dr. Blank replied. "Can you meet with me at your office at six a.m.?"

Sally looked at her watch. That gave her four hours to sleep—that was, *if* she could sleep at all. "Of course," she replied. The question had been purely rhetorical.

* * *

Lincoln High School was in mourning once again. True to her word, Dr. Blank had moved into the newly-remodeled principal's office, and she was calling out orders to Glenda and the mail room clerks when Sally came in for their six a.m. meeting.

"It's going to be a rough ride the next few weeks. I don't have to tell you how upset the board's going to be over this. The community, too."

"And the parents and students," Sally replied. Her own disappointment with Wally over his alleged harassment of Melody Singer notwithstanding, he had always been kind to her, and he had served the school for many years.

"Exactly," the superintendent said. "Since it's just you and me, let's divide duties. I'll deal with the board, community, news media, the other schools. You take over the faculty, staff, and students."

Sally nodded. She had expected this, and whatever trepidation she had about stepping into the major leadership role evaporated when Mr. Stoker's words came back to her. "Are you doing things right, or doing the right thing? I have faith that you know the difference and will let your heart guide you."

"What about the police?" Sally asked. She had seen six police cars in the parking lot, and she suspected the school grounds would be crowded with blue uniforms for the foreseeable future.

"We'll both have to deal with the police. They'll want me for some things, you for others. Let's just make sure we're on the same page with what we give them and what they give us. That reminds me. What were you doing at the police station last night?"

"The police brought in Claude Davis. He was in Alabama with his mom and sister, Shayla. They're holding him as a person of interest in Mr. Stoker's murder, and my husband's representing him."

"Okay, then. Let's meet here at the end of every day to hash over concerns. And call me on the two-way whenever you have a question. Better to communicate too much than not enough."

"I'll activate the crisis plan and set up crisis centers for the kids. Call a faculty meeting for the end of the day. Cancel after-school activities and send the buses home at the end of sixth period." A lot of people were depending on her to do the right thing.

"And, Sally," Dr. Blank continued, "we do have a need for a new principal, not that people are going to be running to take the job now. You might consider it. We can name you as Acting Principal for the remainder of the school year and make it permanent for next year. I'm sure the board would support your appointment."

Sally must have winced, because Dr. Blank rushed on, "No need to answer. Just think about it and we'll talk later."

Sally went back to her office, where she issued a robo-call to be broadcast to all student homes beginning at nine a.m., then she drafted a letter to be sent home with students that afternoon.

Just before the bell for homeroom, Sally sat at her desk, making notes for the speech she would give over the public address system in a few minutes. Engrossed, she barely heard the soft rapping of knuckles against her doorframe. When she looked up, what she saw went straight from her eyes to her heart, and tears filled her eyes. Shayla was leaning against Tyrone, and his arm was wrapped around her waist and resting on her belly. They couldn't have been closer if they had been anatomically sutured to each other. Tyrone's senior ring, back on the chain, was shining from its perch on Shayla's chest. Best of all, the two kids wore full-bodied smiles.

For the moment, Sally forgot all about murders and fires and threatening voicemails. She didn't even think of the obstacles Tyrone and Shayla would have to face in the coming months. She drank in the vision of two kids in love, and she broke into a giant smile of her own. Whatever else had happened, at least something was going right at Lincoln High.

Chapter Fifty-two

THAT SAME MORNING AT THE police station, Ron was given a private meeting with Claude in the "video room." Claude had spent the night locked up. Detective Morris had convinced him and Mrs. Davis that Claude would be safer in jail than out on the street. The fact that Welburton had been killed while Claude was in the station put some points in his column, but there was so much other evidence in the Stoker case against Claude, that it seemed unlikely he would be getting out of jail anytime soon.

Phillips and Morris had wanted to take a crack at getting him to talk, but Ron had specifically instructed them not to speak with Claude, and they hadn't.

As he greeted the detectives on the way in, Ron reminded them, "My client will not speak to you outside of my presence, and I have instructed him to refer all questions to me. Now, is Claude Davis under arrest for the murder of Mr. Stoker, or not?"

Morris shot a look at Phillips, then at the attorney. "Let's just say he is in protective custody for the time being." He fiddled with a toothpick in his mouth, as if plumbing his gums for answers.

"Okay, then," Ron stated, "I would like to spend some time alone with my client."

Now the two were holed up in the video room, sitting inches apart. Ron took in the facial whiskers and the tattooed biceps showing from beneath the black t-shirt and tried to block out the smell of unwashed body. He scooted his chair back a few inches and opened a notebook. He wasn't planning to take notes, unless something came up that he deemed hard to remember.

Claude twisted his wrists against the handcuffs. "Thanks for coming, man. Don't know how I'm gonna pay you." He frowned at his Nikes. "I don't deserve a good lawyer like you. I've done bad. Disgraced my family. The onliest thing, though, I didn't kill nobody."

Ron leaned back and gazed at the young man. Was he telling the truth? He really didn't want to know. "Seems like the police might think you killed Mr. Stoker, though, so tell me your story. Tell me the good, the bad, and the ugly, and don't leave anything out."

Claude began muttering how the Black Devils had wooed him back in junior high, how they'd made him feel important and powerful, like a real man. It had been fun and games with a little money thrown in to make him think he was actually doing something to benefit his family. He'd done some pranks, sold some drugs, carried things from one place to another. He'd started to think of himself as invisible, invulnerable.

Claude's jean-clad knee kept bouncing as he spoke. Ron pictured a Great Lakes salmon, taking the line far out to sea, even though he'd inevitably be reeled in.

"About a year ago," Claude continued, "things started to get crazy. They started demanding some serious shit."

"What kind of shit?" Ron asked.

"Shoplifting, extortion, car theft. They made it sound easy, no-risk. But I knew better. I started to pull back."

"Pull back, how?"

"Invent excuses why I couldn't do it. Said I was sick. Said people were watching me at school or at home."

"What happened then?"

"It didn't work. Ain't no way to fool them guys. They told me if I wimped out, they'd get my mom and my sister. No way I could let that happen, so I started walking the tightrope."

"The tightrope?" Ron asked.

"Yeah, man. Tryin' to stay in the game without hurtin' anybody. It warn't easy, and I did some things I'm not proud of, but," he said, "I ain't never got arrested." He looked around the Spartan room as if reminding himself of where he was now. "Ain't never slept in jail till last night."

"But you did get into some trouble at school," Ron prodded.

"Yeah, just this year. The Lieutenant's been riding my ass ever since school started. He got me to put a note on Coach Donovan's car."

"Lieutenant?" the lawyer asked, thinking at first that he might be referring to a policeman. "You mean a gang leader?"

Claude nodded. "Devils like to stir up trouble. The coach is white, but he works great with Black kids, and everybody respects him. I think they just wanted to see how easy he'd scare."

"But you got caught."

"Yeah, and I damn near got expelled. If it warn't for Stoker, I'da been kicked out, and the Devils woulda made a spectacle of me. As it was, they just gave me a harder task to do."

Detective Morris knocked at the door. Ron signaled to Claude to stop talking, and he scraped his chair on the floor in his clamber to get to the locked door. "Yes?"

"Forgot to mention before, just push this here button when you're ready to get out."

"Okay, thanks," Ron replied, keeping his eyes on Claude's face. As the door closed again, he stood and stretched, then re-took his chair. "Now what was that about a harder task?"

Claude examined his shoes again. "Hard to talk about this. I attacked my sister's boyfriend, Tyrone Nesbitt. He's all rah-rah, quarterback and captain of the football team. Gangs hate those kinda pussies. I think they wanted to test my loyalty, see if I had the guts to kill someone that close to my family."

"But you didn't do it, did you?" Ron said. He couldn't help feeling a little sorry for this misguided kid, although it was looking more and more like the guy was in deep trouble.

"Nah, I couldn't. Didn't have the guts. But I messed him up pretty bad, just to make it look like I tried. He knew it was me, but didn't rat me out. I feel guilty about all of it." Claude covered his face with his handcuff-clad hands. His shoulders shook as though sobs were colliding inside his chest, but neither cries nor tears came forth.

Ron put a hand on the young man's shoulder. "Hey, now. You've covered a lot of ground, but we don't have much more time together, and we haven't even gotten to the Stoker murder."

"Yeah, I know. Well, one thing led to another. It ticked off the Lieutenant that I didn't kill Nesbitt. Every time I failed at carrying out a task, he gave me a harder one." Claude paused to look his lawyer directly in the eye. "This time he told me to kill the principal."

Ron's eyes widened. He hadn't expected this. "Go on," he said, bracing himself in his chair.

"He gave me a gun to use, told me to find a way, to do it soon."

"The gun, was it—"

"—It was a .45 caliber pistol. I didn't want to do it. Mr. Stoker had been so nice to me, giving me a second chance after the Donovan mess. Even gave me a paying job in his office. Nobody at that school had ever done nothin' for me before." Again Claude covered his face and shook with silent sobs.

"You were in a tight spot," Ron said.

"They were going to hurt me, hurt my sister, my mother. I had no choice. I guess I was hoping to find a way to get out of it the way I'd done with Tyrone. I didn't sleep for two nights, trying to figure out something. Finally, I came up with a plan."

"What was the plan?" Ron asked.

"I'd set a fire in the hallway outside the principal's office and pull the fire alarm. I was counting on Stoker to remain in the building until after everyone else evacuated. When I had him alone, I'd shoot him in a leg or something, knock him unconscious, then drag him to a place where he'd be safe from the fire. I—I'd leave the gun and hightail it out of there, run till my feet fell off. I figured I'd have to get out of the state, maybe out of the country, but at least the Devils might consider the job completed and leave my family alone."

Ron stood and paced in the tiny room. "So is that what you did?"

"Not exactly. S—Stoker didn't come out into the hall when I pulled the fire alarm. The office staff went out, but not him. I went in to get him, and we argued. I tried to push him toward the door, but he just stood there staring at me. I'll never forget that look in his eyes, like he couldn't believe I'd turned on him."

"Then what?"

"I kept pushing him, trying to get him to fight back, but he wouldn't. Furniture got knocked over. The office was a mess. Finally, I pulled the gun out of my back pocket and stuck it in his back, using it to shove him into the hallway. By then smoke was coming into the office, and we had to get out.

"As soon as we stepped into the hallway, I swung at Stoker with all my might. My fist connected with his jaw, and I heard a crack. Just like with Tyrone. Stoker fell to the floor, out cold. I was shaking all over, holding the gun, trying to get up the nerve to shoot him in the leg.

"I looked around to make sure no one could see me. I thought there wouldn't be anybody left in the building, but I was wrong. Coming down the hallway from the bathroom was my sister. Shayla saw me holding a gun on Mr. Stoker."

"What happened then?" the attorney asked. He was caught up in the story, despite his efforts to remain calm and think clearly.

A noise in the hallway intruded, reminding Claude this was still a story without an ending. He swallowed and fixed Ron with an empty stare. "So Shayla screamed and ran out. It freaked me out, having her see me with a gun, about to shoot the principal."

"So what did you do then?" Ron asked.

"I looked around at the burning walls, the thick smoke, Stoker lying there, not moving. All that damage, all my fault. I felt like my heart was jumping out of my body, and I couldn't breathe."

"What happened next?"

Claude exhaled with a low growl. "I knew I had to shoot Stoker and run, but I just couldn't. I couldn't do what the Devils wanted me to do. I was suffocating in the bitter smoke, and sweat was dripping from my face onto Stoker's shirt. All's I can remember is dropping the gun and running. I ran to the opposite end of the building and kept on running."

"Did anyone see you?"

"Besides Shayla, you mean? I don't know. There was the fire in the hall and the fire in my gut. All I could think of was to run, and I didn't look around to see who was watching." Claude looked at the floor, and when he raised his eyes, they were dark and wet. "I'm in a shitload of trouble now, right?"

Chapter Fifty-three

DETECTIVES PHILLIPS AND MORRIS SPENT the day at Lincoln High. Dr. Blank had given them the multipurpose room to use as headquarters. They split up to cover more ground: Phillips pursuing Stoker's murder; Morris, Welburton's. "Let's meet here at noon and three," Phillips said, "to see where we are and what to do next. This investigation has already gone on too long, and if we don't arrest the killer soon, I'm afraid Mrs. Pearce and Dr. Blank may be targets."

"I agree," Morris replied. "I'm going to talk to Myrna, Welburton's secretary. I'll find out who was around in the building late yesterday, and I'll interview them. See if anyone saw or heard anything unusual."

"Good plan." Phillips opened his notebook to glance at the names of people he was planning to interview. "Oh, Morris," he called out at the retreating figure, "feel free to wander into Stoker territory if you have the opportunity. Never hurts to get more information."

"You got it," Morris replied, "see ya at noon."

Phillips flipped the cover on his notebook and drained his Dunkin' Donuts coffee cup. He wanted to talk to Glenda O'Malley, the principal's secretary.

* * *

Glenda was tending to her parakeet, Rowdy, when Phillips walked into the newly refurbished office. The smell of fresh paint had all but eradicated the vestigial odor of cinders.

Rowdy flitted around the cage as his mistress changed the newspaper and rang the bell.

221

"Nice bird," the detective said.

"Why, thank you." Glenda batted her eyelashes, an unusual expression for someone of her advanced age. "I'm so glad the fire didn't harm him. I was just frantic standing out there, worrying about my Rowdy. Got sick from the smoke, but a few days in fresh air, and he was singing again." As if to punctuate the claim, Rowdy tweeted a few syllables.

Phillips patted the bird cage and said, "Wish we could say the same thing about Mr. Stoker. Mind if I talk to you a bit?"

Glenda closed the cage door and pointed to the chair next to her desk. "Sure. Have a seat. I was wondering when you'd be getting around to me." She patted her thickly sprayed hairdo and took her own seat, clasping her hands on the desk like a nun about to pray.

"Just for the record, Ms. O'Malley, I came to interview you last week, but Mr. Welburton's secretary told me you were absent, something about minor surgery on your foot."

"Oh, yes. Well, Rowdy and I were out for three days. Thought it'd be good to take care of that while the office was out of commission. Myrna was taking care of Mr. Welburton's business, and, well, I didn't have a boss for the time being."

"I see. Well, let's start by talking about Mr. Stoker. What kind of boss was he?" Phillips opened his notebook and readied his pen to take notes as needed.

"Mr. Stoker? He seemed to be a nice person. Very different from Mr. Morgan, though."

"In what way?"

"Well, it may not be a fair comparison. I was Mr. Morgan's secretary for fourteen years, so I was used to his ways. I only met Mr. Stoker a few times before school started, and he was only here a short time before—"

Phillips looked at his watch. He would have to nudge the lady, or he'd be here all day. "Would you say Mr. Stoker was competent? Well-accepted by the office staff, the faculty, the parents, the students?"

"I'd say," Glenda replied in a tinny voice, "he was a man on a mission to change things, Detective. He didn't care that we had time-honored procedures in this office. He had his new-fangled ideas, and when I tried to explain how we do things at Lincoln, he just *cut me off* and told me how we were going to do them now."

Phillips raised an eyebrow, wondering whether the secretary was throwing a dig at him for having cut her off, as well. "And you weren't happy with the changes?"

"Oh, I suppose I would have gotten used to him, given time. But, of course, we didn't have much time together, after all. Don't get me wrong, Detective. It's a terrible thing that someone murdered Mr. Stoker. He was a nice enough man, and he probably would have been a good principal."

"How did the faculty adjust to Mr. Stoker, in your opinion?"

The secretary drew herself into a vertical line, like a marionette controlled by the heavens. "Not just my opinion—everyone's—was that the man was a loose cannon."

"You mean *no one* liked him?" Phillips asked. He knew from having talked with some of the younger teachers that this was not true.

"'Liked' isn't the best word," Glenda replied, fingering the lace on her collar. "More like they didn't understand him. He came in here like a tornado, pushing for change. Didn't even try to ingratiate himself with the teachers, just the parents and the students. I even asked him about it one day, and ya know what he said?"

Phillips said, "What did he say?"

"He said, 'The teachers get paid for what they do. They have a choice. They can work here or somewhere else, but the students and the parents, they don't have a choice. It's our job to serve their needs'."

"And that was different from the way you were used to?" Phillips replied.

"Oh, yes. When Mr. Morgan was here—"

"—What can you tell me about Claude Davis?" Phillips interjected.

"Claude, he's a perfect example. Mr. Morgan would have expelled that boy in two seconds flat, but Mr. Stoker? He had to 'save' him, give him a job in this office, for Pete's sake. 'Course, it prob'ly cost him big-time."

"What do you mean by that?" the detective asked.

"What do you think I mean? That gangbanger's prob'ly the one who killed Mr. Stoker, and Mr. Welburton, too." With that, the secretary dug into her desk drawer and pulled out a lacy handkerchief to dab at her moistening eyes.

It was Phillips' turn to straighten his posture. His eyes burned into the secretary's. "Ms. O'Malley, this is very important. What makes you think Claude Davis is the killer?"

The lady leaned into Phillips' face, so close that he could smell talcum powder. "Well, you see, Detective, when the fire alarm sounded that day, I went into a tizzy. I usually don't evacuate when we have a fire drill. It takes me away from my work too long, and Mr. Morgan—"

Losing patience, Phillips cut her off. "But that day you evacuated."

"Yes, Mr. Stoker urged me to leave immediately. He knew it wasn't a drill. I wanted to take Rowdy with me, and I was struggling with the cage. Mr. Stoker told me to go on, and he would bring Rowdy in just a few minutes when he left the building."

"And what about Claude Davis?" Phillips prompted.

"Oh, when I left the outer office, I realized there was a real fire in the hallway. I turned around and yelled at Mr. Stoker. 'Fire, fire. Bring my Rowdy and come on out.' And when I turned the corner to exit the building, I glimpsed a foot sticking out from behind the machine in the copy room. I'm not one to just ignore the little things, so I opened the door to the copy room and shouted, 'Fire, fire!'"

"Did anyone come running out of the copy room then?"

"No, not at all. And I didn't bother to go in and get the person to come out either. It was a real fire, and I always say, 'It's every man for himself,' at times like that."

"Could it be you just imagined the foot?"

"Uh-uh," Glenda said. "I know what I saw, all right. It was a foot, and it was that boy, Claude Davis' foot." She slapped her desk as if to substantiate the truth of her statement.

"How did you know it was Claude's foot?" Phillips asked. He thought he knew the answer, but that wasn't what concerned him most.

"I recognized his shoe, that's how. These kids are poor as church mice, but they wear two hundred dollar shoes like Michael Jordan. I had commented to Mr. Stoker about those shoes when the boy was working in the office."

Phillips scooted his chair an inch or two away from the talcum powder smell. "Okay, Ms. O'Malley, let's say Claude Davis was hiding in the copy room across from the main office. How do you think that proves he killed Mr. Stoker and Mr. Welburton?"

Glenda looked at the detective as if he were a pathetic child. "That's easy. Claude set the fire and hid in the copy room, waiting for Mr. Stoker to come out. When he did, he shot him dead."

"And Mr. Welburton?" Phillips knew full well Claude hadn't committed that murder.

"The second one was easier. The boy just hid in the bushes near Mr. Welburton's parking spot and ambushed him when he left the building."

"One more question," Phillips said. "You said Mr. Stoker was going to bring Rowdy in his cage when he evacuated the building. What happened to the bird when Mr. Stoker was killed?"

Glenda stood and jabbed a finger into the cage to pet the bird's head. "My poor Rowdy. He just stayed in the office and inhaled all that nasty smoke. Nearly killed him." Her whine rose several decibels. "Mr. Stoker was supposed to have brought him out!"

Chapter Fifty-four

WHILE DETECTIVE PHILLIPS INTERVIEWED GLENDA, Detective Morris visited with Welburton's secretary. Myrna blotted her face with tissue after tissue as the tears kept coming. The features in her lined face disappeared behind each new white rectangle. Sobs alternating with hiccups sallied forth, but so far, the detective had failed to elicit anything useful.

"I—I—j-just c-can't believe he's gone," Myrna wailed. "I—I knew something bad was g-going t-to ha-happen." Myrna set the current tissue down on top of a pile of maybe thirty used ones. "I—I—j-just feel t-terrible."

Morris took a deep breath, sniffing menthol and magnolia. "Mrs. Short, I know you must be in shock, and grieving for Mr. Welburton."

Myrna wailed again and drew another tissue from the flowered box. "Of course I'm grieving. I've been working for Wally for more than twenty-two years. He was like a son to me."

Morris did the math. Twenty-two years as assistant principal would probably make Welburton fiftyish. His secretary looked to be around seventy. It was possible she could be his mother, age-wise. He decided to treat her as if she actually were the victim's mother.

"Mrs. Short, you have my deepest sympathy and that of the entire police force. We want you to know we are here for you at this terrible time, and we are going to do everything we can to bring Mr. Welburton's murderer to justice." He patted her desk instead of her arm.

Myrna sniffled and moved the pile of used tissues to the trashcan.

She fiddled with the gadget in her ear, too. "I—I appreciate your sympathy."

"Yes," Morris continued, "and we need your help, too. No one at this school knew Mr. Welburton better than you. You knew his habits, how he spent his time, who his friends were."

Myrna raised an eyebrow. "And who his enemies were? Is that what you want me to tell you?" She shivered, and Morris caught another whiff.

"Well, yes, if you get right down to it, ma'am. It would be helpful if you could tell me who might have had a grudge against your boss."

Grabbing a worn sweater from the back of her chair and slipping her arms into it, Myrna grimaced. "Nobody, Detective. Nobody had a grudge against Mr. Welburton. He was popular with the faculty and other administrators. The only person who might not have liked him was Mr. Stoker, but *he* couldn't have killed him, could he?"

"Why would Mr. Stoker not have liked your boss?"

"Huh, I'd think that would be obvious. The faculty wanted Mr. Welburton to be principal. He and Mr. Morgan ran this place so smoothly. We didn't have murders and mayhem here then. Everything was disciplined. Everyone knew what to expect."

"So you think Mr. Stoker had it in for Mr. Welburton?"

"W-well, I can't say *that*. Mr. Stoker didn't seem to care about Mr. Welburton one way or another. Mr. Stoker was so focused on changing everything, even when most of us thought things were fine just the way they were."

"What about the students, the parents?"

Still sniffling, Myrna replied, "Hmph. That's a laugh. When you're in charge of discipline, you upset some kids and their parents. The bad ones, that is."

"Who are 'the bad ones,' in your opinion?"

Myrna blew her nose before replying. "You know, the gangbangers, the troublemakers. Wally, I mean Mr. Welburton, went after the gangs on a regular basis. That's why—"

"Why what?" Morris sensed there was more, although he was beginning to think this would be another dry well.

"Well, that's why I was surprised Mr. Stoker was killed at first, and not Wally. Stoker was so student-oriented, giving that Claude Davis a pass when he should have been expelled. Even hiring him to work in the main office, of all places. I would have thought the gangs would love that kind of principal."

Morris mumbled, "Gangs and love don't often reside in the same sentence."

"What was that?" Myrna asked, fiddling with her hearing aid.

"Oh, nothing." Morris asked, "So is it your opinion that Mr. Welburton was killed by gang action?"

Myrna sat up straighter and leveled her eyes with the detective's. "I have no doubt that is the case. You saw those threatening notes Wally received. It's been a fear of mine for a long time that they would come after him, and now it's happened."

Morris was hoping for something more helpful than fulfilled predictions. "Can you tell me who was in the building late last night, what meetings were scheduled? In other words, who might have been on campus around the time of the killing?"

Myrna pointed to the desktop calendar in front of her. "Grievance committee, curriculum committee, and parent advisory committee. Mr. Welburton was with the parents."

Finally, Morris felt he was getting somewhere. "How quickly can you get me a list of who attended each of the meetings? Also, I'd like a copy of Mr. Welburton's calendar for the past week. It's very important."

Myrna's mouth formed a thin line, and she nodded. "Won't take me long at all, Detective. I'm glad to help. The only thing is—"

"Yes?"

"I think it's a waste of time looking at the faculty. I'll bet dollars to doughnuts the killer is a gangbanger."

Chapter Fifty-five

WHILE POLICE OFFICERS WORKED IN the roped-off parking lot, and detectives interviewed Lincoln High personnel inside, Sally was working her butt off trying to handle the publicity nightmare of having another murder at school. Even with Dr. Blank presiding over the main office and handling the press, the sheer number of phone calls and demands for information had Sally dancing a merengue without any music. The crisis plan had been reactivated, so counselors and social workers were working staggered schedules to staff the crisis center locations. Hallways during passing periods were uncharacteristically quiet as students moved from class to class.

Attendance was down by at least a third, and over thirty parents had come to withdraw their youngsters in the first two hours of school. "It's not a safe place anymore," one parent said to Sally. "In fact, I'm surprised you're staying here, bein' white and all."

The comment pierced Sally's gut like a long, sharp javelin, but she forced her face to remain expressionless. "Color has nothing to do with anything," she replied. "Lincoln High is my professional home, and these unfortunate events won't influence my commitment. The school is still a good place. The kids are good kids."

"But is it safe?"

The question echoed in Sally's ears long afterward. She understood the impulse to transfer one's child to another school. Her role was to stabilize the school community as quickly and effectively as she could, given the circumstances. If she abandoned the ship, who would be willing to come aboard and lead the faculty and students back to purposeful teaching and learning? And what other superintendent would want to hire her if her solution to trouble was to flee? Besides, she had cast her fate with Lincoln High long ago, when she knew her gifts were best suited to the urban setting.

While Sally met with parents and planned an after-school in-service for teachers, her secretary Pat gathered data for the state reports, due in two days. When Shayla came in to work at sixth period, carrying a foil-wrapped rectangular package, Sally realized she needed a break. Her stomach grumbled, and her shoes were pinching her feet.

"My mama baked you some banana bread. She says thanks for all you and Mr. Pearce are doing for us."

"How thoughtful of her. Let me get a good look at you, Shayla," she said, a weight being lifted from her chest, like a helium balloon destined for the clouds. A quick hug, and she sank into her chair and kicked off her heels. She grabbed a plastic knife from her desk drawer and opened the package. Her eyes and nose feasted on the moist cake and the sweet aroma. She sliced into the loaf and started to break a bite-sized piece off to eat, then remembered her manners and offered another piece to her aide.

"No thanks," Shayla replied. "I ate lunch, and I have to watch my weight these days."

"What's new with your mom and brother?" Sally asked, as she opened a bottle of water and took a swig.

"Don't you know? I thought Mr. Pearce would have told you."

"Mr. Pearce doesn't discuss his cases with me. Lawyers can't do that."

"Oh, well, Claude's been transferred to the city jail. They say it's for his own protection, but Mama's worried. He's in solitary, except a guard goes with him whenever he goes out of his cage."

"Solitary? Have they charged him?"

"Not yet. They say he's just a person of interest. Mama don't trust 'em, though. She thinks they're gonna give him the death penalty." Shayla bit a fingernail and went on, her voice rising an octave. "He didn't kill Mr. Stoker. You believe that, don't you?"

Sally took her time swallowing the last bite of banana bread before answering. "I do believe that, Shayla, but there's something I'd like to talk with you about, if it's not too painful."

Shayla's hand flew to her belly, as if the physical protection would equal the emotional. "Sure," she replied, her voice giving lie to the word.

"It's about what you saw the day Mr. Stoker was killed. You told me you saw someone with a gun, and whoever it was, you seemed traumatized. Was Claude the person you saw with the gun?"

Shayla crumpled in her chair, elbows on knees and head in hands. She began to cry.

"You don't have to answer me if you don't want to," Sally whispered. "It's just—well, I am beginning to have my own theory of what occurred that day, and what you saw might be important."

Shayla lifted her head and made eye contact with Sally. "No, I want to tell you. You helped Claude get a lawyer, so I owe you—"

"You don't owe me anything, but I am curious about what you saw."

Shayla took a deep breath and puffed it out before speaking. "It was dark and smoky in the hall. It stunk, and my eyes and throat were burning. I was hurrying past the main office hallway toward the auditorium exit." She coughed and wiped her eyes, as if reliving the experience. "I was so focused on getting out of there, I almost didn't look. I almost made it down the stairs without turning my head, but something caught my attention. Maybe it was a sound. I don't know."

Sally scooted forward. Shayla's voice was low, and Sally didn't want to miss a syllable.

"Anyway, I did look, and what I saw was Mr. Stoker lying on the floor. Someone was standing over him, pointing a gun at his head." Shayla continued in a monotone. "At first I couldn't tell who it was, but then I recognized the shoes. Even with the smoke and all, I could tell from the shoes. Mama had just given those shoes to Claude for our birthday the week before. They were Michael Jordan Nikes."

Shayla wiped at the perspiration on her brow with her forearm. Sally thrust the box of tissues toward her.

"I knew it was Claude. Not just the shoes, but the clothes, the shape, the size. I couldn't believe my eyes, but at the same time, I knew it was true."

"Did Claude see you?" Sally asked.

"I didn't think so. I just ran outside and sat down on the curb across from the auditorium. That's where I was when you found me. I know it looks bad for Claude. I'm sure you think he killed Mr. Stoker, but he didn't."

Sally had her own reasons for thinking someone else had killed the principal, but she replied, "How do you know that, Shayla?"

"Because, when I finally got home, Claude was there, and I point blank asked him. 'Did you kill Mr. Stoker?' and you know what he said? He said, 'I tried to. Lord, help me, I tried to kill him, but I couldn't. I couldn't make myself pull the trigger.'"

"So Claude didn't kill Mr. Stoker," Sally repeated. Another question had been gnawing at her gut. "But what did he do with the gun?"

"I asked him that same question," Shayla replied, her lips curling. "He told me he punched Mr. Stoker in the jaw and knocked him out. Then he dropped the gun and ran out of there. Whoever killed Mr. Stoker, they must've used the same gun after Claude dropped it."

"And Claude never saw the gun again?" Sally pictured the gun, glinting under the stairs of the Davis house, where she and Tyrone had found it.

"He never saw the gun again. That's what he says, and I believe him."

Sally patted Shayla on the arm. "You know what? I believe him, too."

Chapter Fifty-six

DESPITE DR. BLANK'S BEST EFFORTS to control the media coverage of the events at Lincoln High, the campus was swarming with reporters and mini-cams. School violence sold newspapers, and the murders of two principals in quick succession attracted almost as much attention as the Rodney King trial had, several months earlier.

By the time students were dismissed at 3:35 p.m., there wasn't a stretch of sidewalk or parking lot unmarked by copy-hungry interviewers, looking for quotes. Thus it happened that a reporter from *Time* magazine accosted Tyrone on his way to football practice.

"Hey, son," the twenty-something redhead called out. "Can I have a word?"

Tyrone kept his eyes on the sidewalk and kept moving toward the gym. No way was he gonna get himself on the six o'clock news, not for this.

"Aw, come on, son. With three deaths tied to Lincoln High, surely you have something to say."

Three deaths? Tyrone slowed his stride and made eye contact with the reporter. He hated to bite on such obvious bait, but the word, "three," had hooked him. "What three?"

Keeping pace at Tyrone's side, the reporter replied, "Jim McDonald, *Southside News*. Two principals and a student. Last one just happened an hour ago."

"Look, I'd know if a student had been killed an hour ago, mister. I was in my econ class. Now let me get to practice."

"Not so fast. It didn't happen here on campus. It happened at the city jail. Claude Davis, Lincoln High senior. Do you know him?"

A bolt of lightning nailed Tyrone to the sidewalk. *Claude, dead?* He couldn't believe it was true, but Shayla had told him about Claude's being transferred to the city jail, and why would this guy make up something like that?

The reporter grabbed Tyrone's arm. "Hey, do you know Claude? Can you comment?"

Tyrone's tongue felt encased in sand, while his thoughts flew in a thousand directions at once. He needed to go to practice. He needed to find out if it was true about Claude. He needed to go to Shayla. Finally, he pulled his arm away from the grim messenger. He muttered, "Sorry, I got to go," and he ran off in the direction of Mrs. Pearce's office. Maybe Shayla hadn't left for home yet. Maybe he could catch her.

Tyrone darted around the building to the main entrance, where he knew he could get back into the building. From there it was just fifty feet to Mrs. Pearce's office, but he gasped and then sped up when he heard a loud wail coming from that direction. When he turned the corner, he saw the door to Mrs. P's office flung open, and inside Shayla and her mother clinging to each other and sobbing. Detective Phillips stood nearby, a somber expression on his face.

Behind the trio, Sally caught a glimpse of Tyrone first, and she ran to meet him at the door. "We've had terrible news—"

"Is it true? About Claude?" Tyrone searched the assistant principal's face.

Before Sally could ask how Tyrone had heard, Shayla broke away from her mother and ran to throw her arms around Tyrone.

As Tyrone enfolded his girlfriend in his arms and accepted her grief into his own heart, he couldn't think of another time in his life when so much had gone wrong. He pressed Shayla's spine, patted her hair, all the while murmuring syllables into her ear. Gradually, the shaking stopped, though Shayla continued to cling to him.

Meanwhile, Sally had led Mrs. Davis into the inner office, where she and the detective had seated themselves in the guest chairs. Sally took several bottles of water from the small refrigerator and distributed them. "Come on in here, Tyrone and Shayla. Please sit down and have some water."

Tyrone heard footsteps running toward the office and turned to see a tall man with a full head of silver-streaked hair rushing into the office.

"Sally?" the man called out, as he turned the corner and entered through the open doorway. He stopped short when he saw Tyrone standing there, his arm still around Shayla.

Mrs. Pearce ran out to meet him. "Oh, Ron. What terrible news." She looked back at Mrs. Davis and over at Shayla and Tyrone. "Detective Phillips says Claude's been killed."

Ron took Mrs. Pearce into an embrace, briefer and less intense than that of the young lovers, but probably no less comforting. "I came over as soon as I heard." He took Mrs. Davis' hand in his own and expressed condolences.

Mrs. Pearce moved all of the guest chairs into a small circle, as if setting up a meeting of a curriculum subcommittee. "Let's all sit down. Perhaps Detective Phillips can shed some light on what's happened."

"We don't have all the details yet. The state's attorney and the warden haven't released a written statement yet, but apparently Claude was the victim of gang violence."

Tyrone addressed Shayla. "I thought you said he was going to be in solitary."

Phillips responded, "He was in solitary. The guard was taking him for a shower and must have turned his back or left the room for a minute. One of the other prisoners, a Black Devil, jumped him and thrust a shiv into his kidney. They took him to the county hospital, but the internal bleeding was too severe. I'm so sorry."

Mrs. Davis cried out, "You tol' me he would be safer in jail! You lied to me, Detective. You brought Claude back here from Alabama, straight into danger. You all killed my boy."

Phillips flinched, but he kept his composure. "I understand how you feel. I'd feel the same way, myself. We did put Claude in solitary, because we knew the Devils were after him." He ran his hands through the short-cropped hair at his temples. "Ain't nothing simple when it comes to gangs."

Ron broke in. "For what it's worth, Claude told me he was innocent of murdering Mr. Stoker, and I believe him."

Sally and Shayla exchanged looks.

Mrs. Davis said, "The Black Devils killed them all! They killed Mr. Stoker, Mr. Welburton, and then they killed my baby. Oh, when are these kids gonna grow up and realize violence don't solve nothing? They's just killing they own, ruining any hope for any of them to climb out of this neighborhood." She began sobbing again.

Sally walked over and put an arm around Mrs. Davis, handing her a box of tissues.

Phillips said, "How 'bout I give you and Shayla a ride home now? Maybe you can get some rest, and tomorrow we'll help you make arrangements." He offered a hand to the grieving mother, who grabbed it and held on for a moment, clutching a wad of tissues in her other hand.

"Tyrone, you want to come home with us? I b'lieve Shayla'll feel better if you stay with us a while."

As Phillips led Mrs. Davis, Shayla, and Tyrone out of the office, Tyrone heard Sally and her husband talking.

"Do you think it was the gang that killed Mr. Stoker and Mr. Welburton?" Ron asked.

"They may've killed Claude, and they may've killed Wally, but I'm pretty sure they didn't kill Mr. Stoker."

"What makes you think that?"

"I don't think it. I know it," Sally replied. "I know it because I know who did."

Chapter Fifty-seven

WHILE DETECTIVE PHILLIPS MANAGED THE aftermath of the Claude Davis incident, Detective Morris interviewed the people who had stayed late for school meetings the previous night. Perhaps someone had seen or heard something of value in the parking lot.

If Phillips and Morris together were a pair of hungry rat terriers, Morris alone was a ravenous Chihuahua. "Exactly when did the curriculum meeting break up, Ms. Singer?" he snapped.

Melody pulled on a corkscrew curl before answering. "I'm not sure. Sometime after 8:30."

"Did you leave immediately, or did you make a stop before exiting the building?"

"I went back up to my classroom on the third floor to drop off my grade book and notes from the meeting. Then I stopped at the bathroom."

"So what time would you say you actually left the building and went into the parking lot?"

"Maybe 8:45? Something like that." Dark semi-circles detracted from Melody's youthful complexion. "If I had known something horrible was going to happen, I would have paid more attention."

"Horrible? Why do you use the term 'horrible'?" What was keeping this white girl from sleeping? Did she know more than she was saying?

Melody rolled her eyes. "Wouldn't you consider it horrible if someone you worked with was killed in the same parking lot that you had to use every day?"

Morris ignored the question. "What did you see or observe when you got to the parking lot?"

"Nothing. A few other meetings were disbursing at the same time, so there were several of us leaving. It was dark outside, and the streetlights lit up certain areas of the lot. I did notice the security guard's vehicle was not in sight. Maybe he was cruising the gym area at the time."

"Who else was leaving the building at the same time as you?" Morris was practically salivating with each question.

"The only ones I know for sure are Mr. Johnson, Ms. Dunn, and Mr. Gottschalk. There were only about fifteen cars in the parking lot by then."

"Do you know where Welburton parked his car?"

"Sure. Administrators park on the west side of the lot. There's a sign with his title on it in front of his spot."

"How close were you parked to his spot?"

"On the opposite side and way down. I'm just a first-year teacher. No parking privileges for me."

Morris leaned forward. "First-year teacher? How well did you know Mr. Welburton?"

Melody shivered. "Not that well. He was my evaluator, so I had a couple of meetings with him."

Morris bookmarked the body language in his brain. "What did you think of him, then?"

Melody shrugged, and her eyes focused on a spot on the ceiling. "Not my idea of a great administrator, but okay, I guess."

"You're a first-year teacher, and you already know what makes a great administrator, eh?" Morris flicked a piece of lint from his shirt cuff. "Who, would you say, is a great administrator?"

"That's easy. Mr. Stoker was great. He cared more about the students and what they were learning than he cared about himself, and he knew a lot about current curriculum and teaching methods. When he died, it was a huge loss for the students, the school, and even for me."

"Ms. Singer, do you know of anyone who had a beef with Mr. Welburton? Anyone who might have wanted him dead?"

Melody shifted in her chair and looked uncomfortable. "Not really. I'm probably not the best person to ask, though. After all, I'm just a first-year teacher."

* * *

Derrick Johnson sat at the head of the table in the multipurpose room, hands folded. Looking at his three-piece suit and shiny black Oxfords, Morris thought he might have been interviewing a Harvard professor. The man even had an East Coast accent.

"I 'ppreciate your time, sir. It's about what you observed after the curriculum meeting last night."

"Last night?" Mr. Johnson replied, eyebrows raised.

"Yes, but why are you so surprised?" Morris leaned forward, his pen ready to capture whatever crumbs of information the economics teacher might toss his way.

"Hmm." Johnson cleared his throat. "It's just, well, I thought you might be interviewing me about the day of Mr. Stoker's death." He smoothed an imaginary wrinkle from his lapel. "There are so many murders occurring at this campus one tends to become confused, or disheartened, at the very least."

"Well, how 'bout we start with last night? When did you leave the meeting and enter the parking lot?"

"My dear man, I can only guess at the time. The battery in my watch is dead, and I have to do without until the weekend, when I have time to replace it. That said, I believe it was around 8:40 or so. When I passed by the cafeteria, I saw the parent meeting breaking up, and Mr. Welburton was shaking hands with someone at the door. So I'm guessing he was just a few minutes behind me. Quite a shame what happened to him."

"Yes, a shame. Now did you exit through the auditorium lobby into the faculty parking lot?"

"Indeed I did."

"Did you see or hear anything suspicious? Anything that strikes you now as significant in light of Mr. Welburton's death just minutes later?"

"Actually, I thought I heard a person whistling, just a single tweeting sound, when I approached my car, but I dismissed it as sheer fantasy until later."

"Could you determine the direction of the whistle?" Morris asked, jotting down something in his notebook.

"Possibly from the west side of the lot. I can't be sure, though. I know that's where Mr. Welburton and the other administrators parked their cars."

"Now, Mr. Johnson, what did you mean when you mentioned the day of Mr. Stoker's death? Did you see or hear anything unusual on that day?" Morris wondered, if that was the case, why he hadn't come forward before now.

"Well, ah, well. When the signal sounded to evacuate the building for the fire drill, which, in fact, turned out not to be a drill at all, I was in my sixth period class. I ushered my class out of the third floor classroom, and led them to the planned exit at door two, all according to the fire drill procedures. But then I realized—"

"Yes?" Morris leaned forward.

"I realized I might be caught outside in the practice field for quite some time, and I had to urinate." Johnson looked about as if checking for unfriendly ears. "So I stayed behind to use the men's room adjacent to the teacher's lounge, planning to rejoin my students before anyone noticed my absence." A glimpse of ultra-white teeth poorly represented a smile.

"How long did you stay in the building?" Morris asked.

"Well, on that day the battery in my watch was still working, and I happened to check the time when I made it outside. It was 3:17."

Morris narrowed his eyes and asked the jackpot question. "Did you see or hear anything or see anyone else in the building between the time that your students evacuated and the time that you, yourself, left the building?" He held his breath.

"When I went into the restroom, there were still classes evacuating the building, but when I came out, the building was empty, and eerily quiet. The hallway doors had closed as part of the sprinkler system, and I thought I could detect the smell of smoke, though at the time I brushed the thought aside as merely the power of suggestion."

"Were you alone in the building, then?"

"Well, I thought so, but then—"

"But then?" Morris had to force himself to stay put. He wanted to jump up and wring the teacher's neck for making him wait.

"But then I saw one of my colleagues behind the closed doors in the main office hallway." Mr. Johnson stood with an abrupt scrape of chair on floor, and he began to pace, thumbs hooked in suspenders.

"Which colleague?" Morris whispered, though he thought he already knew.

Johnson made another circle before responding. "I couldn't believe my eyes. I thought my eyes were playing tricks on me. The person I saw behind the double doors was the faculty association president. It was Norma Dunn."

Chapter Fifty-eight

SALLY'S HAND SHOOK AS SHE reached across Dr. Blank's desk to grab the latest gang missive. The handwritten letters had become uncomfortably familiar.

> Hey, Supe! You can thank us for making LHS famous. Its in all the papers and mags now. WW had to go, too hardass, and CD, too weak. Now maybe you realize we are the ones in charge. By the way, your parking lot security gaurd is a pushover.

Sally's gut was knotted from all the events and repercussions of the last few weeks. What an introduction to school administration! The classes she had taken in leadership and supervision had prepared her for this job as well as jumping jacks prepared one for bungee jumping.

Dr. Blank's stare demanded a response, so Sally said, "Sounds like they are claiming responsibility for Wally and Claude. But what about Stoker?"

"I thought the same," the superintendent replied. She patted her corn-rowed hairdo and leaned back in the leather chair. "I wondered all along about Stoker's death. The messed up office, the fire, the broken jaw—they all seemed a bit adolescent—but they lacked the characteristic emblems of a gang hit. No note, no symbols."

"What about Wally?" Sally asked, her voice almost a whisper. She wasn't sure if she really wanted to know.

"Police found a drawing of a pitchfork etched in the gravel by Wally's car, and the right pants leg rolled up on his body. Black

Devils, people signs. We had none of that with Mr. Stoker."

Sally thought for a moment before replying. She was heartsick over the three deaths, all people who meant something to her. Now, though, the obvious concern was for the safety of the school community going forward, her own personal safety included. "I'm afraid we are going to have more upheaval when the police make an arrest for Stoker's murder."

"Yes," Dr. Blank replied, biting her lip. "Detective Morris told me how you've assisted them. They appreciate your cooperation more than they will ever tell you."

Sally thought of the various parts she had played in the investigation. She wasn't particularly proud of any of them, except perhaps yesterday, when she had starred in a video. "And Claude? Do they know who killed him?"

"Another Black Devil, serving time for manslaughter. The jail is full of them. They bribe the guard for an opportunity, and they do the Devils' work, even behind bars."

Sally clasped her hands in her lap, the knuckles showing white. "I feel so bad for Claude's family. He didn't deserve to die."

Dr. Blank reached over and patted Sally on the forearm. "No, he didn't. Apparently, he got caught up in the wrong world at a young age, and when he got smart enough to want to get out, he couldn't."

"It's all too common a story these days. It's one of the reasons I'm committed to working at Lincoln," Sally said. "I hope to help our kids make better choices."

"You do?" the superintendent replied, "even with all of this?" A smile teased at the corners of her lips.

"I know it sounds strange, at least right now. Having no children of my own, I throw myself into parenting other people's children. The families at Lincoln High have accepted me as someone who cares about their kids. It doesn't seem to matter to them that I'm white. They just know I'll do everything in my power to help the kids succeed, despite all the obstacles, gangs included. I wish I'd been able to help Claude."

Now a full smile broke out on Dr. Blank's face. "You're sounding more and more like R.J. Stoker." She fiddled with some papers on her desk. "Have you thought any more about taking on the principalship? I can't promise you carousels and cotton candy, but I promise you it will never be dull. That, and I'm going to beef up our security detail. There will never be another murder here again, at least not on my watch."

Contradictory feelings bubbled inside Sally's heart: gratitude and sadness, humility and responsibility. How could she be excited in the face of all this turmoil? "Dr. Blank, I've already discussed your offer with my husband, and I've convinced him that this is where I'm supposed to be. I'm honored to accept this principalship. I promise I will give the job my all."

Chapter Fifty-nine

"**O**N WHAT GROUNDS ARE YOU holding me here?" Norma Dunn screamed, her voice reverberating off the walls in the small rectangular room at the police station, in the same seat where Claude Davis had sat just a day and a half ago.

"I explained it to you, Ms. Dunn. I showed you the warrant. I read you your rights. Now just calm down." Detective Phillips felt like a cowboy who'd lassoed a wild calf, knowing the battle wasn't even half over. He wished Morris would get back with the video soon. The lady's perfume was overpowering in these tight quarters, and her shouting was giving him a headache.

"I want a lawyer. I want a lawyer right this minute! You can't keep me here like this. I'm an educator, a leader, for God's sake. You can't just treat me like common vermin." She struggled with the steel handcuffs on her wrists to tug on the hemline of her tight skirt, which had ridden halfway up her thigh.

"No one is treating you like vermin. You have the right to counsel, and here's the telephone. Go ahead and call." Phillips pushed the phone closer to the handcuffed suspect. "Just push the speaker button, and make your call."

"I have no idea whom to call, you scum, and I didn't kill Mr. Stoker. I demand to be uncuffed and let go."

"I'm afraid that will be impossible. We have ample evidence to charge you. It would be in your best interests to cooperate with us. Otherwise, you may end up with the death penalty."

"Don't you threaten me," Norma shouted, her voice becoming hoarser by the word. "Why don't you tell me what evidence you have?"

"I'd be glad to oblige, Ms. Dunn, if only you would stop shouting and agree to talk with us. But have it your way. We can put you in a cell and wait until you get a lawyer to start our discussion."

"A cell?" Norma looked at her aubergine skirt and jacket, her mauve silk blouse, and her alligator pumps. "This is outrageous!" She bent her head to sip at the cup of water placed before her and took a deep breath. "Okay, okay, I'll talk. I have nothing to hide anyway, and I can't bear to go into a *cell*."

The detective pulled a pocket-sized tape recorder from his jacket. "I'll turn this on to document our discussion, then. It is for your protection, as well as mine."

Norma tapped her foot on the floor. She stole glances at the tape recorder, but she didn't stop the proceedings.

Phillips spoke into the recorder. "Today is Monday, September 27, 1993. This is Detective Phillips, and I am speaking with Ms. Norma Dunn, teacher at Lincoln High School, regarding the murder of Principal R.J. Stoker on Monday, September 13. Ms. Dunn has been read her rights, and has waived her right to an attorney in this interview. Is that correct, Ms. Dunn?"

Norma's voice sounded like chalk screeching on a blackboard, except muffled. "That is correct, but I reserve the right to cut the interview off at any time."

"Of course," Phillips said. "Now, Ms. Dunn, can you please tell me about your relationship with Mr. R.J. Stoker, the victim of the murder?"

Norma said, "Before I answer the question, could you remove these handcuffs? I swear, I can't even think, I'm so uncomfortable." She twisted her wrists against the metal bonds as if to demonstrate the claim.

Phillips hesitated, more for show than for fear that his prisoner would bolt. "I could do that, but with the understanding that you remain under arrest, and any attempt to take advantage of your wrists being freed would be met with immediate incarceration. You realize there are other officers outside this door."

"I won't try to escape. I want out of here, but not like that."

Phillips removed the handcuffs, but kept them open on the table, a physical reminder of his power over her. "Now, please answer the question. Your relationship to Mr. Stoker?"

"He was my boss. That's all. We didn't have any other relationship."

"In your role with the faculty association, did you have dealings with Mr. Stoker?"

"Yes, but that was true with all of the Lincoln principals. Teachers would have grievances, and I would represent them."

"Were you handling grievances against Mr. Stoker?"

"Unfortunately, yes. Mr. Stoker apparently had little regard for his teachers. In his passion to befriend the students and parents, he tromped all over the faculty. I didn't like him, but I didn't kill him, either."

"So, you're saying you had no interest in Mr. Stoker beyond the business of teacher grievance?"

Norma's eyes shifted from the tape recorder to the door. "That is correct. I didn't consider Mr. Stoker to be worthy of my time or attention."

Detective Phillips opened a thick folder in front of him and extracted a lavender envelope marked, "Stoker." Ignoring the tiny gasp from the other side of the table, Phillips proceeded to remove the letter from inside. "Did you send this note to Mr. Stoker, asking him to meet you on the third floor?"

Norma shifted in her chair and smoothed her skirt before answering. "I did not. I've never seen that letter or envelope before in my life."

"Now, Ms. Dunn. What would you say if I told you I have testimony from someone that you indeed were the author of this letter, and that you invited Mr. Stoker to an after-hours meeting on the third floor?"

"Who would say something like that?"

"Actually, it was Mrs. Pearce. She identified the envelope as having come from you, and she said Mr. Stoker had asked her to be present whenever you came to his office alone."

"Well, she must be mistaken. I did not write that note."

Phillips took a different tack. "Let's talk about September 13. There was a fire alarm near the end of the school day. Can you tell me where you were and what you did when the fire alarm sounded?"

"Why, I did what every other person in the building did. I evacuated the building." Norma fanned herself with her bare hand, and Phillips noticed tiny beads of moisture on her forehead.

"Did you take your class outside?"

"No, I don't have a sixth period class. I descended the stairs from the third floor, and I evacuated the building."

Phillips leaned back and gazed at his suspect through half-lidded eyes. "Did you make any stops on your way to exiting the building?"

Norma wiped her brow and pulled at her skirt. "No, I did not. I went straight outside like all of the other people."

"Which door did you exit, and where did you stand during the evacuation?"

Norma hesitated. "I believe I exited through door two, and I stood in the teacher's parking lot."

Phillips leaned forward. "Did you speak with anyone while you were out there? Is there anyone who can corroborate your statement that you were there?"

Norma narrowed her eyes and raised her voice. "What are you implying? That I'm lying? Why would I lie about that?"

Phillips kept up the pressure, as the calf twisted and turned against his rope. "Perhaps because you did not exit the building. Instead you were seen in the hallway outside the main office, exactly where Stoker's body was found."

"That's ridiculous. No one saw me there, because I was outside in the parking lot with hundreds of other people." Norma chewed on a fingernail. "Who told you I was there? Was it that jerk, Derrick Johnson? If it was, he's the most unreliable witness ever. He's just trying to get back at me because I refused to go out with him."

"Ms. Dunn, have you ever handled a gun before September 13?" Phillips hoped the change of flow would jostle the feisty suspect.

"Don't think I don't see what you're doing, implying I handled a gun on September 13. Well, I didn't. I don't even have a gun, and if I did, I wouldn't bring it to school. It's a gun-free zone."

"That was not my question. Have you ever handled a gun *before* September 13?"

Norma tapped her foot and glanced at the door again. "Well, yes. Some of the teachers here belong to gun clubs, and they invited me to shoot targets with them. I have a firearms owner ID card. But I don't have a gun, and—"

A light tap at the door interrupted Norma's reply, and Detective Morris entered, smelling like a combination of cigarettes and donuts, and carrying a manila envelope. "Excuse the interruption, and sorry I'm late. Here is the item you asked me to pick up." He slid the envelope onto the table in front of Phillips.

"Let the record reflect that Detective J.J. Morris has entered the room," Phillips spoke for the benefit of the tape recorder. "Please have a seat, Detective Morris."

Norma shot Morris a sideways glance. "As I was saying, I do not own a gun."

Phillips continued, "Do you recall being fingerprinted last week in Mrs. Pearce's office?"

"Yes, of course, I do. Messy operation. The ink got all over my good blouse."

"Then how would you explain the fact that your fingerprint was found on the murder weapon?"

Norma gasped, then covered her mouth as if yawning. "That's preposterous. You must be making this up. I don't believe you in the slightest."

Phillips and Morris exchanged glances, and Phillips prepared his next question with care. "Perhaps the fingerprint transferred to the weapon when you hid it under the stairs at Claude Davis' house?"

Norma's voice rose to a screech, "Oh, I see. You guys are framing me for what Claude Davis did. Claude's dead, so you've got to find somebody else to pin the murder on. Well, it wasn't me. You've got to believe me. It wasn't me."

Phillips nodded to Morris, who jumped into the conversation. "Ms. Dunn, with all due respect, I'd like you to view something that's been shared with us by Miss Minnie Marshall. Miss Marshall's grandson is taking a photojournalism class at the community college, and he happened to be shooting a project with a borrowed camcorder. When Miss Marshall witnessed something highly unusual, she called her grandson to photograph it."

"What does this have to do with me?" Norma almost shouted.

"You'll see," Morris replied. He set up the projector and screen in the narrow room and flicked the lights out. The screen lit up with a scene of a street, a dogwood tree, a plain wood-frame house with a small porch and three stairs, a cat, and most importantly, the shapely backside of a light-skinned woman in a navy blue suit and pumps, kneeling on the ground and shoving something under the stairs. The figure took several seconds to make sure the object was well-placed. Then she rose from the position and ran out of the picture. The whole video took less than ten seconds to play.

Norma put her face into her hands and began to sob.

Morris donned his pit bull voice. "Fortunate for us, unfortunate for you, Ms. Dunn. We have proof that you took the murder weapon from the school and hid it at the Davis house to make Claude look like the guilty one." He fixed the suspect with an icy stare. "You might as well admit it. We've got you six ways to Sunday."

"Okay, okay. Get me a lawyer. I killed Mr. Stoker. I didn't mean to. I didn't plan it. I just saw him lying there unconscious, a loaded gun by his side, and... and... and, he had *dissed* me. Do you understand? He had rejected me! I just wanted him *gone*."

Chapter Sixty

THINGS QUIETED DOWN AT LINCOLN High School once Mr. Stoker's murderer was apprehended and given a speedy trial. Wally's murder remained unsolved, except that the Black Devils were generally given credit, or blame. Sally and her secretary Pat moved into the principal's office, where Sally hung a portrait of R.J. Stoker. Her first order of business was to re-focus on teaching and learning. She asked Melody Singer to lead a series of after-school staff development sessions based on new teaching methods. She worked with the counselors to initiate a weekly scholarship seminar with the goal of placing every Lincoln senior into an affordable postsecondary institution. The new faculty association president, Derrick Johnson, occasionally dogged her with some concern or another, but for the most part, she'd heard the faculty and staff regarded her as a welcome breath of fresh air.

On May 2, Glenda, who had kept the title of Principal's Secretary, was feeding her bird, Rowdy, when two important phone calls came in close succession. Sally took the first. It was Coach Donovan, sounding giddy with an Irish lilt in his voice. "Hey, Pearce. You must've written a helluva recommendation letter. Syracuse has accepted Tyrone with a full ride."

"Oh, yeah!" Sally shouted into the receiver, punching the air with a fist. "Great job, Coach. I knew he was star material, but your reputation and influence didn't hurt either. Does Tyrone know yet?"

"Not sure. He's not at school today, and I tried to get him at home—no answer."

"Thanks for letting me know, Coach. I'll try to find him—"

The buzz of another incoming call caused Sally to say goodbye to Donovan and punch the other extension. "Lincoln High School, Mrs. Pearce speaking."

"Mrs. Pearce, it's Shayla."

"And Tyrone."

"We're calling you from the hospital. Our baby is born. He's a handsome little guy, eight and a half pounds and twenty-two inches long. We're naming him Claude."

Sally's eyes filled with tears at the thought of a new Claude in the world, one whose life would likely be happier and more fulfilling. "Congratulations, you two. I can't wait to meet the little guy."

Shayla bubbled on, as if childbirth hadn't tempered her energy one bit. "I'll be home with him tomorrow. Maybe you can come visit after school."

"I'd love that," Sally replied, thinking of the gift-wrapped boxes of layette items and the high chair she had waiting in her basement. "I know you two are going to be wonderful parents."

Then she remembered, "Tyrone, are you still on the line?"

"Yes, Ma'am."

"Do you have some other good news for me?" Sally hinted.

"Other good news?"

"You haven't heard? Syracuse accepted you, and they've given you a full scholarship."

Shayla spoke first. "Tyrone! Congratulations! Syracuse was your first choice."

"Yeah, thanks. But—"

Sally thought she knew what Tyrone was going to say next.

"It's just—well, I've got a family now. I've got responsibilities."

"Yes," Sally said, "and you owe it to your family to get your college degree and become the best person you can possibly be. That is your biggest responsibility from now on."

"But I won't leave Shayla and my little man. I can't do that."

"Well, then," Sally replied, "you'll just have to take them with you to New York."

* * *

Three weeks later, Sally was helping Shayla don her cap and gown in the main office before lining up for graduation. The recent news that Norma Dunn had been convicted of voluntary manslaughter and sentenced to eleven years in prison did little to disrupt Sally's focus on launching this amazing group of seniors into the world. She didn't even pause to wonder whether Norma had ever figured out that the woman hiding the gun in Ms. Marshall's grandson's video had actually been Sally.

"I'm so proud of you, Shayla. Despite all of the obstacles you've had to face this year, you managed to graduate on the honor roll."

"Thanks, but a lot of the credit belongs to you. You got me the homebound tutor and helped me get my applications in order. Without you pushing me along, I probably would've given up." Shayla hugged her mentor. "Besides, I have a graduation surprise for you."

"A surprise for me?"

"I got a letter from Syracuse this morning. I'm in with a partial teacher scholarship. Claude and I are going to college with Tyrone, and I'm going to be an educator, just like you."

Just then Tyrone burst in, his purple gown and gold tassel flying behind him. His eyes glowed with excitement. "I thought I'd find you in here. Did you tell Ms. Pearce the good news?"

Shayla nodded, and the three of them formed the tightest and happiest group hug possible.

* * *

There is something about graduations that lifts the spirits beyond the ordinary date and place, beyond the strains of "Pomp and Circumstance" and the bleachers full of flowers and balloons. On Graduation Day, even the modest circumstances of the students in an urban high school are lifted to the realm of the royal.

As Sally delivered her first commencement address as principal, she expressed gratitude to R.J. Stoker for selecting her as his assistant and for inspiring her every day. She expressed gratitude to the faculty and staff for their yeoman's service in moving the school from tragedy to accomplishment in this rough year. And finally, she expressed gratitude to the students and their families for daring to pursue their aspirations beyond the walls of Lincoln High.

"Each of you has left your mark on Lincoln High School, and each of you will be missed, but with your diploma you accept the charge to keep learning, keep achieving, and make us oh, so proud."

As Sally returned to the principal's office and removed her cap and gown, she thought there would never be another year like this, or another graduating class like this one. She glanced at the portrait of Mr. Stoker, and she could have sworn his lips moved, and his voice filled her ears.

"That's right, Sally—that is, until next year."

Acknowledgments

WHILE *A MURDER OF PRINCIPAL* is purely fictional, I've had an exceptional career as a teacher and administrator in School District 205 in South Holland, Illinois; Galveston Independent School District in Texas; St. Louis Public Schools; and Brentwood Schools in Missouri. I am utterly grateful to the many students, parents, fellow teachers, fellow administrators, department chairs, counselors, deans, faculty association officers, coaches, administrative assistants, and other support staff who made up my work family. Like the Lincoln High School Warriors, these individuals face challenges every day and meet them with strength, compassion, and a positive spirit.

I am also inspired by my colleagues from the Southern Regional Education Board's High Schools That Work. As school improvement consultants, they work with under-performing high schools, always striving, like R.J. Stoker, to "do the right thing" for students.

I'm grateful, as always, to my husband Ed for being this book's first reader and my constant consultant throughout the writing process. I'm also indebted to the members of my writers' critique group for catching errors and suggesting fine points for improving the manuscript. Most importantly, I appreciate the staff at Encircle Publications, including Eddie Vincent, Cynthia Brackett-Vincent, and Deirdre Wait, for believing in this story and giving it wings.

Finally, readers, thank you for joining me on this book's journey. As J.K. Rowling said, "No story lives unless someone wants to listen." I'm grateful that you did.

—Saralyn Richard

About the Author

AWARD-WINNING MYSTERY AND CHILDREN'S BOOK author **Saralyn Richard** has drawn from her experiences as an urban high school educator to write *A Murder of Principal*. Her previous books—*Naughty Nana, Murder in the One Percent*, and *A Palette for Love and Murder*—have delighted children and adults, alike. An active member of International Thriller Writers and Mystery Writers of America, Saralyn teaches creative writing at the Osher Lifelong Learning Institute, and continues to write mysteries. Reviews, media, and tour schedule may be found at www.saralynrichard.com.

If you enjoyed *A Murder of Principal*, please leave an honest review at: https://www.amazon.com/Murder-Principal-Saralyn-Richard/dp/1645991326/ref=

9 781645 991328